AFTER THE WORKSHOP

AFTER THE WORKSHOP

A MEMOIR BY

JACK HERCULES SHEAHAN

A NOVEL BY

JOHN MCNALLY

COUNTERPOINT

BERKELEY

Library of Congress Cataloging-in-Publication Data

McNally, John, 1965–
  After the workshop : a novel / by John McNally.
    p. cm.
  ISBN 978-1-58243-560-2 — ISBN 1-58243-560-X
  1. Authors—Fiction. 2. Publishers and publishing—Fiction. 3. Iowa City (Iowa)—Fiction. I. Title.
  PS3563.C38813A69 2010
  813'.54—dc22
                                            2009038163

Cover design by Silverander Communications
Interior design by Megan Jones Design
Printed in the United States of America

COUNTERPOINT
2117 Fourth Street
Suite D
Berkeley, CA 94710

www.counterpointpress.com

Distributed by Publishers Group West

10 9 8 7 6 5 4 3 2 1

For AKB

It plagued us all during our time at Iowa, the question, there was no escaping it. Did I, we all wondered constantly about ourselves, have a future as a writer?

—William Lashner

AFTER THE WORKSHOP

WAS A MEDIA ESCORT.

That was how, twelve years after graduating from the Iowa Writers' Workshop, I was earning my keep. I worked freelance, negotiating my fees with publicists at the major publishing houses, but I was occasionally thrown work by a woman named Barbara Rizzo, who had escorts waiting, like operatives, all across the country.

My duties?

I picked up writers, novelists mostly, from the Cedar Rapids Airport, drove them to Iowa City, dropped them off at the hotel, took them to their various media interviews, made sure they arrived at their book signings on time, and then drove them back to the airport the next day. If they wanted, I would join them for dinner or drinks (all of which I would bill to the publisher), but this rarely happened. Most writers, exhausted by early flights and bloated itineraries, were happy enough to hole up in the hotel and order room service—that is, until the next time they needed me to take them somewhere, even if the destination was a block away.

The only time I ever met other media escorts was at BookExpo America, the annual conference at which nearly every publisher, large and small, launched their forthcoming books to the world; and every year at the BEA, way off in one of the far-flung corners of the convention center, the media escorts announced their annual Bull's-Eye Award.

The Bull's-Eye was given to the author who had been the biggest pain in the ass to escort. The original idea was to hold a mock-award ceremony during which a laminated shooting range target would be unveiled, with a photo of the author's head glued atop the silhouetted torso, but this proposal was wisely nixed. The name of the award—the Bull's-Eye—stuck, however. Naturally, the winning author would never be informed of his or her honor.

One year the award was given to a feminist icon who terrorized all her media escorts, mostly middle-aged women, and referred to them, regardless of age, as "girl." Another year it went to one of the hip young writers—his first book has a title too long for me ever to remember it correctly—for making absurd requests, such as the time he insisted that the bookstore play a recording of humpback whales during his event, or how he refused to give anyone, even the poor schlub driving him around, a straight answer.

"I have pancreatic cancer," he told one escort in St. Louis named Marissa, whose own father had recently died of a malignant brain tumor. "I have only ten weeks to live," he continued, remaining poker-faced, "so please don't mess up anything tonight, okay? I want this to be a special event."

The Bull's-Eye Award was Barbara Rizzo's very own creation. I liked Barbara, but whenever I worked for her, she would harangue me for not owning a cell phone ("You need to go out there today and get a cell phone. Will you do that for me? Tell me you'll do that for me!"), or for not having a better network of contacts in Iowa City ("What do you mean you don't know a good masseuse?"), or for not owning a bigger car ("When are you going to upgrade, Jack? Have you seen the new Hummers? You really should take the day off and go look at the Hummers, Jack."). She sent out frequent lists of dos and don'ts. The dos included, among other things, vacuuming your car before picking up a client, shaving (for men), and wearing pantyhose and a skirt (for women). The don'ts list specified that we shouldn't tell the authors our problems ("Don't get personal with the clients!"), we shouldn't ask to borrow money from them for parking ("Always bring change for meters!"), and that we were never, under any circumstances, to engage in any form of sexual activity with a client ("We're not THAT kind of escort service!").

Over time, I broke nearly every "do" and "don't" on Barbara's list, culminating with the night I did shots of Absolut with Sherry LaGris, author of *Planet Penis*, a best-selling book about the male-centric world we live in. We ended up in her hotel room, in her bed, and we had sex—drunken sex that included me getting poked in my right eye with an elbow and Sherry falling head-first off the bed during one of my more enthusiastic thrusts—and yet all appeared as though it were going to be okay (that rarest of things: an uncomplicated fling) until she confessed that I was the first man she'd slept with since her husband of twenty-five years had walked out on her for her negative ("But honest!" she insisted) portrayal of him in her book. Naked, slightly woozy, I tried to comfort her. "Now, now," I kept saying. "Everything's going to be all right." The next morning, our clothes reeking of cigarette smoke and sweat, Sherry perfunctorily signed my copy of *Planet Penis* on our way to the airport. "Good wishes," she wrote and scribbled her name. I made sure she got through security without a hitch, but only after I had borrowed five bucks for airport parking.

Fortunately, Barbara Rizzo never found out about this particular breach of protocol, and she even invited me to attend the BEA in Chicago, all expenses paid, for providing the best anecdote about that year's Bull's-Eye Award winner, Maria Castaneda. Maria Castaneda, best known for her derivative magical realist novels, was the darling of multicultural studies across America. Her books were assigned in hundreds of courses on Latino/Latina literature, courses on feminist theory, and courses about both "real" and "imagined" borders, whatever that meant. She commanded large speaking fees and had even convinced her publisher to bring out a book of her poetry, a slim volume titled *You Seek Answers to Questions I Have Not Heard.*

In order to win the Bull's-Eye Award, you needed to garner the most votes, and in that particular year, Maria Castaneda won it hands down. According to the other escorts, she had been dismissive of the groups of young girls, mostly Latinas, who came out to see her ("Cheerleaders," she called them, rolling her eyes); she had berated bookstore workers for not recognizing her upon sight, and then mumbled insults under her breath when these same workers, after learning who she was, didn't treat her with the proper reverence; she insulted their cities ("This sure is an ugly place. Where am I again?"); she barked orders at her media escorts and then, like a family pet, curled up in their backseats for naps, no matter the distances they were driving; she made at least two media escorts come to her hotel room and massage her feet.

At BookExpo, in front of a small crowd of media escorts, along with a few curious passersby, Barbara Rizzo stood in front of a microphone and eloquently enumerated the long list of complaints filed against Castaneda. Rizzo read the list as though it were a string of accomplishments, encouraging her escorts to applaud after each deed. And then Barbara called me up to the microphone to tell my story.

My grievance was, in the larger scheme of things, a small one: Maria Castaneda wanted me to take off my baseball cap while I was in her presence. Since Barbara Rizzo herself wouldn't have approved of the baseball cap, I revised my complaint, claiming that she berated me for not wearing a tie and insisted that I wear one the next time she saw me. I wasn't comfortable with my modified anecdote, so I hurried quickly through it, taking listeners up to the point where I had finally—gratefully—dropped Maria Castaneda off at the airport, wishing her a safe flight to her next destination.

"But when I got home," I said, "I decided to look up all her books on Amazon. And that's when the idea came to me. I spent the next ten or so hours setting up different accounts, using all the credit cards I owned, so that I could log on ten negative reviews for each of her books. And then I emailed all my friends to do the same. By the end of the day, Maria Castaneda's books each averaged one-and-a-half stars!"

My fellow escorts roared; they were eating it up.

"And then I started leaving comments about her every time I found a blog that mentioned her," I continued. And I was about to regale the audience with some of the nastier comments I had left on blogs, many of which were libelous, when I saw Barbara Rizzo peering warily up at me, and I remembered that I hadn't told her this part of the story. Some of the other escorts were giving me looks that suggested I'd pushed my reprisal a little too far, so I quickly wrapped up my speech.

"Just a few blogs," I added, shaking my head. "Nothing too awful."

My speech petered out here, and I stepped away from the microphone, but as I climbed down from the small platform, I saw Maria Castaneda. Arms crossed, she stood at the back of the crowd, glaring at me. Was it really her?

"Look, look," I said out of the corner of my mouth to the people closest to me, "she's here. I think it's her, at least." But no one paid any attention. I was either speaking too softly, or everyone was embarrassed for me. Had I gone too far? I wondered. Was I a terrible person?

The next time I looked, Maria Castaneda was gone, swallowed by the herd of anonymous conventioneers—or perhaps, like a character from one of her own novels, she had stormed out of the building and, buoyed by humiliation, floated up through the earth's atmosphere, never to be seen again.

PART ONE

There are no second acts in American lives.

—F. SCOTT FITZGERALD

M OST PEOPLE FAIL to recognize the moment they've touched the ceiling of their potential, that point at which they've reached the height of their intellectual prowess or the summit of their popularity. It can happen anywhere, at any point in their life—away at college during a study session the night before a final, or on a high school football field while catching the game-winning touchdown. For some poor souls it happens as early as grade school, often inconspicuously: surrounded by friends on the blacktop on the first day back to school, or saying something funny in class that makes even the teacher smile. And then, after that, it's all downhill.

My swift rise began when the director of the famous and often-maligned Iowa Writers' Workshop, a man named Gordon Grimes, awarded me a much-coveted Teaching-Writing Fellowship. The TWIF, as it's called, was a plum appointment given only to the most promising writers in the program, and much to my own surprise, I had been deemed one of them. A month later, my short story "The Self-Adhesive Postage Stamp" appeared in *The New Yorker*. The following year, as I was finishing my thesis, that same story was reprinted in the most prestigious anthology, *The Best American Short Stories*. Success on that scale altered the way I came into contact with the world around me: Walking felt like floating, street lamps buzzed extra bright, and every song drift-ing through the open window of an apartment or automobile became the soundtrack to my life. I was twenty-four years old. The world—the publishing world, at least—was mine for the taking!

But then an odd thing happened. I never published another word.

I stayed in Iowa City after graduation and worked on my novel. I worked feverishly on it those first few years after the Workshop, maintaining the single-minded focus of a bee in a hive. On those rare nights when I would sneak away from my novel and go to the Foxhead, I was surprised to learn that the new students recognized my name when I wrote it on the chalkboard wait list for the pool table. (In full disclosure, I would write my entire name on the board—Jack Hercules Sheahan—and although it sometimes took an entire game of eight-ball before the student made the connection, we became fast friends once the tumblers of who I was and where I had published clicked into place.)

"Hey, you wrote 'The Self-Adhesive Postage Stamp,' didn't you? Dude. I friggin' *love* that story. You turned the civil-service-job short story on its *ear*. On its friggin' *ear*!"

I had even fallen into bed, on two separate occasions, with Workshop women who wanted to sleep with someone whose work had appeared in a magazine they themselves hoped one day to publish in. One of the women lived in a dingy apartment about to be condemned, com-posing poetry on an electric typewriter that sat atop a stack of stolen milk crates while she sat cross-legged on a dubiously stained sofa pur-chased at Goodwill. (I later learned that she had gone to Berkeley as an undergrad and received a hefty monthly allowance from her trust fund, though you wouldn't have guessed it from some of her poems with titles like "Scabs" or "My Mother's Pimp" or "Chemo Dreams." Her name is Pauline Frost. Maybe you've heard of her.)

But my celebrity—small and dismal as it was—was short-lived. Five short years after I had graduated, no one knew who I was; no one had heard of my story "The Self-Adhesive Postage Stamp"; and if the occasion arose to tell a fresh-faced Workshop student my name and casually mention my publication, they regarded me with suspicion, as if I were making it all up—a crazy local trying to infiltrate and taint their exclusive little circle of talent and promise. What I realize now but didn't— *couldn't*—grasp back then was that my peak had come when the complimentary copies of *Best American Short Stories* arrived in the mail. I ripped open the padded envelope before I could get back inside my apartment, just so that I could see my story reprinted alongside acknowledged masters of the form. And that was my peak right there: holding that book open and staring down at a series of artistically strung-together words that had sprung from some elusive part of my own brain.

Twelve years after I had graduated from the Workshop, I was still living in Iowa City. I had become friends with the Foxhead's regulars over the years—non-writers who grudgingly suffered the Workshop students whenever they burst through the front door and talked loudly (always loudly) about Jonathan Franzen or Mary Gaitskill or drunkenly scribbled Barry Hannah quotes on the bathroom walls. These men (all the regulars were men) used to ask me how my novel was coming along, but eventually they forgot that I had been working on one—that, or they knew deep-down the sad truth: I had given up my dreams, as they had given up theirs. I knew that Joey, who always sat near the pay phone as if he were expecting a call that never came, had once played guitar in a pretty good local band; and that Sand Man, who took a stool at the corner of the bar for a bird's-eye view of the pool table, had won a few major eight-ball tournaments in Vegas in the early 1970s; and that Larry McFeeley, who lived on a steady diet of Slim Jims and Hot Tamales, had been a weight lifter of Olympic caliber, breaking the state's high school records for both the clean-and-jerk and the snatch. "It happens to the best of us," they might have told me if I'd asked them how someone so promising could fall so far—but I never mentioned the novel again, and they quit asking. We all just silently, mercifully, let it go.

I T WASN'T OFTEN that two authors came to town on the same day, but if I could juggle it, I would agree to pick up both of them, and that's how this story begins: On a gray snow-promising day in early December, I took on two such jobs when I should have taken only the one.

The first author scheduled to arrive that morning was Vanessa Roberts. Her niche was the quasi-literary novel, mostly ones about child abuse, and she had just published her first memoir, *The Outhouse*, a hundred-and-twelve-page tale of how she and her younger brother fondled each other for the first time while visiting relatives who lived in a house with no indoor plumbing. The press release, which I quickly flipped through at the Cedar Rapids Airport while waiting for her plane to land, described *The Outhouse* as both "shocking" and "explosive." I opened the book, looking for the dirty parts, but then quickly shut it when a priest walked up next to me, also waiting for a passenger to arrive.

"Father," I said and smiled.

He glanced over at me, frowned, then looked back up to the monitor that gave arrival estimates. Even though I was a lapsed Catholic, I still felt inexplicable twinges of guilt and reverence around priests and nuns. I also felt the desire to start confessing my sins, something I hadn't done since my eighth-grade confirmation, which was the last time I had stepped foot inside a church—any church. I wanted to ask him if he thought there was any relationship between the implosion of my career and my cavalier attitude toward God, but when I turned back to inquire what parish he presided over, I realized that he wasn't a priest at all. He was just an old guy wearing a white turtleneck underneath a dark sport jacket.

He looked over at me and said, "Is there a problem?"

"No problem," I said. I walked closer to the security guard who kept people from entering the gate area, a man so large he looked like he might have had trouble tying his shoes, let alone chasing down someone with ill intent. I glanced over my shoulder at the man in the white turtleneck and sport jacket; he was still staring at me. Lately, I'd begun mistaking words and phrases when I saw them, mostly on street signs or billboards. At a quick glance I might think "No Stopping" said "No Groping," or "Watch Out: Bump Ahead" said "Watch Out: Bum Ahead." Only on a second, more discerning look would I see the words for what they were. But today was the first time I had mistaken a person for someone other than who he was, and I feared that I was in the early stages of some horrific disease, like the villagers in *One Hundred Years of Solitude* who, suffering from mass amnesia, begin hanging signs on things, like cows, to remind themselves of what they were looking at.

A plane started deboarding, so I held Vanessa Roberts's book in front of my chest—her cue that I was her media escort. One thing I had learned: Never rely on an author photo. If it hasn't been Photoshopped to death, it's probably twenty years old. One time, I stood waiting with the book held up, looking for a sexy, woodsy woman in her late twenties to amble up to me, and I became increasingly irritated when a heavy-set, middle-aged woman eating an enormous cookie stepped in front of me and blocked my view. She finally lowered her cookie and said, "Should we get my bags or what?" "Oh," I said, "hello!" and when she smirked at me I could see, if only fleetingly, the younger, spunky woman inside the older one, and how the woman standing in front of me had decided, at some critical juncture, to just let herself go. She was wearing sweatpants that day, and her hair stood on end. Cookie crumbs dotted a stained T-shirt that advertised the Bermuda Triangle Writers Conference.

Another time, I chased a black man across the airport, thinking that he had failed to see me holding up his book, but when I caught up to him and tapped him on the shoulder, asking if he was indeed the book's author, even going so far as to show the author photo to him and point at it, he said, in a good-natured way, "If I say yes, do I win something?" Before walking away, he laughed and shook his head, muttering something under his breath that I couldn't hear. I didn't blame him, and as a guy who prided himself as being sensitive to racial issues, I was mortified that I had followed the wrong man across the airport.

So I had quit looking at author photos altogether. I read the press material, and I skimmed the book, but I refused to be led astray.

A woman holding a baby approached me. The baby, still red-faced and wrinkled, looked fresh out of the womb. It was, to the best of my recollection, the smallest human I'd ever seen before.

"Vanessa Roberts," she said. "I'd shake your hand, but . . ." She held up the infant to prove that her hands were full. "Oh, hey, could you take the baby for a minute?" she asked.

I'd recently had a nightmare in which a stranger handed me her baby and I accidentally dropped it. As dreams went, this one landed somewhere between forgetting my locker combination and falling off a cliff: a classic anxiety dream, the subconscious flotsam of a chronic worrier. Fortunately, I jumped awake before the baby hit the floor.

I took Vanessa's baby. I cooed, but the baby seemed barely sentient. I made a face, poking out my bottom lip and widening my eyes, but the baby simply moved arms and legs back and forth, like a toppled-over insect.

Vanessa set down various bags, purses, and satchels, rummaged through a few of them, then pulled out a bottle and handed it to me. After picking up all her detritus, slinging some of the bags over a shoulder, she hitched her pants and straightened her blouse, then motioned for me, by wiggling her fingers, to give back her child.

"Here," she said, annoyed. "I'll hold; you can feed."

"Are you sure?" I asked.

"The nipple goes in the mouth," she said impatiently, and I must have turned red, thinking about the author's memoir—naked siblings fondling each other in an outhouse—because she said, "Forget it," and jerked the bottle from me, doing the task herself. "Where's baggage claim?" she asked. "I checked the baby seat."

I pointed to my left, and off we went.

ITH ONLY TWO exceptions, the authors I picked up never asked me if I was a writer, and I never brought it up. It was no different with Vanessa Roberts, who sat in the backseat without putting on her seatbelt and then fell sound asleep while the baby, belted in place like an astronaut about to be blasted into outer space, looked around wide-eyed.

I hit a bump, and my muffler fell off. Vanessa woke up and asked me what that noise was.

"What noise?" I asked. I saw cars in my rearview mirror swerving to avoid running over the muffler, but then a semi-trailer flattened it, sending debris bouncing toward the side of the road.

"And that smell?" she asked. She coughed a few times. "What's *that?*"

"I don't know," I said. "I don't smell anything."

The exhaust fumes were burning my eyes, but I admitted nothing. *We're almost there*, I thought. *Just a few more miles to go.*

The baby started wailing. Vanessa, coughing, rubbed her own eyes. "Now, now," she said to her child. "Everything's okay." To me, she said, "What's wrong with this car?"

"Nothing's wrong with this car," I lied. "The pavement's ridged along this stretch. That's the noise you're hearing. What you're smelling is an old milk truck with an oil problem. It sped by us while you were napping."

"Dammit," Vanessa said.

"What?"

"I lost something." She rummaged through her bags. "It must have fallen out in the overhead bin." She shut her eyes. "*Shit!*"

Vanessa was silent the rest of the way to the hotel. I zipped into the semicircle and killed the engine as hotel guests stopped to stare at me and my loud car. I needed to work fast—the next author pickup was in an hour—so I carried the baby to the sidewalk.

"Does she stay in the chair, or do you want to carry her?"

"*He. Him.*"

"What?"

"The baby is a boy," she said.

"Oh. *Him*, then," I said and smiled. I set his chair on the sidewalk. I looked down and said, "Hey, li'l guy. How ya doin'?"

The baby started bawling.

"Look," she said, "I need a favor." She pulled a Montblanc pen and a leather-bound journal from her purse and started writing. Maybe this was what I had needed to get me through my writing slump—a $200 pen and a pad of paper sheathed in the skin of some exotic or unlikely animal, like a bobcat or a hedgehog. Maybe the cause of my creative impotence lay in the fact that I had used black Bics and legal pads purchased in bulk at Office Depot.

Vanessa tore the sheet from her journal and handed it to me. What she'd written was a product name, but the words meant nothing. They looked foreign or made up.

"I need you to get that for me," she said. "Bill it to my publisher."

"Where do I find it?"

"The drugstore," she said.

I nodded. I glanced at my watch, worried about my next author pickup. "When do you need this?"

She looked down at her howling, pinch-faced baby and said, "As soon as possible."

"Okeydoke," I said. "Good enough."

I started to pick up the baby again, but when I saw one of the bell-boys, I motioned him over and said, "Could you? Do you mind?"

He smiled at Vanessa but frowned at me, reaching down and taking hold of the baby seat as though it were an old piece of Samsonite.

"Be back soon," I said. Vanessa merely nodded. She followed the stranger lugging her child away. The huge glass double doors swept open, and an agreeable blast of ventilated heat hit me before the doors swept shut again, leaving me in the skin-charring cold.

CHEERFUL, ANTISEPTIC MUZAK version of "Psycho Killer" wafted like nerve gas through CVS's ceiling. I looked down at the sheet of paper that Vanessa had given to me. The only words on the page were "Advent Isis iQ Uno."

"Excuse me?"

A portly woman stocking shelves stopped what she was doing to hear what I had to say, but she wasn't pleased that I had interrupted her.

"I was wondering," I said, "if you carry this?" I showed her the sheet of paper.

She read it, then looked up at me. By her expression, I half-expected her to pull out her walkie-talkie and announce a Code Red in aisle four, but then she turned without uttering a word and walked away. I followed. When we reached an aisle stocked full of baby supplies, she pointed to a box on the top shelf. What I had asked for, apparently, was a breast pump.

"Oh," I said. "Perfect. Thank you."

The woman, still not speaking to me, returned to her appointed aisle. Her revulsion clung to me, though. I wanted to find her and say, "Look, it's not like I came to CVS looking for a *penis* pump. This is for my *wife*! It's for our *child*!" But it wasn't for my wife or child, and maybe she sensed this. I wasn't wearing a wedding band, and I was slightly out of breath. I may even have been panting.

I grabbed a Starbucks Frappuccino from the freezer on my way to the checkout. More than anything, I needed a fix of caffeine right now. Or, perhaps, I *desired* the Frappuccino, whereas I *needed* a new muffler. It had been my experience, however, that desires almost always trumped needs.

Behind me in line, someone said, "Jack?" It had been over three years since I'd last seen Alice, ten years since we'd been a couple. Even though we resided in a town of sixty thousand, it was entirely possible to live your whole life here and not see everyone, so it wasn't particularly surprising that Alice and I traveled in entirely different orbits: She was a scientist; I was . . . something else. I couldn't say that I was a writer. And yet I couldn't quite pin down my occupation—my reason for being—since what I did for a living struck me as more of a hobby than a profession. In an earlier life, back when I *could* have said what it was I did (or, at least, what it was I *thought* I was doing), Alice and I had been engaged to be married.

"Alice!" I said, trying to convey in my smile a complicated commingling of fondness and regret, though almost certainly expressing bewilderment and worry instead. Alice shut her eyes slowly and opened them, the way a cat sometimes does when you say its name. She had green eyes and skin so pale it was almost blue from her veins. Strange as it sounded, I fell in love with her translucence before I fell in love with her.

"It's funny," Alice said. "I was just thinking about you the other day. A friend of mine was going on and on about a play that I should see, and I remember how much you hated plays. Remember? You used to say, 'The acting. It's so . . . *theatrical*!'" Alice laughed. "Remember that?"

"No. Did I say that?" I asked, wagging my head, though I knew perfectly well that I had. I was the king of witticisms back when my *New Yorker* publication meant (or seemed to mean) that I was destined for larger things, but now that I knew the truth, that I was a one-hit wonder, I quit making ridiculous pronouncements and regretted that I had been such a pompous asshole.

Alice, making a pained expression, said, "So, how have you been?"

"Oh, not too bad," I said, but when this sounded to my own ears like a pathetic appeal for sympathy, I said, "Actually, pretty good. Great, really."

"Oh good," Alice said, brightening. "I'm so glad."

"And you?" I asked.

She made an exaggerated frown. "I've put on a few pounds," she said. "You know. Old age. Metabolism. *Ugh.*"

"Stop it," I said. "You look great. You could use the weight. Seriously. Don't get me wrong. You were gorgeous before. But you look even better now." I could see that I was heading into dangerous territory, so I quickly added, "And I'm older than you. Remember?"

"You're sweet," she said.

I raised my eyebrows, shrugged. I looked down at my shoes. I was still in love with Alice, but I didn't want her to know. And yet I couldn't think of anything else trivial to say or ask.

"Are you all right?" she whispered.

"What?"

"You look so sad," she said.

"I do? No, I'm great. No, no, everything's great."

"NEXT!" It was the cashier; I had failed to see that my turn had finally come. I stepped forward, and Alice moved up behind me.

"Do you want to get coffee sometime?" I asked. My heart had begun to thump harder, causing me to take quicker breaths.

The scanner beeped twice—once for the Frappuccino, once for the breast pump—and the cashier said, "That's two hundred and sixteen dollars and forty-three cents."

"*How* much?" I asked.

Alice, eyes lighting up, said, "What did you *buy*, Jack?" and then she looked down and saw the breast pump. "Oh," she said. "Congratulations?"

"It's not what it looks like," I said, but as soon as I said this, I realized that it sounded even worse. If a breast pump wasn't going to be used for its intended purpose, then to what use would I be putting it?

"Credit?" the cashier asked. She pursed her lips, waiting.

"Uh . . . just a sec," I said. My credit line was close to being maxed out, but in my bank account sat less than three hundred bucks—barely enough to last me the month. My choices were to humiliate myself with a credit card purchase that would be denied, float the check, or return the merchandise.

"Do you take checks?" I asked.

"Do you have an I.D.?"

I pulled out my driver's license and wrote a check.

The cashier bagged the pump, threw the receipt inside, and yelled, "NEXT!"

I drank my Frappuccino and waited for Alice by the exit, hoping to salvage our talk, but she pretended to be in a hurry when she saw me.

"I've taken *way* too long of a lunch break," she said.

"Do you know who Vanessa Roberts is?" I asked.

"Is she the one who wrote *The Bathroom*?"

"*The Outhouse*," I said.

Alice nodded.

"Well, this is for her," I said. I raised the bag with the breast pump in it.

"I really need to go," she said. "But it was great seeing you, Jack. Take care of yourself, okay?"

"All right," I said. "Okay." I lifted up the bag, spun the breast pump to tighten the plastic sack's opening, and then carried it out of the mall like a hunter clutching a dead goose by its limp neck.

Back at the hotel, standing at the front desk, I used the house phone to call Vanessa. Her phone rang and rang, but no one answered.

"Are you sure this is the right room?" I asked.

The man working the front desk shut his eyes and nodded. Displays of visible irritation were not uncommon in Iowa City. Nearly everyone in town had an MFA or a PhD, and yet most were relegated to jobs that paid barely above minimum wage. For all I knew, I was probably talking to the next great post-abstract-expressionist.

I hung up and said, "Listen. She *needs* what's in this sack. Could you give it to her as soon as possible?" I handed over the pump and said, "This is urgent. A child's life depends on this." To further make my point, I added, "A *baby's* life."

The man took the bag with no emotion.

"Thank you," I said. "I mean that." My hope was that sincerity might breed competence.

The man looked over my shoulder and said, "Checking in?"

I looked over my own shoulder: A family of eight had somehow snuck up on me.

"Welcome to Iowa City," I said, "the third best small metropolitan area in the United States!" I stepped aside, gesturing for them to proceed to the front desk. "According to *Forbes*," I added.

N THE CORNER of Summit and Burlington I lived in a turn-of-the-century house that had been divided into four apartments, two large, two small. I lived in one of the small ones—hardwood floors, gas oven, built-in bookshelves, arched doorways, a claw-foot tub. Each year, the owner jacked up the rent; a letter, informing tenants of the new rates, appeared under our doors in the middle of the night. My annual income had long since plateaued, so it was only a matter of a few years before I would get the boot.

The first thing I saw today when I stepped inside my apartment was the blinking light of my answering machine. There were half-a-dozen messages waiting for me. I punched "play" and listened while I made myself a baloney sandwich. All of the messages were from Vanessa Roberts's publicist, Lauren Castle. Lauren was head of publicity for Roberts's publisher, and, like most New York publicists, she seemed to think that if I wasn't busy running errands for the publishing house, I was out slopping pigs or birthing calves. This was Iowa, after all. What else would I be doing?

Publicists usually worked for a season or two, and then they disappeared, never to be heard from again. Mostly they were women in their early to mid-twenties, and when they called, they barked orders at me, wondered why I didn't have a cell phone, and told me what wonderful human beings the authors were that I would be taking care of, even when it wasn't true. Oh, most of the authors *were* lovely people (polite, gracious, funny, even apologetic), but more than a few had been terrors, like the famous Canadian author, Coop Dunfield, whose list of demands specified that he required a wooden podium for his reading (metal would not be acceptable), a 1.76-ounce tin of cinnamon-flavored Altoids (unopened), Fiji water (no other brand would be consumed), three black Sharpie Ultra Fine Points, and four moist towelettes (the kind given to patrons of Kentucky Fried Chicken for cleaning their greasy fingers). There were detailed dietary restrictions, too, and a message that I was to relay to the bookstore: Mr. Dunfield would not be signing any books after his event.

Dunfield wasn't the only pain in the ass. Another was Kit Austin, who had written one acclaimed short story collection followed by a lame, uninspired novel. I sometimes made small talk with the author to pass the time ("Read any good books lately?" "Are you at the beginning or the end of your tour?"), but whatever I happened to say to Ms. Austin, she countered with a combative comment: "Define *good*," or "What difference does it make if I'm at the beginning or the end of my book tour?" I was prepared to dump Ms. Austin off at her hotel with directions on how she could find the bookstore on her own (it was only a two-block walk from where she was staying) when she requested that I join her for dinner. ("I wouldn't know where to eat around here," she said. "Meet me at 5:30.") What I learned about Ms. Austin was that her editor had hated her new book, had even tried talking her out of publishing it ("She thought it would kill my career"), but then, finally, relented. The initial deluge of reviews was indeed bad, some of the worst I'd ever seen, but then Janet Maslin weighed in with a glowing review in *The New York Times*. Austin stabbed her rare rib eye, sawed off a hunk, lifted it to her gaping maw, and said, "I guess I knew what I was doing after all." She popped the steak into her mouth, chewed, and said, "Have you read the book?"

"Which book?" I asked.

"My new one. The novel."

"Oh. Not yet. No."

She nodded, clearly disappointed. "Well, I'd be interested in knowing what you think when you read it. I mean, Janet Maslin loved it. Janet fucking Maslin of *The New York* fucking *Times*." She swallowed, coughed, turned red, lifted the napkin up to her mouth, coughed out whatever she was chewing, took a long swig of wine, and sawed off another slab of meat. "Yeah, I guess I knew what I was doing after all," she repeated.

And so it went: For every half-dozen decent authors, I would get saddled with a real piece of work. I rolled with it, though. What else could I do?

Today's messages from publicist Lauren Castle began with her wondering if the plane had come in on time and if everything was going all right, but by the third message, she wondered what was wrong with my car.

"Vanessa thinks you're lying to her," she said. "She thinks you don't even have a muffler."

By the fifth message, Lauren was pleading with me to call her.

"Are you there? Why won't you pick up the phone? Vanessa told me she had you run an errand an hour ago. I don't understand. How could you not be home by now? Call me the second you hear this."

While the answering machine beeped one last time, letting me know that the last message was over, the phone started ringing. I picked up.

"Hello?"

"Where have you been?" demanded Lauren.

"I just got home," I said. "I'm making myself a baloney sandwich."

"Why didn't you call me? Never mind. Listen. What's wrong with your car? Do you have time to get it fixed? Are there service stations where you live?"

"Service stations?" I said. "What are those?"

"Are you making fun of me?" Lauren asked. "Forget it. I want you to get your car fixed before you take her anywhere else. Can you do that?"

"Well," I said, "there's a little problem." I took a bite of my sandwich. "Ms. Roberts had me run an errand, and I had to write a check for two hundred and sixteen dollars, and now I'm broke. I was actually just about to call *you*."

"Whoa!" Lauren said. "Back up. Call *me*? Explain."

"She told me to bill you," I said.

"Bill us? For what?"

"A breast pump."

"Did I just hear what I think I heard? Did you just say a *breast pump*?"

"She lost hers," I said.

"Well, then," Lauren said. "I hate to be the bearer of bad news, but that's between you and her. We don't reimburse for breast pumps. Sorry."

"It's for her baby," I said.

"Hey. I don't care if it's for her pet monkey. We have a strict policy here for what we can and cannot reimburse for. Number one, top of the list—you want to guess what it is?"

"Hookers?"

"Nope. We'll reimburse for hookers. Guess again."

"Breast pumps?"

"Bingo," Lauren said. "Get the money from her, and then get your car fixed. Are we on the same page?"

"The same paragraph," I said.

"Good," she said, and hung up.

FOUND MY SECOND author at baggage claim, waiting for me.

"Tate Rinehart? Oh, hey, sorry I'm late."

Tate said nothing. Bored, maybe perturbed, he stood and cracked his knuckles, one hand and then the other. Then he grabbed hold of his head and twisted it one way, popping something in his neck, and then twisted it the other. His only luggage was a messenger bag strapped over his shoulder.

"This way," I said, leading him out of the airport and into the parking lot.

I'd had my fill of Tate Rineharts: all of them guys from New York, early thirties, black plastic–framed glasses, black T-shirts, torn jeans. They were often finalists for, or winners of, National Book or National Book Critics Circle Awards, frequent contributors to *The New Yorker* and *Harper's*, their bored expressions gracing the covers of *Poets & Writers*, their enthusiasm for camp culture well-documented, their own writing often experimental and gratuitously gloomy but penetrable.

I hated these fuckers. I'll admit it. I hated all of them. But maybe I hated them because I'd had a shot at becoming one of them but had blown it. Or maybe I hated them because they were worthy of being hated. It was hard to say, really.

I relished the fact that Tate had underdressed for the Iowa weather, and when we stepped outside, he quickly zipped up his vintage service station jacket, the name Leroy stitched in red inside an oval over his heart. The jacket was too thin, and I swore I heard him whimper.

"Almost there," I said, though I'd had to park, out of necessity, at the far end of an aisle.

Inside my car, Tate flipped open his cell phone and speed-dialed a number, but as soon as I started the engine and the car began to roar, Tate cut his eyes toward me and shut his phone.

"Muffler fell off this morning," I said. "And then a semi ran over it."

"Hm," Tate said.

Halfway to Iowa City, Tate said, "Is there any way to quiet this car? I need to call a friend of mine who lives in town. Vince Belecheck?"

"I know Vince," I said.

"Really?"

"Yeah, we were classmates together."

"Undergrads?"

"No. The Workshop."

Tate was sizing me up now. I could see, out the corner of my eye, the two skinny rectangles of his lenses facing me.

"You were in the Workshop," he said matter-of-factly. "So you're a writer?"

I nodded. I knew better than to go there, but the hook was waiting for me—or, more precisely, for my ego.

"I've been working on a novel," I said, but before he could write me off as "one of them," I quickly added, "I had a story in *The New Yorker*. Got picked up in *Best American*." I shrugged. "But it's the novel I've been focusing on."

I looked over and saw that he was smiling. I was no longer simply his escort. I was a writer. The real deal. I had validated myself. And yet

I hated him even more now. The awful thing was, I *wanted* him to like me. I *wanted* his respect. That was the sick part of it all.

"So you're friends with Vince!" he said.

I hadn't said that we were friends—what I'd said was that I knew him and that we had been classmates—but I nodded anyway. Vince Belecheck was one of the trust-funders who pretended he'd come from a blue-collar background, going so far as to wear old plaid work shirts from Goodwill and a pair of well-worn brown leather Danner work boots, the kind no actual blue-collar worker I knew growing up could ever have afforded. This was all part of the Belecheck myth, you see, that he was the child of laborers and that he himself had kicked around in a series of day-labor jobs after college until he'd applied to the Workshop. His characters were foul-mouthed roofers and hard-drinking bricklayers, whereas Belecheck's own parents were university professors and Belecheck himself drove a Jaguar with a vanity license plate advertising his best-known novel: STEELTOE.

"What did you say your name was?" Tate asked.

"Jack Sheahan," I told him. "Jack Hercules Sheahan is what I publish under."

Tate said, "And when were you in *The New Yorker*?"

"Oh, it's been awhile," I said. "Maybe I should have written a few more stories, made more of a name for myself, but the novel . . ." I looked longingly through the windshield, as though the pages of my novel were speared atop a hood ornament. "The novel kept calling to me."

Tate said, "You gotta go where the muse calls you. I'm the same way."

"Really," I said.

"Absolutely," Tate said. "What's the name of your story? The one in *The New Yorker*?"

Each time he said "*The New Yorker*," I felt compelled to reach over and slap him. I could tell he loved saying it. Tate Rinehart had published there at least a half-dozen times, but he'd also won *Paris Review*'s Aga Khan Prize and done a fashion shoot for *Esquire*'s literary issue, in which he wore a sand-colored tweed jacket with matching tweed pants while two scantily dressed "librarians" helped him locate a book.

"'The Self-Adhesive Postage Stamp,'" I answered. "But it was years ago."

"No, wait; wait," he said. "I remember that story. I do." And then he told me the plot, point by point, just to make sure that he was indeed remembering the correct story. "Is that the one?"

"The very one," I said.

"Yes, I remember it," he said.

And then he fell silent. He had remembered the story so vividly— in fact, he remembered the story better than I remembered it, recalling details that I had long forgotten—that I assumed he would follow up with a compliment. I didn't expect him to *gush*; I wasn't even expecting more than a kind word or two; but, no, the fact that he remembered it had been duly noted, so the discussion of my story was over.

The temperature had already dropped a good ten degrees since morning, and now the sky, never particularly colorful in Iowa in December, had turned to slate. Tate pulled out an advance review copy of Vince Belecheck's forthcoming novel, *Where the Nail Goes*, and read it for the rest of the drive. Every few miles, Tate offered a grunt of satisfaction. I had read Belecheck's early books and found them all to be not only patronizing but poorly written. In the one workshop we'd taken together, his similes were overworked ("like the stripe on a skunk after a car had run over it at sixty miles per hour") and his language weirdly redundant, as if to convey some kind of gravity that the content lacked

("Freddie Johnson rolled the round ball back and forth in the flat palm of his hand"). But what did I know? Belecheck had since been published in every major magazine and anthology, and he'd won nearly every major award, short of a MacArthur "Genius" Grant, which I was sure he felt he deserved. Part of the Belecheck shtick was that the "establishment" overlooked poor schlubs like him, your "working stiffs," your "everymans."

"Here we are," I said, pulling into the hotel's semicircle for the second time that day. "Your reading's tomorrow, right?"

"Right, but . . ."

"But?"

"But I may need you to drive me around tonight. You can do that, can't you?"

I wanted to remind him that Iowa City, not unlike New York, had taxi service, but I needed the money.

"I have another author in town," I said, "but as soon as I'm done with her, I'll be available."

"Who's the author?"

"Vanessa Roberts?"

Tate's face lit up. "*The Outhouse*! Oh my God, what a book. Have you read it?"

I shook my head. I didn't tell him that I had skimmed it looking for the dirty parts.

"An *amazing* book," Tate said. "Scary, honest, sad." He wagged his head and said, "Human."

"Human," I repeated flatly. "I can't wait."

Tate said, "Tell you what. I'll meet you at Vanessa's reading tonight, and we can take it from there. Maybe she'll even want to go out with us."

"She brought her baby along," I said.

"Of course she did," Tate said, thinking about it. "Naturally she would be a protective mother, given all that she's gone through."

"That's what I was thinking," I said.

"I'll see you tonight, then," Tate said. "At the reading."

"Tonight. Will do."

I T WASN'T UNTIL after I had gone back to my apartment for a nap that I remembered that I was supposed to ask Vanessa to write me a check for the breast pump. I should have taken care of it when I dropped Tate off at the hotel. I could have driven to my bank, cashed the check, and brought my car to House of Mufflers, but I was already beat.

The answering machine was blinking again when I got home, probably with another half-dozen messages from Lauren Castle, so I unplugged the phone. For reasons I couldn't articulate, I kept every phone book I'd owned since living in this apartment, one for each year. I sometimes flipped through the oldest one, startled by restaurants, now long gone, that I had completely forgotten about, or the dog-eared pages with asterisks scribbled next to old friends who had either moved on or died. The oldest phone book was a document of a city that no longer existed, an ever-increasing graveyard of people and places. And yet here I was, still chugging along.

At the bottom of the pile of phone books was a manuscript box. Inside was my never-completed novel. I slipped it out. I hadn't looked at it in seven years, hadn't added a word to it in ten. I carried it over to my sofa, sat down, and blew dust off the lid. I had written the title along the side of the box with a thick black Sharpie, the way they do at publishing houses and literary agencies: AFTER THE FALL. Granted, it wasn't the most original title. Only later, after I was well into writing the novel, did a woman at a bar inform me that it was the title of an Arthur Miller play.

"It's just a working title," I told her. "Plus, titles aren't copyrightable. I could name it *Moby Dick*, if I wanted. Or *The World According to Garp*."

"You couldn't name it *The World According to Garp*," she told me. "You'd get sued."

"No, I wouldn't. John Irving can't copyright that title."

"Are you crazy?" she asked me. We were both drunk, and, until then, I had been hoping to go home with her, but a dark mood descended upon us, and I could tell, by her cross look, that she was more likely to slap me across the face than go to bed with me.

"Fuck it," I said. "You know what? I'm going to call it *The World According to Garp*. Just to prove my point."

"Good," she said, gathering her stuff from the bar—cigarettes, lighter, change, lip gloss. "I hope John Irving comes over to your house and kicks your sorry ass."

"I'd like to see him try," I said.

She sneered at me and shook her head. "You wouldn't have a chance," she said. "He was a *wrestler*. A goddamned *wrestler*."

"Oh," I said, feigning fear. "A *wrestler*!" I laughed wildly and said, "I'm scared now. I'm quaking in my boots."

She reached over and snatched the book I'd been reading before she came in—the Black Sparrow Press edition of Paul Bowles's stories—and started tearing pages out of it.

"What the fuck are you doing?" I asked.

She ripped out several pages at a time and threw the book at my head. I ducked, and the book hit the man sitting next to me, an alcoholic carpet-installer named Bobby T.

"You son of a bitch," Bobby T. said.

"It wasn't me," I said. "It was *her*." I pointed at the woman I'd only a few minutes ago been trying to imagine naked.

Bobby T. narrowed his eyes at the woman standing behind me and then cut his eyes back at me. "Writers," he said. "I wish you'd all just die."

I tossed a few dollars from my pile of bills at the bartender and gestured with my head toward Bobby T. A free drink would smooth away any trouble between us. And it did. I finished the night sitting next to Bobby T., straightening out the torn pages from Paul Bowles's stories, returning them to the place in the book where they belonged.

A few weeks later, I met Alice. Three years after that, I was alone again—and have remained alone ever since.

I lifted the lid to the box and pulled out my manuscript. The dot matrix print and the continuous-feed paper, with its fuzzy perforated edges where I had torn away sprocket-holed sides and then separated one page from the next, all made the novel itself seem dated, even before I read the first word. The pages themselves were actually starting to turn yellow.

"Jesus," I said, and I caught my breath, surprised by the welling up of what I'd assumed were long-snuffed emotions. I might as well have opened up the carton holding the cremated remains of a beloved pet. All the longing to become a writer that I had once felt, all the promise I was told I'd had, came bubbling back to the surface at the sight of my manuscript. "Goddamn it," I said. I had opened the box to read over what I'd written, but now I couldn't do it. I shut the box and tossed it onto the coffee table, then reclined on the couch and closed my eyes, falling into a deep and troubled midday sleep.

PART TWO

The writer should remind himself of how his writing went when he first began:
torturous labor and revision and gradual improvement, and first drafts at least as bad
as the ones he faces now—except that in those days he saw the faults less clearly,
felt more excited by the possibilities, and was tricked by the exhilaration of a new love.

—JOHN GARDNER

H ERCULES IS MY real middle name, though I wasn't named after the son of Zeus, as you might think. Hercules is a city on San Pablo Bay, located between San Francisco and Napa, where my father knocked up my mother.

One summer, when I was nine, before I knew that I had been named after the city in which I had been conceived, my parents planned a trip from Minneapolis, where we lived, to Hercules. It was a big deal to me, this trip. My friends were always going away on vacations. They would come home wearing Mickey Mouse ears or carrying chunks of meteorites from Arizona, their parents suntanned and smiling, but the only trips we ever went on were to the Wisconsin Dells, a few hours to the east, or to the Amana Colonies in Iowa, a few hours to the south. My notion of what a family vacation should have been was based primarily on a short eight-millimeter movie my parents owned. It was a travelogue that featured families driving through tunnels cut out of the trunks of sequoias, brown bears walking right up to their cars and patting their hoods, and couples spreading out elaborate picnics within sight of Niagara Falls.

The first indication that our vacation would not be anything like the one in the movie was when my father realized he'd been using a map so old that one of the roads we were on had been closed for years. I was in the backseat, counting cows and making a list of license plates from states other than Minnesota, when my father pulled over and said to my mother, "Let me see that map again."

My mother, who had been reading a romance novel until she started feeling carsick, opened the glove compartment and retrieved the map.

My father said, "Don't we have one that's newer than this one?"

Mom said, "Don't yell, Gus."

"I'm not yelling," my father said, raising his voice. "I'm *asking*."

"This is the only map of Iowa in here," Mom said.

"Okay then," Dad said. "That's all I needed to know."

By the time we reached the Nebraska state line, I had seen cars with license plates from Kansas, Illinois, Iowa, Nebraska, Wisconsin, and Missouri. I had also seen one lonesome soul from Alaska. I had never seen an Alaska license plate before and couldn't help bouncing up out of my seat and pointing toward the speeding car.

"Look!" I yelled. "Alaska!"

"Keep it down back there," Dad said.

Mom shot my father a look, then twisted around in her seat and said, "That's exciting, honey. Now, write it down."

Later that night, the temperature dropped, and rain pounded our car. Eventually, the rain turned to ice pellets. I kept thinking we were going to stop at a motel for the night, but my father didn't like to talk about his plans, and my mother sometimes didn't know what my father had in mind.

When he finally took an exit ramp in Nebraska for a city named Cozad, my father yelled, "Hold on!" Even as my father spoke, the car slipped off the ramp and into the ditch, landing on its side. My head bounced off the window; my father fell on top of my mother. She let out a soft "oof" as if the air had been knocked out of her, and then she made a moan that scared me until it ended with the word *shit*.

"Everyone okay?" my father asked.

"Sure," I said.

"I guess," Mom said. "What the hell happened?"

"Ice," Dad said. He stood on the passenger-side window and, his feet straddling Mom, opened the driver's-side door, as if it were a hatch. The glass shattered under his weight. "Great," he said. To Mom, he said, "Don't cut yourself. That's the last thing we need." He hoisted himself up and out of the car and then helped my mother out. Finally, it was my turn. "Careful," he said. "It's slick." He pulled me out by one arm, yanking it in such a way that caused it to hurt worse than any pain incurred by the actual car accident, but I didn't say anything.

Dad popped the trunk, which was sideways, and two suitcases fell out. Dad picked up both suitcases and started walking. Pellets of ice hit us, so we walked up the exit ramp with our heads facing down. At the top of the ramp was a sign for a motel: 4.3 MILES, the sign read, with an arrow pointing to the right.

"I can't walk that far," Mom whined.

"Quiet," Dad said. "Just keep on the grass. The road's too slick."

"Don't talk to me that way," Mom said. "You're not my boss."

Dad stopped walking. He looked at me then at Mom. "Let's not start in here, okay? Not here. Not now." He turned around and continued walking. I waited to see what Mom was going to do, and when she started following him, I fell in line, trailing a few steps behind her.

It took us over an hour to reach the Do Drop Inn—a horseshoe-shaped motel with a neon sign of a horse rearing up on two legs. The night clerk at the Do Drop was an old woman who had been sleeping in a bed in the small room off to the side until we'd rung the bell and woken her. While my father filled out the form, the woman lit a cigarette, flicking ashes into an ashtray the shape of Nebraska.

"Make of car right here," she said, tapping the form with a red-painted nail.

"It's in a ditch," Dad said. "We walked here."

Mom and I were starting to shiver, and the old woman nodded. She'd heard worse stories.

We slept that night in a single bed, the three of us together. I slept between my mother and my father, the only time I could remember doing so. The next morning, while my father was out trying to find a service station, my mother took the longest shower I'd ever heard her take. The entire room filled with steam. On one of the windows, I started writing what would be my first short story. It began, "The old man from Alaska found a bear standing in the middle of the road." Standing on a chair, I filled all three windows with words, starting at the top of each one and writing all the way down to the bottom, and when I finished, I shut the curtains so that I could surprise Mom. When Mom finally came out of the bathroom wearing only a towel, I slowly opened the curtains, like a stagehand revealing the opening act of a play, but the words had already fogged back over. You could sort of see the words, but mostly you couldn't. For all practical purposes, my entire story had disappeared. I tried telling my mother what I had written, but the story didn't seem the same. I kept forgetting words and images, and by the time I finished telling her what I could remember, I felt like weeping.

"Now, now," she said. "Don't worry. You'll see another car from Alaska. You will," she insisted. I tried explaining to her that I wasn't sad about the car from Alaska, but before I could finish, Mom said, "Look," and pointed out the window at the tow truck pulling our car. My father was in the passenger seat of the truck, talking to the driver.

"Could you do me a favor, Jack?" Mom asked. "Could you turn around until I say so?"

I did what she asked. I turned around, but there was a mirror in front of me now, and in that mirror I saw the back of Mom and, through the window, Dad sitting in the tow truck. When the tow truck driver wasn't looking, my mother opened up her towel and did a little dance, and then she quickly shut the towel. My father smiled. The tow truck driver, looking up again, saw nothing.

"Okay, sweetie," my mom said. "You can turn back around now. Turn around and wave at Daddy."

I turned around and waved. Dad winked at me. Two hours later, we were back on I-80 and heading home. A sheet of cardboard covering the broken window ripped free and blew away behind us, causing us to shiver for the rest of the drive. According to my father, we didn't have enough money to make it all the way to Hercules. In fact, we barely had enough now to make it back to Minneapolis.

"This'll have to do," he said, his teeth clacking together. He looked in the rearview mirror, smiled at me, and said, "You can tell all your friends you vacationed in Nebraska. I bet there aren't a lot of 'em who could make that claim."

My father nudged my mother, and Mom smiled, pressing herself against my father to keep warm. I didn't know what was so funny, but I smiled, too. Nebraska, I thought. And I was already imagining all the enviable things I would tell my friends—some of it true, like tipping our car over into a ditch, but most of it, like meeting the old man from Alaska who traveled the country with a retired circus bear, not.

I PEERED THROUGH THE peephole to see who had woken me by relentlessly pounding on my door. "M. Cat?" I said, quickly unlocking the door and opening it. M. Cat spent most of his days in his apartment across the hall smoking dope by the pound, and only an event of the direst consequences, such as a fire, was likely to rouse him from his sofa. His fraternity buddies had given him his nickname after he'd taken, and failed, the MCATs three times before finally giving up, but all of that was twenty years ago now. These days, M. Cat worked as a bartender at the Deadwood Tavern when he wasn't home getting baked.

"M. Cat," I said. "What the hell's going on?"

"Some chick keeps calling me asking for you," M. Cat said. "I told her she's got the wrong number, but she keeps calling and yelling for me to go and get you. This chick is wack, dude."

I followed M. Cat across the hall and into his dark, pot-reeking lair, picked up his phone, and said, "What?"

"Jack?"

"Yes, it's Jack. Who's this?"

"You know who this is," she said, and I did: It was Lauren Castle, Vanessa's publicist. "Where have you been? Why aren't you answering your phone? Do you have any idea how much trouble I went through to get this number? I finally had to call the police."

"You're crossing a line," I said, trying to remain calm.

"Maybe if you'd get a cell phone," Lauren said, "I wouldn't have to call your neighbors."

M. Cat took a long pull from his bong. Holding smoke in his lungs, making a face of calamitous pain, he reached out and offered the bong to me. I shook my head and mouthed, *No, thanks.*

"So what's so urgent?" I asked.

"Muffler fixed?"

"Yes," I lied. "Is that why you called?"

"No. Vanessa's husband phoned. He's worried about her. He's afraid she's going through postpartum depression right now."

"And?"

"And he wants you to make sure that nothing happens to the baby."

I laughed. I said, "She is *not* going through postpartum depression. Would someone going through postpartum depression have me run out and buy her a breast pump?"

M. Cat moved the bong from his mouth, squinting at me, wanting to hear the rest of the story. The combination of the words *breast* and *pump* had piqued his interest.

"I wouldn't know," Lauren said. "I hate kids. I would never be in her position in the first place."

"Vanessa's fine," I said. "The baby's fine."

"How do you know? Did you deliver the breast pump to her personally? Well? Did you?"

"No," I said. I shut my eyes. "Okay, okay, okay. I'll go back to the hotel and check on her." When I opened my eyes, M. Cat was right in front of me, waiting for me to wrap it up so that I could fill him in on what was happening.

"Actually," Lauren said. "Her husband didn't say 'postpartum depression.' What he said was 'postpartum psychosis.' Do you want to hear the symptoms?"

"Do I have to?"

"Delusions, hallucinations, sleep disturbances, and obsessive thoughts about the baby. She may also experience rapid mood swings, from depression to irritability to euphoria."

"Are you serious?" I asked.

"I Googled it," Lauren said. "Listen up. Don't let anything happen to her. Do you hear me? Vanessa Roberts has written one of the most important books of this decade."

"Have you read it?"

"No."

"I'll go to the hotel right now," I said.

"Good," Lauren said. "Call me back this time. Don't make me call the police again."

"Fine," I said. "I'll call you back." I hung up.

M. Cat, reaching up under his shirt to apply a few swipes of Speed Stick, said, "What's up with the breast pump, dude?" He hesitated. He unconsciously held the deodorant up to his mouth like a microphone. "What *is* a breast pump?" he asked.

"I'm really sorry about this," I said, "but she might call again. She's crazy." I patted him on the shoulder and returned to my apartment, reluctantly plugging my phone back in.

M OST WRITERS FLEW into town, gave a reading, signed their books, and flew out early the next morning. The majority were pleasant and unassuming. They appreciated it when I presented them with a bagel and coffee for their trip back to the airport. They never expected anything and often, when they made a modest request, asked if they were inconveniencing me. One of the perks of the job was getting a free copy of the book from the publicist, and most authors graciously signed theirs for me. "With gratitude for making this a pleasant trip" and "Thanks for the lift" were not uncommon sentiments.

But then there were those writers whose personal lives I knew too intimately. A best-selling novelist who wrote books that tapped into the mass consciousness of whatever year the book was being published needed me to run out and get him some Imodium AD as quickly as possible for what he described as "the worst fucking diarrhea I've ever experienced." Throughout his entire reading, to an audience of over five hundred, I was the only one in the room, other than the author himself, who knew that the man's stomach was a bubbling volcano waiting to blow.

Lucy Rogan, a romance writer doing a book signing in Cedar Rapids (my one and only romance writer during all my years as a media escort, and the only writer I ever took to a bookstore that wasn't located in

Iowa City), asked me on our way to the event if I had any children—a segue, it soon became clear, for her to tell me about her recent miscarriage. The miscarriage then became a segue to talk about problems in her marriage: She'd married too soon; he wasn't a writer and didn't *really* understand her or—worse—didn't really care about what it was she did, as when she tried talking to him about a problem she was having with one of her plots, or how characters sometimes took on lives of their own, or how people looked down on romance writers when what she was doing, though not Shakespeare, was still a craft that took time to develop. I kept looking over at Lucy to assure her that I was listening. According to her bio, she had won several local beauty contests when she was a child, but I could see now why she didn't continue to compete or, if she did, why she didn't win—and yet it was *these*, her losing attributes, that I found the most compelling: the small puggish nose, the too-thick eyebrows, the hair that couldn't be tamed. I doubted she was even five feet tall.

She wept openly twice while talking to me during the fifteen-minute drive from the airport to the bookstore, and I was genuinely moved by her tears, so much so that I told myself that I was even going to read her novel, which featured on its cover an illustration of a brawny man with thick windswept hair and a pair of firm, muscular tits. He was clutching (rather violently, I thought) a much younger woman whose own breasts were popping out of a sheer, low-slung nightgown.

At literary events, an author who isn't a best seller would be lucky to scare up twenty-five people; in front of the bookstore in Cedar Rapids, however, a line of women trailed out the front door and all the way down the street. When I took Lucy inside, there were mountains of her books, maybe six hundred copies of a single title. Lucy's spirits were lifted at the sight of her fans—"Oh, look!" she said, brushing away tears—and once we were inside and she had settled behind her desk, pen poised to begin a day of marathon signing, she looked up at me and said, "You're a sweetheart," and squeezed my arm, even though I had said practically nothing the entire drive. I'd merely listened while guiltily fantasizing about a life in which I swept her away from her uncaring husband, carved out a life for us together in Iowa, and made fervent love to her every night: in cornfields, in haylofts, in cars parked on dusty rural highways. She was, in a word, bewitching. It was as though I had finally found someone who might understand *me*, who might even be able to offer some insight into why my own dreams to become a writer had short-circuited.

But no sooner had I gotten home and begun reading her book than I wondered what the hell I had been thinking. Her novel was full of clichés and plot contrivances, and the characters were all paper-thin. I read two chapters before tossing it aside. It wasn't so much that I was an elitist (though I probably was); it was just that my expectations had been higher, and though I knew that the romance genre was formulaic and that its main point was to fulfill its readers' expectations and not subvert them, I had hoped, after all the talk about her own struggles, to find something, *anything*, in her writing that would suggest a deeper connection between us. All I could imagine, after reading what I did, was a life in which I grew to resent her each time I drove her to a bookstore and saw all those eager fans, the same readers who would find my own work "too dark" or "too depressing" or "filthy" because I'd used the word *fuck* one too many times, even as they read books that glorified rape and treated women like inflatable dolls.

This was what I'd told myself—that is, until the next day when I picked Lucy up from her hotel to take her back to the airport, and I fell under her spell all over again. Inside the airport, she hugged me goodbye—a long, deep hug. Afterward, I stood there watching as she passed through security and disappeared amid the other midday travelers.

Her books were best sellers now, and there was never any mention of her husband in her bio. Each time she published a new book, I picked it up and stared longingly at the author photo, wondering if, like one of her bronzed and well-endowed heroes, I should have grabbed her before she passed through Cedar Rapids Airport security, spun her around, and carried her back to my Corolla.

Having returned to the Sheraton, I asked the woman now working the front desk to please connect me to Vanessa Roberts's room. She typed something on her keyboard, examined her screen, then typed something else.

"Vanessa Roberts?" she asked.

"Yes. She checked in this morning. An early check-in."

The woman typed away. The more the keys clattered, the hollower my stomach felt. She finally looked up and said, "I'm sorry, but she checked out an hour ago."

"That can't be right," I said.

The woman nodded sympathetically and said, "No, I'm sorry, unfortunately it is right. She checked out."

"Do you know *who* checked her out?"

"It wasn't me." She studied the computer screen, then said, "Charlie, come here."

Charlie, with his shaggy hair and sad little goatee, looked like a beatnik, as did a lot of guys in Iowa City who were Charlie's age— twenty-two, twenty-three, done with college but not sure what to do or where to go.

"Did you check out a Vanessa Roberts?" the woman asked Charlie.

Charlie said, "She have a baby?"

"Yes," I said.

"Yeah, I checked her out then." Charlie studied me a moment then asked, "Is there a problem?"

"Yeah, there is," I said. "I'm her escort." When Charlie's eyebrows raised, I said, "*Media* escort."

Charlie smiled and said, "I was gonna say, dude, you don't want to go announcing that in here." When I didn't return his smile, he said, "Yeah, she and the kid checked out. There was a bag back here waiting for her. For confidentiality reasons, I can't tell you what was inside, but she took it out of the bag and tucked it under her arm."

"Did she say where she was going?"

"Uh, no. Why would she do that?"

"Did she take a cab?"

"I didn't look. Typically, we don't follow our customers out the door."

"I'm sorry, but are you getting smart with me?" I asked.

"I'm just saying . . ." Charlie said. He drummed his fingers. That's when I saw the prison tats across his knuckles and realized I had seriously miscalculated who I was dealing with. One set of knuckles spelled LIFE, the other, DETH. I wanted to ask him how he had managed to get a job with tattooed knuckles, not to mention the rather egregious misspelling, but he was already making his way around the front desk to confront me face to face. "These questions," he said. "I'm not sure you have a right to ask me. Do you have a badge or something? Oh, no, wait. You're an *escort*."

There are times when you know intuitively that it's in everyone's best interest to back off, and this exchange was almost certainly one of them. I'd seen it too often in bars, two men talking shit, the ante upped too quickly, everyone puffing up, and then a moment of eerie calm before someone throws a punch. These were explosive fights in which anything at hand became a weapon (beer bottles, pool cues, a dartboard), people ended up in the hospital or behind bars, half the furniture became next day's kindling. Usually, innocent patrons ended up injured, sometimes from a thrown shot glass, though more likely from the losing pugilist tumbling into them, knocking them off a high stool. And so I saw this moment in the Sheraton for what it was: a fight, barely dormant, waiting for the first jab. And I wasn't going to throw it.

"Thank you!" I said. I backed up, grinning. My teeth were pressed so hard together they squeaked. I was probably pumping my fists, too, but no matter: I was leaving. Everything would be fine.

I needed to make a few calls, but, as Lauren Castle had pointed out on numerous occasions, I didn't own a cell phone. And as I had discovered recently while trying to call Lauren collect from the airport to inform her of a canceled flight, most pay phones didn't work anymore.

"Shit," I said, standing outside, cinching my coat tighter. The wind had picked up; clouds churned overhead. For lack of a better plan, I walked over to the bookstore to give them a heads-up that tonight's literary luminary might not be showing up for her book signing after all, but once I arrived at the store and stared in at the elaborate window display of Vanessa's book, I changed my mind. What if she had merely checked into a different hotel? What if I inadvertently set off a manhunt for a woman who wanted only better room service?

I slipped next door to Mickey's, one of Iowa City's many overpriced restaurants, and slid into a booth near the back. After ordering my food, I slumped down and spaced out. Back when I still believed that I was a writer, I spent all my time watching people. I used to bring a notepad with me, jotting down random details, like "crushed fedora," "gimpy leg," or "the forgotten dab of mustard on her chin." These days, I merely stared ahead, into space, until my focus blurred.

"Jack?"

I looked up. It was Alice, my ex-fiancée, and she was covered in large snowflakes. Before today, I hadn't seen her in years, and now I was seeing her everywhere I went.

"Alice!" I said. "It's snowing?"

"You'd be surprised," she said. She started taking off her coat but paused to ask if I was expecting anyone. When I told her that I wasn't, she continued slipping out of it. And then she joined me. "Jack, I'm sorry about this morning. I kind of freaked out. When I saw what you were buying, I thought . . ."

"That it was for *me*?"

"Not *you*, per se. Your *wife*. Thinking that you were married and I didn't know about it just . . . well, it kind of freaked me out a little."

My *wife*. I smiled.

Alice said, "But then I remembered your job. The whole escort thing. And then I realized what you were trying to tell me. And then I Googled what's-her-name."

"Vanessa Roberts?"

Alice nodded. "I saw that she was married and had a baby. And that she was on a book tour." She looked like she wanted to say something else.

"What?" I asked.

"Oh, nothing. I guess I just started feeling guilty. I mean, here I am feeling shitty that you might be married, and yet—"

"What?"

Alice shook her head. Whatever she was about to tell me, she had decided not to. I didn't press. She said, "That book. It looks *terrible*." She made a face and shivered.

"It is," I said. "I mean, I haven't actually *read* it yet, but I can just imagine."

Alice said, "The publisher says it's a memoir in the same league as Richard Wright's *Black Boy* or Elie Wiesel's *Night*. Who writes this garbage?"

"The author, usually," I said. "Or the author's editor."

"*The Outhouse!*" Alice said and harrumphed. "What a load of crap."

I smiled. This was the Alice I had fallen in love with, a woman who cut quickly through bone and gristle, pulled out the still-pumping heart, and held it up for everyone to see.

"*The Outhouse* indeed," I said. I was cheered that Alice had sought me out, so I asked, "How did you find me?"

"I didn't," she said. "I came in to grab a bite to eat and saw you sitting here. You looked so sad."

"Really? I did?" I smiled to prove her otherwise. "I'm fine," I said. "No worries. Just a long day."

When the waitress took Alice's order, I asked for another draw of Bud.

"I'll take one, too," Alice said. And it was like old times again, the two of us meeting at Mickey's for dinner, settling in for the day's gossip over ice-cold beer. I ordered four more Buds over the course of the afternoon. To my surprise, Alice matched me mug for mug. When we paid up and stepped outside, I helped her on with her jacket. The flakes of falling snow were preposterously large and sticking to every surface, including my face.

"Oh, damn it," she said. "I'm parked all the way across the river."

"My car's just over here," I said, pointing to the hotel. "In the parking garage. Want a lift?"

It was less than an hour now before Vanessa's event. I peeked into the bookstore's window, but I had a good buzz going, and my eye was easily distracted. Instead of Vanessa Roberts, I saw Tate Rinehart standing near the front table of new releases, reading a copy of his own book. When he looked up, I smiled at him and he smiled back, but then his brow furrowed and he cocked his head. He'd recognized me, or, more likely, *thought* he'd recognized me but couldn't quite remember who I was, despite the two of us having spent thirty minutes together only a few hours earlier.

In the parking garage, Alice and I were forced to walk up one ramp and then another instead of taking the stairs, like civilized humans, since I had foolishly forgotten where I'd parked.

"Click the button to unlock your doors," she said. "Maybe you'll hear it beep."

"The locks are manual."

In a voice that was more playful than critical, she asked, "Are you still driving that old Toyota?"

"Yup," I said. "Only 155,000 miles on it."

"Good God!"

"And there it is!" I wheezed, pointing.

Inside the car, I shoved my key into the ignition, but instead of starting the car, I turned and caught Alice staring at me.

"What?" I said, smiling.

"What?" she repeated.

It wasn't, I supposed, the best place to rekindle a romance, but I knew if I didn't do something right then, I might not get another chance. I leaned over the emergency brake and kissed Alice, and Alice kissed me back.

"Who'd have thought this morning," I said, "that we'd be here now doing this?"

"Shhhh," she said, unzipping my coat. "No talking."

"It's cold in here," I said.

"Start the car."

"And these bucket seats," I said. "They're not very—what's the word—*conducive*."

"We'll use the backseat," she said.

"Well, look at you," I said. "Xavier Hollander."

"Who?"

"No one," I said.

"Just get the heater going," she said.

And I did. We slipped into the backseat and, with our pants pulled either partway down or entirely off, and with buttons and clasps and zippers manipulated by cold, stiff fingers, we somehow managed, in such cramped and unkempt quarters, to engage in a kind of sex more appropriate for couples half our age: teenagers with no place to go and not entirely sure what they're doing, confused by both the complexities and realities of anatomy. We weren't confused so much as we were tipsy, and Alice had to whisper, "No, no, not there" and "Are you still inside me?" more times than I would have liked, and on two occasions Alice stepped down hard onto something sharp on my floorboard. "Ouch!" she yelled the first time. "I think I cut my toe on a bottle cap," and then, a few minutes later, "Is it possible you have a cheese grater back here?" "It's possible," I said, remembering that I had bought one at Target a month earlier but couldn't find it when I had gotten home and unpacked my purchases. I had even called the store manager to complain. And now here it was, slicing my ex-fiancée's foot as she tried positioning herself for better leverage.

When we were done and lying across the Toyota's backseat (designed, I was fairly certain, without two overdressed Iowa lovers in mind), Alice whispered into my ear, "My big toe is throbbing."

"I would imagine," I said, catching my breath. "Are you bleeding?"

"Maybe," she said. She crossed her leg and examined her foot. "Yes," she said, "I'm bleeding."

"Oh," I said, but neither of us took any action. I worried that the reason we were so lethargic wasn't because of the sex but because deadly blue-gray exhaust had been seeping through a crack in the floorboard and we were now starting to asphyxiate—but then Alice sat bolt-upright and said, "Whew! That was refreshing." She clasped her bra and buttoned her blouse. "Wait a minute. Aren't you escorting today? Didn't you need to bring what's-her-name to the bookstore? It's already past seven."

"Oh, yeah, I didn't tell you," I said. "She checked out of her hotel."

"Really?" Alice said. "Where did she go?"

"I dunno," I said.

"Oh well," Alice said, pulling up her underwear. "You can write your own memoir now. Call it *The Backseat*."

"Get this," I said, and I told her about Vanessa Roberts's husband calling the publicist, worried that his wife was suffering from postpartum psychosis. "Do you believe that shit?" I said.

Alice stopped putting on her shoes and raised up. "And you don't know where she is?"

"Not a clue!" I said, smiling. But even as I said this, I realized that these were simple dots to connect, and that I had been less than diligent, especially since I hadn't even called Lauren back to tell her that Vanessa had checked out of the hotel.

"And you think this is *funny*?" Alice asked. "I mean, she has her baby with her, right?"

"Yeah, but . . ."

"No," Alice said, putting up her hand. She didn't want to hear any more. "This woman's probably in trouble, God only knows what kind of danger that poor baby is in, and here we are screwing in the backseat of your car."

"Well, for starters, we're not really screwing right this second," I clarified.

Alice finished getting dressed, opened the door, and flung herself up and out of the Toyota. I had expected the passenger door to open and for Alice to slide back inside so that I could drive her across the river to her own car, but she was already halfway down the parking garage ramp when I opened my door and climbed out.

"Hey!" I yelled. "Don't you need a ride?"

Alice kept walking. I got back into my car, slammed the door, and backed out of the space, hoping to catch up with her, but by the time I rounded the corner, Alice had either ducked into a stairwell or disappeared into thin air. She was nowhere to be seen.

LEFT MY CAR in the parking garage and trudged back to the bookstore. Snow was already ankle-deep, and college students, usually sidled up to a bar by now, were outside playing in it. A few hard-packed snowballs whizzed past my head. Whether or not I was their target, I couldn't tell.

There are few pleasures quite like walking into an independent bookstore on a snowy evening, and tonight was no exception. Once inside, I stomped my feet and said hello to Eileen, who was working the cash register and had been an employee there before I was a student at the Workshop. Other fellow night travelers had come in from the snow, wearing knit caps and scarves, their gloves tucked into their pockets as they perused the latest New York publishing had to offer. Here we were, all lovers of literature, gathered together on a night straight out of a Dickens novel. I half-hoped to look out the window and see Tiny Tim atop Bob Cratchit's shoulders, but no: All I saw was an undergrad writing SUCK ME in the snow that covered somebody's car while another guy bent over and pressed his ass against the car's front door, hoping for an accurate imprint.

I climbed the stairs to where the author readings were held, but the only people up there were one of the store employees folding chairs and Tate Rinehart.

"Where is she?" Tate asked.

"I don't know," I said. "I looked everywhere."

"What do you mean, you don't know?" Tate said.

I shrugged. "She checked out of the hotel. That's all I know."

Tate's lips tightened into two worms spooning. He flipped open his cell phone and speed-dialed a number. "Vince? Yeah, Tate. Listen, the reading was canceled. Yeah, I don't know what happened. I'm here with someone you know, though." Tate looked up at me. "What's your name again?"

"Jack Sheahan," I said.

"Jack Sheahan?" Tate said into the phone. "She? *Han?* Says you two were in the Workshop together? Yeah, well, anyway . . . he's my escort, so tell me where we should meet, and he can take me there. Sounds good, brother. See you shortly." He closed the cell phone and said, "You know George's?"

I nodded. Of course I knew George's.

Tate picked up his canvas messenger bag and slipped it over his shoulder. "Vince is meeting us there," Tate said. "I hope you don't mind hanging out with us tonight. It'll probably be just a drink or two, and then you can take me back to the hotel. Sound good?"

"Sounds great," I said. "But I need to make a call first."

I walked behind the abandoned information desk, picked up the phone as though I worked there, and called my neighbor, M. Cat.

"Yo," M. Cat said, picking up before the phone could even ring on my end.

"M. Cat? It's Jack."

"Jack who?"

"Your neighbor."

"Dude," he said. "*Dude!* That lady—the one from New York—she's been calling here every fifteen minutes looking for you. Apparently, that chick you're in charge of checked out of her hotel, and now this crazy chick—the one from New York—is fucking *pissed*, dude. She is *pissed*."

"All right, all right," I said. "Easy. I *know* she checked out."

"Do you have any idea just how *pissed* this insane New York chick is?" M. Cat asked. "She wants to string you up by your *cojones*. And for a chick, she swears a lot. You need to call her cell. You got a pen? You got some paper?"

"Listen. I'm not calling her," I said. "But I need your help. There's two hundred bucks in it for you."

"Two hundred?" I heard M. Cat take a long hit on his bong. In a high-pitched voice still full of smoke, M. Cat said, "Do tell."

What I told him was that I needed him to find Vanessa Roberts. I needed him to call all the hotels and motels, and once he found her, he would have to drive out there to make sure that she was okay. If need be, he should spend the night in the lobby to make sure she didn't go anywhere she shouldn't be going.

"Now here's the thing," I said. "According to Lauren"—I cleared my throat—"you know, the crazy New York chick Vanessa, may be experiencing postpartum psychosis. Do you want to hear the symptoms?"

M. Cat said, "Hey, man, I almost went to medical school. I *know* what postpartum psychosis is."

"So you know how serious it is?" I asked.

M. Cat snorted. "Dude, I'm on it." Before I could ask him to keep me updated via my answering machine, he hung up.

I turned to Tate, who was holding a recently reissued Stanislaw Lem novel that he'd written the introduction for. "Ready?" I asked.

Tate glanced down at the book, as though expecting me to acknowledge his contribution, but when I didn't, he sighed and returned the book to the shelf.

"Okay," he said. "Let's go."

12

THE SNOW WAS coming down so hard now I put on a ski mask. Tate regarded me at first with suspicion until the onslaught of snow forced him to duck his head in order to see where he was going.

"Just follow me," I yelled into the wind as it ripped down Washington Avenue.

By the time we reached my car, Tate was shivering and knocking free the snow that had clung to his thick hair. His glasses had steamed over, but he couldn't seem to clear the fog no matter how many times he rubbed at them with his shirttail.

Inside the car, Tate leaned back and sighed. "My God," he said. "Is the weather always this bad?"

"Only in the winter," I said. "And in the summers when the tornadoes come through," I added. "Otherwise, it's pretty nice here."

Tate started sniffing. "What's that smell?" he asked.

"What smell?" I said, though I knew perfectly well what smell he meant. I smelled it, too. It was sex.

"It's . . . *familiar*," he said. "But I can't place it."

I shook my head and shrugged. "Huh!" I said. "I don't smell anything."

"Maybe you would if you took off that ski mask," he said. "Can you see well enough to drive?"

"Does a cat have nine lives?" I asked.

"No," Tate said. "It does not."

We said nothing else to each other. Each time I turned a corner after exiting the parking garage, the car fishtailed. With the ski mask on, I felt as though I were driving a getaway car. If I owned a prop gun, I could have held it up to Tate's head and pretended I'd taken him hostage.

It was unusual for an escort job to continue beyond the walk back to the hotel. When Booker Award–winning British writer Clive Darling was in town several years ago, a young woman approached him after his reading and invited him to a farmhouse on the outskirts of Iowa City for an after-hours party. When we arrived, there were only seven or eight Workshop students there and none of them had gone to Clive's reading. With the exception of the host, everyone feigned indifference to Clive's presence. When the host introduced me to the group as "Clive's keeper," Clive visibly bristled. He cleared his throat and said, "This is Mr. Jack Sheahan. He is a graduate of the Workshop. A writer. He has published in *The New Yorker*. A story of his was anthologized in *The Best American Short Stories* series. He is not my *keeper*. Please pay him the respect he deserves." The students had paused whatever it was they were doing (drinking, mostly; playing cards; poking fun at Nathan Englander's jacket photo) to listen to Clive's speech, but when he was done talking, they gave each other looks (Who the hell *is* this guy?) and returned to their activities, refusing to acknowledge either of us for the remainder of our time there.

Clive and I stood in a small kitchen and drank two beers each. The kitchen was full of appliances from the 1940s and 1950s, most notably a colossal stove that required a match for lighting the oven and a too-small refrigerator decorated with literary magazine rejection letters with comments like, "We liked this one but couldn't find room this issue" and "This one too violent—try again?"

Clive was one of the few writers I'd escorted who had asked me what it was I did besides escort writers, and I was so grateful for his interest that I'd unloaded a complete curriculum vitae, even as Clive stifled several yawns. I was happy nonetheless. Clive had put the little bastards in their place. "Thanks for what you said in there," I said as we stood together, finishing our beers. Clive, still miffed, pursed his lips and wagged his head.

Before we left, Clive disappeared into a bedroom, presumably to retrieve his coat. When he came out without a coat, I remembered that he hadn't brought one, and I suspected that he had remembered this, too, while digging through others' coats—but this proved not to be the case. "I jimmy riddled all over their stuff," he told me on our drive back to the hotel. When I asked him what he meant, he said, "I piddled on their bed, in their closet, and across their bureau." "You *pissed* all over their stuff?" I asked. Clive nodded, then pointed to a semi pulling out in front of me. "Mind the truck," he said, and I braked too hard, leaving a trail of black rubber across the asphalt.

"Have you ever read Clive Darling?" I asked Tate now through my ski mask to break the silence.

"A little too fussy for my tastes," Tate said. "A little too . . . *British*."

"A word to the wise . . ." I said.

"What's that?"

"Don't offend the man," I said. I pointed to George's. "We're here!"

Once inside George's, I peeled off my ski mask. My hair, alive with static electricity, stood on end. I tried patting it down, but each time my hand came near my head, my hair crackled and rose even higher, so I gave up.

"Tate!" someone yelled from the back of the bar. It was Vince Belecheck wearing an insulated jumpsuit, industrial-brown and of the variety that pole climbers for the electric company would wear in the winter. I half-expected to find a hard hat resting on the table, but no luck.

Tate and Vince hugged and shook hands, the way old army buddies would, although they had met only once, for a photo shoot in New York for a now-defunct magazine's coronation of America's best male writers. (There was some quirky and idiotic stipulation attached. The writers had to be over a certain height or under a certain weight. I no longer recalled the magazine's criterion, even though it had been trumpeted on the cover.) It had been a big deal, though, this particular issue of the magazine, catapulting a few relative unknowns into the literary limelight, earning them six-figure advances for their next books.

After a few fake arm punches on Vince's part, along with sly allusions to the bacchanalia that followed the photo shoot, including money well spent at the Pussycat Lounge (*"Duuuuuude,"* Vince kept saying, pointing at Tate and laughing. *"Duuuuuude"*), Tate and Vince finally sat in a booth across from each other.

"Oh, yeah," Tate said. "This is Jack Sheahan."

Vince regarded me with a studied mixture of superiority, pity, and disdain. "Hey," Vince said. "Have a seat, buddy." I slipped in next to Tate, who made a show of moving over.

Tate said, "Jack here says you two were in the Workshop together?"

Vince raised his eyebrows. I told him which class we'd shared. I even recalled one of the stories he'd turned in, the one about the racist roofer who accidentally tarred himself and then fell off the roof, landing on a torn feather bed lying next to a Dumpster.

Tate's eyes widened. "Whoa! That's a *great* fucking story, Vince. Whatever happened to it? You publish it anywhere?"

Vince shrugged. "Nah. I was writing a lot of allegorical and symbolic stories back in the day."

"Well, you should *definitely* pull that one back out," Tate said.

Vince perked up. "You think?" He frowned and nodded. "Maybe I will. *I* always liked it." Vince looked over at me now. "I *do* remember you now," he said. "You didn't like that story, did you?"

"I honestly can't remember," I said.

"Weren't you the one who had all kinds of logic problems with it?"

"Maybe," I said.

"Logic," Tate said derisively and snorted. "Imagine García Márquez in a workshop!" He rolled his eyes.

Vince sniffed. He scrunched up his lips, playing the role of tough guy to perfection. "You published a story in *The New Yorker*, didn't you?"

"A long time ago," I said. "Yeah."

"What're you up to these days?" he asked. "Working on anything?"

"A novel," I said. "I'm taking my time."

"Attaboy," Vince said. "You want to hit the first one out of the park, don't you? Well, good for you. Me? I just write 'em as they come to me. I don't have the leisure of waiting for the muse. Don't get me wrong. I wish I did." He leaned over the table and slapped my shoulder. "Win one for the team. Make us proud."

The waitress came up, and Vince ordered two beers and two shots.

"You're driving, right?" he said to me. "Otherwise . . ." He turned his attention to Tate. "So, man, tell me what you've been up to? You sold film rights to *The Duke of Battery Park*, didn't you? Is it in development?"

Tate shook his head. "They're having casting issues. One producer wanted Brad Pitt; another wanted Tobey Maguire. Personally, I'd like to see someone like Vincent Gallo in that role. Or maybe a theater guy. Someone from off-Broadway. Or off-off-Broadway."

"It's your book, bro," Vince said. "You should put your foot down. You know what I'm saying? If you don't, they'll cast Jim Carrey or Eddie Murphy in the role, and *then* how're you gonna live with yourself?"

"I know, I know."

Vince said, "You know what? We should write a screenplay together."

When the drinks came, Vince and Tate downed their shots, and Tate said, "A collaboration. Absolutely!" For the next hour, Vince and Tate hammered out a blow-by-blow plot treatment in which a bricklayer, through a series of unrealistic and clichéd contrivances, trades places with a New York club-goer and all-around hipster.

"I mean, *that's* what movies are all about," Vince said. "Opposites. Think about it. *Pretty Woman. Sixteen Candles. Planet of the Apes.* They're all about opposites."

"The 'other,'" Tate said, raising his hands and making rabbit ears.

Vince, lost in thought, nodded.

"Imagine the New York hipster trying to fit in with all these bricklayers!" Tate exclaimed.

"Or the bricklayer going clubbing!" Vince countered, nodding. "This is gold, bro. Pure fucking gold." At Vince's insistence, the two men high-fived.

"I need to take a dump," I said. "I'll be at the Dairy Queen. Cleaner toilets over there. Anyone need anything?"

Vince and Tate, their reverie interrupted, glared at me without saying a word.

"Everyone's good?" I asked, sliding out of the booth. "No Dilly Bar? No Snickers Blizzard? No Moolatte?"

"Bring us some fries," Vince said. "You got an expense account, right?"

I nodded.

Vince said, "One large fry."

"Tate?" I said.

Without looking at me, he shook his head.

I snaked my way out of the bar, trudged next door to the Laundromat, and called M. Cat. I let his phone ring twenty times before I hung up. Either he didn't own an answering machine or it was so full of messages from Lauren Castle that it had ceased to work. I considered checking my own messages, but I wasn't up to wading through the muck of Lauren's accusations and pleas.

I walked over to DQ and ordered a large fry from a pocky white teenager who was trying to look like an inner-city gang-banger. His pants were twice his size, and his Dairy Queen visor was turned sideways.

"We all outta fries," the kid said. "You want O. rings?"

"What are those?"

"*Onion* rings, homes," he said, sighing.

"Sure. Give me the onion rings." As the kid dumped two handfuls of onion rings into the grease basket, I told him the plot of Vince and Tate's movie. "Would you go see a movie with that plot?" I asked.

"Sounds like it sucks ass," the kid said. "I mean, who wants to see a movie about a bricklayer?"

"I could actually see a good movie about a bricklayer," I said. "My point is, the *plot*. You've seen it before, right?"

"Maybe *you* have," the kid said. "*I* haven't. A movie about a brick-layer and some hip-hop artist? Nuh-uh."

"A *hipster*," I corrected. "Not a hip-hop artist."

"What is this?" the kid asked. "One of those surveys? Yo, I don't do surveys. They collect all kinds of information about you that they can use against you later."

"Like what?" I asked.

"Like *what*? What planet you from, homes? In-fo-*may*-shun. *Personal* information. Hel-*lo*? You ever heard of identity theft? You ever heard of phone scams?" He handed me the bag with the onion rings in them. "Who did you say you were again?"

"Nobody," I said, opening the door to leave, the bell tinkling over my head. "I'm nobody."

"Nuh-uh," he said, shaking his head. "You somebody."

I HAD LANDED THE job of media escort because the guy who had it prior to me (a writer named Max Kellogg who'd graduated from the Workshop a full ten years before I did) got drunk one winter night, drove through a guard rail, and drowned in the Iowa River. Witnesses said his car sank like a stone. When the police fished him out, they found inside his car an itinerary for Joyce Carol Oates's upcoming visit to town and an unfinished novel manuscript with Max Kellogg's name on it. The police labeled the cause of death an accident, but I knew without a doubt that it was his damned unfinished novel that had killed him.

It was the owner of the bookstore, Bobby Dunn, who hooked me up with this job, calling me only a day after the police had found Max Kellogg's body. He'd warned me about the publicists ("By and large, a bunch of rich daddy's girls that went to Sarah Lawrence and Vassar," he'd said. "A hundred bucks says not a one of them could even find Iowa on a map"), but when he told me how much money I could make, I didn't hesitate. It sounded easy. Too easy. And, by and large, it *was* a cushy job. But then there were days like this one when everything went wrong.

Armed with onion rings, I stepped back inside George's. Pink Floyd's "Shine on You Crazy Diamond" radiated from the jukebox. It didn't matter what bar you went into in Iowa City, sooner or later "Shine on You Crazy Diamond" came on. My theory was that most people who played it didn't actually like Pink Floyd; they played it to get as much bang for their buck as possible. The song lasted damned near fourteen minutes, depending on the version. These same people were also likely to play Frampton's "Do You Feel Like I Do," Skynyrd's "Free Bird," Don McLean's "American Pie," and the Doors' "The End," all of which, running back to back, lasted almost an hour. And if you found a juke-box that played five songs for a buck, you were way ahead of the game. I knew all too well that this could have been my life if I hadn't taken the media escort job: sidled up to a bar at midday while mentally calculating the lengths of songs, the amount of beer I was likely to consume, and the sum total of loose bills and pocket change piled in front of me—the alcoholic's calculus. And I might have had it all figured out perfectly, how to stretch the night out until last call—that is, until I ordered that first shot of rail whiskey and threw all of my calculations irreversibly out of whack.

In addition to the freshly drained shot glasses and beer bottles on Vince and Tate's table, two women were now sitting with them. They were laughing at something either Vince or Tate had said, and Tate's hair looked slightly mussed and his glasses crooked. When I was in the Workshop, the only groupies were mentally unstable men who showed up in town without warning and pitched tents in the visiting writers' back yards, intending to share with them their latest Vietnam opus with the hope of getting it published. These days, the groupies were closer to what I had fantasized about when I was twelve years old and considered becoming a rock star. The funny thing was that the new groupies and the old ones shared the same endgame: They, too, wanted book con-tracts, except these days the contracts would be for their victim mem-oirs, or they wanted to be included in the Best New Voices anthology, or they wanted a tenure-track teaching position on either the East or West Coasts. And where the old groupies usually ended up spending a night in jail for trespassing, the new ones spent it in the writer's bed, hoping by daybreak that their hard, feverish work had not been all for naught. Shortcuts to fame: Everyone wanted one.

There was no room for me to sit down in the booth, so I stood at the end of the table and, forcing a smile, peered down at the revelers.

Vince said, "Girls? This is Jack. He's Tate's escort. Jack? These are the girls."

The women regarded me with suspicion. Was I a male prostitute? Was Tate gay?

"*Vince*," I said softly. "Come on, man."

Vince looked up at me, genuinely confused. "What?"

"Me and you," I said, "we were classmates. There's no need for that."

Tate said, "Oh, hey, Jack. Vince said he could take me to my hotel tonight." He looked at Vince for reassurance.

"Yeah, yeah," Vince said. "No prob."

"Are you sure?" I asked.

"We're what . . . three blocks away? Yeah, I think I can handle that."

"But go ahead and bill my publisher for the night," Tate said. "I mean, I dragged you out here and everything."

"Alrighty," I said. "I'll do that." I tossed the bag of onion rings to the center of the table and said, "Oh yeah. I almost forgot. They all outta fries."

WHEN I GOT back to my apartment, I pounded on M. Cat's door, but I couldn't hear anything inside and finally gave up. My answering machine blinked a few dozen times before pausing and blinking a few dozen more times. I removed my phone from its charger and carried it to the couch, considering giving Lauren Castle a late-night update, but then thought better of it and turned on CNN instead. After ten minutes of listening to Anderson Cooper, I fell sound asleep.

The next time I woke up, it was two in the morning. I picked up the remote and turned off the TV. Too tired to drag myself to bed, I tried fluffing a spongy foam sofa pillow. Curling up without any blankets, I drifted into an uncomfortable slumber.

The phone, clutched in my hand, started ringing just after three in the morning.

"Jack?" a voice said.

"Yeah?" I sat up but kept the lights off and my eyes shut. "Who is this?"

"I'm not sure if you remember me. It's S. S. Pitzer."

S. S. Pitzer was a famous writer who had, after writing twelve critically acclaimed books in twelve years, disappeared after his last novel, *Winter's Ghosts*, became his first *New York Times* best seller. I had escorted him ten years ago, shortly after I had taken this job; *Winter's Ghosts* had just come out in paperback. Once the tour was over, he disappeared. *Poof*, and he was gone. Neither his agent nor his editor claimed to know where he was, and although his estranged wife hadn't seen him either, she had told the press that she still received monthly checks drawn from a secret account in the Bahamas. The odds of S. S. Pitzer calling me in the middle of the night were at best one-in-ten-thousand, and I almost hung up, but there was something about the tenor of the man's voice that made me stay on the line to hear him out.

"S. S. Pitzer, huh? Nice try," I said.

"I'm at the bus station," he said. "I know this is an imposition, but I was wondering if you could come get me."

"The bus station? In Iowa City?" I didn't believe him, and I almost said so, but then he told me something that only he could have known.

"I still remember the first sentence of your novel," he said.

The only person I had ever shown any of my novel to was S. S. Pitzer. We'd gone drinking after his reading, and we'd ended up at my apartment, listening to old Tom Waits CDs while polishing off whatever had been hiding in my cupboards. In a moment of weakness, I told him what my novel was about. To my surprise, S. S. wanted me to read the first chapter aloud to him. I turned off the stereo. Reclining on my couch, S. S. Pitzer had listened to me with his eyes closed, as though he were hearing music. When I finished, he opened his eyes and said, "It's brilliant, Jack. This is going to put you on the map in a big way." And when I told him to quit fucking with me, he said, "No, no. That first line . . . Good God, man. You've got what it takes. You do." Naturally, I was flying. If S. S. Pitzer thought it was brilliant, it had to be! When I drove him back to the airport the next day, he signed my copy of *Winter's Ghosts*, "For Jack, To Whom the Gods of Literature Have Whispered. Your faithful reader and loyal friend, S. S. Pitzer."

"Would you like me to recite it to you?" he asked me now.

"No, no," I said. "I'll come get you."

"Please hurry, though," he said. "There's no heat in here."

I had to dig my car out of the snow and then spend a good fifteen minutes backing up and pulling forward to rock it out of the drift that had built up along the sides, but the tires eventually found traction and rocketed me into the street.

Pitzer's words, all those years ago, should have given me the courage to finish my novel, but instead they'd had the opposite effect. He had planted a poisonous seed inside my head, and with each new word I added to the manuscript, the seed bloomed until all that remained were expectations that I could never meet. I had tried to make every sentence as brilliant as the first, but at the end of a long day's work, all I was left with were wooden paragraphs and lifeless scenes. The plot eventually petered out as well. No matter how many times I sat at my kitchen table and pored over the manuscript's pages, I couldn't revive it. The novel had flatlined.

And so I boxed it up and never wrote another word. Over the years, I had come to loathe S. S. Pitzer, even though I knew in my heart of hearts that I alone was really to blame. Still, I was secretly glad that he had quit writing books.

A Greyhound bus idled as plumes of exhaust rolled like fog past the station's windows. I saw S. S. Pitzer standing inside the bus station alongside a few homeless men I recognized from around town. In his early sixties, Pitzer still had a thick mane of white hair. Wearing a tweed suit and a long wool overcoat, as though he were heading cheerily to a university production of *Othello*, he was the only living person I knew for whom the word *dandy* still applied. I honked my horn, and Pitzer, holding his overcoat closed, stepped out of the station. When he opened my passenger-side door, enough snow blew inside to chill my bones.

"The buttons popped off somewhere between St. George, Utah, and Lincoln, Nebraska," he said. "It's good to see you again, Jack. You wouldn't believe the trip here. I started out in L.A., and the weather just got worse and worse, state by state. The earlier drivers, why, they'd pull over and wait for the storm to subside, but this last driver, my God, he wouldn't stop. We couldn't see ten feet ahead of us, none of us, but the driver kept pushing ahead. It was as though he were possessed." He looked over at me and said, "You must be tired, old friend. We can chat more about this in the morning." He said nothing about the awful sound my mufflerless car was making, and for that I was grateful.

"So, what brings you to town?" I asked. Once I'd thrown the question out there, I could feel the air around us shift ever so slightly, but it was too late: I couldn't retract it.

"Oh, just passing through, son," he said. "Just passing through."

"And where am I taking you?" I asked.

"The thing is," he said, "I didn't book a room. I was wondering—hoping, really—that I might could rent your sofa. Is it available? If it's an inconvenience, please let me know and I'll get to work on other accommodations."

"No, no, it's fine," I said.

"Are you sure?" he asked, but before I could answer, he said, "Thank you, Jack. I owe you. I most sincerely do."

PART THREE

Everywhere I go, I'm asked if the universities stifle writers.
My opinion is that they don't stifle enough of them.

—Flannery O'Connor

HAD LONG BELIEVED that I'd been let into the Workshop due to a clerical error, or because the outgoing director wanted to screw with the incoming director by admitting some of the worst applicants in the Workshop's long and illustrious history. The short story I had submitted was one that I had written for my undergraduate workshop, a story about Manny Grouse, a retired optometrist with failing eyesight who considers suicide until he sees a billboard advertising the annual optometrist's convention at a local lodge. Manny goes to the convention with the hope of seeing a few old friends for the last time, but he recognizes nobody inside the old, dimly lit building with its paneled walls and flooring of cracked asbestos tiles. The keynote speaker, a man twenty years Manny's senior and with a white beard and large old wire-frame glasses from the 1970s, talks not of new developments in optometry but rather of health, happiness, and prosperity; he talks of peace of mind; he talks of being as enthusiastic about the success of others as you would be of your own success. "Remember," he intones, "that if you give adequate time to the improvement of yourself, you will have no time to criticize others!" Manny takes these words to heart, and, noticing several folding tables at the back of the hall, behind which men and women are offering opportunities to volunteer in the neighborhood, Manny wanders over to find out more. Childless and widowed, he signs up to help out an inner-city baseball team; he also writes a check for $500 so that the community center can purchase new equipment for the kids. On his way out, the keynote speaker stops Manny and introduces himself. "We haven't seen you here before," the man says, and Manny, as though kneeling inside a confessional and staring into the dark scrim at the priest's obfuscated head, admits that it's been awhile. Nodding, the old man smiles, puts a hand on Manny's shoulder, and says, "Welcome back to the Optimists', my friend." Manny, confused, thanks the old man, then walks outside and into the dark parking lot, but before getting into his car, he turns toward the dingy trailer sign parked next to the road. Beneath the blinking arrow, against a yellow background, are the words: WELCOME OPTIMISTS' CLUB! Manny, unsure if what he's reading is what's actually on the sign, walks across the gravel lot and reads the letters, one by one, and then looks up into the sky, sees the constellation Cassiopeia, the vain queen who boasted of her unrivaled beauty, and begins to weep in gratitude for his spared life.

It wasn't a good story. In fact, it was a pretty bad one. Any reader with even a passing knowledge of fiction writing could have pointed out the ridiculous plot contrivance. It was an overly clever story in which my presence hovered obtrusively. The plot's saving grace was that I had been inspired by the early, ironic short stories of Chekhov rather than the gimmicky work of O. Henry, but I had also lifted, for the story's finale, a little bit of James Joyce's "Araby" and a dash of John Cheever's "The Swimmer." I hadn't been aware of any of this as I wrote it, but when I started boning up on the classics after graduation before heading to Iowa, re-reading my Intro to Lit anthology from cover to cover, I saw with no small amount of horror what I had done. That no one who'd read my application pointed this out to me, and that the renowned Iowa Writers' Workshop had actually *accepted* me on the basis of an overly ironic short story with not-so-subtle allusions to two stories that had appeared in nearly every short-story anthology published in the last thirty years, pretty much cemented my suspicions that my acceptance had been either an accident or a practical joke. To my credit, the story was full of strong imagery, and there was a precision to the language that naturally pulled the reader into Manny's world even as my plot worked to push the reader out. If my admission into the Workshop *hadn't* been an accident or a joke, it was because someone saw something in the story that transcended all that smacked of amateurishness. I had applied to Iowa on a whim. I never really expected to get accepted.

Which was why I felt compelled to work as hard as possible to become the best writer I could. I was fueled by guilt. I didn't want anyone reading my stories for workshop wondering why I had been let in; I certainly didn't want anyone going back to my application, reading my sample story, and saying, "What the fuck is *this*?" I was protecting both myself and the reputation of the Workshop. Even so, the entire time that I was there, I felt the distinct possibility that I might be called into the office of the Workshop coordinator, a woman named Leslie Buttons who had survived the reigns of four previous Workshop directors, and told to pack my bags, that the error had been caught, and that the only solution was for me to leave town as soon as possible. This, I supposed, was why I had become friends with the director himself, a writer named Gordon Grimes. I needed protection from the inside, a bulletproof vest, and Gordon Grimes was the only person who could provide that for me.

Grimes was in his early fifties when I met him, though he had a boyish face and a thatch of hair that hung perpetually over his forehead, making him look more like a rakish teenage boy in search of trouble than a professor of creative writing. He'd published only one book, twenty-two years before becoming director of the Workshop, an autobiographical novel about growing up in Hollywood and being forced by his mentally unstable stage mother to audition for bit roles in motion pictures. That book alone, though its sales were modest at best, garnered enough critical attention for him to parlay its success into a series of prestigious jobs. A few weeks before meeting him, shortly after I finished reading his memoir, I had actually seen one of his movies on TBS, a patriotic film of World War II, typical of the period, called *The Tinseltown Chronicles*: Gordon Grimes, eight years old and wearing overalls and a floppy hat, the same style of hat Jackie Coogan wears in Chaplin's *The Kid*, selling newspapers on the corner of Hollywood and Vine and yelling as loud as he can, "Extra! Extra! Read all about it! Japs bomb Pearl Harbor! U.S. goes to war! Extra! Extra!" During a six-year period, Gordon Grimes appeared in thirty-two feature movies, but he was never in more than a single scene, and his only other talking role, besides *The Tinseltown Chronicles*, was in his final movie, a low-budget science fiction serial titled *Little Green Men Conquer Earth!* In that scene, Gordon shouts, "Look, Mommy. The Little Green Men are here!" In the next shot, using their laser guns, the Little Green Men bloodlessly annihilate the house in which both mother and son live, appropriately concluding Gordon Grimes's career, such as it was, as a child actor.

By the time I had met Gordon Grimes, the year he'd taken over as the Workshop's director, he was on the brink of renewing his old drinking problem, a problem, we were all to learn later, that had once reached epic proportions, but in those first few weeks in town he stuck to nursing imported beer and, in a futile attempt to quit smoking, chewed the living shit out of one stick of gum after the other. I happened to come across him, before the semester began, sidled up to the bar in the Miss Q. I was still exploring Iowa City, having just arrived from a state college in northern Michigan, where it wasn't uncommon for hunters to get drunk and accidentally shoot each other, and where an overzealous bouncer had recently been jailed for choking a patron to death. Iowa City, by comparison, had seemed like a real university town, where you found students reading books like *Gravity's Rainbow* or *The Electric Kool-aid Acid Test* in bars in the middle of a sunny afternoon, or you heard someone using the word *postmodern* or *hegemony* in passing. You saw the torches of intellectual pursuit flickering in the students' eyes, rather than the rheumy fog of a hangover or near-overdose.

"Mr. Grimes?" I said, approaching him cautiously, as if he were a cornered possum. I was unsure how he would react, and, to be honest, he scared the daylights out of me.

After I had explained who I was, he motioned dramatically to the barstool next to him and said, "Sit, sit!" His accent was a curious blend of northeast prep school and W. C. Fields. That first night, he ordered me to read the entire nineteenth century.

"What books in particular?" I asked, and he looked back at me, astonished.

"All of them, of course!" he replied. "Dickens. Flaubert. The Russians. Read *all* the Russians." He picked up a book of matches, turned it over in his fingers, and said, "The nineteenth century. That's all you'll ever need."

"What about the twentieth century?" I asked.

"Yeah; sure," he said, waving his hand dismissively. "Of course you need to read your contemporaries. Hemingway and Faulkner, too. And Joyce . . . but only early Joyce. The first two books. He got worse the older he got."

This was news to me: My Irish lit professor had spent an entire semester illuminating the genius of *Ulysses* and *Finnegans Wake* as opposed to what he had called Joyce's juvenilia, *Dubliners* and *A Portrait of the Artist as a Young Man*. Grimes's words cheered me immensely, since I secretly preferred the earlier stuff. This was the first time I saw how differently writers and literature professors viewed the written word, and I wanted to hug Gordon Grimes for confirming what I had lately been suspecting—that a story with a beating heart was infinitely better (and more noble) than a story that made its reader scratch her head.

"What about *Finnegans Wake*?" I asked him.

"Crap," he said, depositing the tooth-gray nugget of spent gum in the ashtray. He unwrapped a new stick and popped it into his mouth. I expected him to say more about *Finnegans Wake*, but he didn't.

Gordon Grimes was notoriously rough in workshop. One time he held up a particularly bad story with the tips of his forefinger and thumb, and asked, "What smells like shit in here?" Another time, he spent an hour berating a student who had misspelled the word *fluorescent*, which also happened to be the story's title. "Don't you own a dictionary?" he asked. "Imagine Faulkner misspelling 'sanctuary,' for Christ's sake. Imagine Hemingway not taking the time to look up the proper spelling of Kilimanjaro." On yet another occasion, he spent the entire four hours of workshop reading aloud, sentence by sentence, a story that he most likely hadn't read *before* coming to class. He now painstakingly questioned every choice made by the author, a young woman named Betsy McKay. "Why is there a semicolon here? Why is the relationship between *this* sentence and *that* one so important that it *requires* a semicolon? Can anyone explain this to me? Oh, and why the paragraph break here? Can anyone show me where the transition is? If the reader starts thinking that your choices are random, well, then, you're through. You're *done*! The reader is going to toss your precious work into the fireplace. Who wants to read a story in which the author hasn't questioned every word, every comma, every break in paragraph?" Not even the sound of Betsy weeping moved Gordon to stop the assault. Only after Betsy, unable to take any more, left the room did Gordon, broken from his own trance, finally look up. His bloodshot eyes searched the room for his victim. We were well into the fourth hour of the interrogation. Without acknowledging Betsy's abrupt departure, Gordon said, "Okay, then. I guess that's all for today."

Gordon's were workshops of either tough love or masochistic persecution, depending upon the quality of light in which you viewed it. But Gordon liked me, and, more importantly, he liked my fiction. Most nights, we ended up at the Foxhead at about the same time and wrote our names on the chalkboard for the pool table.

"Sheahan!" he often yelled. "Are you sure you want to make that shot? The side pockets are the hard pockets!" Or else, in an attempt to throw me off my game, he would yell, "Are you sure that's the English you want to put on the ball? *Think* about it before you shoot!"

Once, when he accidentally separated an otherwise tight-knit group of solids while leaning over to shoot another solid, Gordon raised up, smiled at the new, more promising configuration of pool balls, and said, "Hey, whaddya know?" as if the balls had separated of their own volition. By then, he was back to drinking whiskey and smoking. Groups of workshop students surrounded him—he had a guru's following—and he would make offhand comments about how *this* writer or *that* one was whoring himself by working in Hollywood or writing thrillers under pseudonyms. "I'm not saying it's wrong," he added. "Everyone whores himself every now and then." But you could tell that he *did* think it was wrong, even though he himself had spent considerable time doing hackwork.

I occasionally sat with the group, but mostly I remained in a booth across from everyone, alone, separating myself from all the bootlickers, even though I knew deep down that I too was one. I focused on the pool table instead, on whatever game was being played, ignoring the whoops of my classmates each time Gordon Grimes insulted one of his contemporaries or even, after a long night of drinking, one of our own classmates.

Gordon Grimes was responsible for awarding me the much-coveted teaching-writing fellowship—the TWIF—given to only four fiction writers each year, and he was the one who had sent my short story, "The Self-Adhesive Postage Stamp," to an editor at *The New Yorker.* The story appeared in the magazine three months later, which, as I later gathered, was practically unheard of. He also guest-edited the volume of *Best American Short Stories* in which my story was reprinted. In other words, Gordon Grimes was single-handedly responsible for my meteoric rise. When he finally succumbed to cirrhosis, his wife Jenna, whom I had met but didn't really know, called to ask if I could say a few words at his wake, and though I agreed, I went to the Foxhead instead and drank until I could barely walk and then got arrested for public intoxication after calling a cop "a little pinheaded Nazi," all of which, I believed at the time, was what Gordon would have preferred. I later apologized to the cop, but I couldn't ever bring myself to call Jenna Grimes. What kind of man stands up his mentor's widow, abandoning her at the funeral home? A shit-heel. That's what kind.

Why all of this was swirling through my head the morning I awoke after the disappearance of Vanessa Roberts, I didn't know. Gordon Grimes had been dead for over two years. My days in the Workshop were a lifetime ago: a rapidly receding memory.

S. S. Pitzer was sitting on my couch, holding my manuscript box in his lap. Half the manuscript's pages were face-down on the coffee table.

"No, no," I said. "You don't want to do that."

S. S. looked up. "*This,*" he said, looking down at what he was holding and then back up at me, "is a masterpiece."

"Please, no," I begged. "I really wish you wouldn't."

"I can't stop now, for God's sake!" he yelled. "But I have to ask you. Where's the rest of it?" He held up the box, as if to prove how light it was.

"I never finished it."

"You *what?*"

"I got stuck. And then I finally gave up." I considered telling him that he was responsible for me giving up, but as soon as the words formed in my head, they seemed too preposterous to say aloud. A lie.

"That can't be," he said, physically wilting, as though I had just told him about the death of a mutual friend.

I shrugged. I made a face to show that these things happen.

"Did you start writing another one?" he asked.

"No," I said. "Not really."

"Short stories?" he asked. "Poems?"

"No," I said.

"Oh-oh, I know," he said. "Creative nonfiction. A memoir! Those are hot now, aren't they? Or perhaps their time has already come and gone."

"Nothing," I said. And then to end the conversation, I added, "I gave up. Now if you'll excuse me." I could see that S. S. had wanted to pursue the subject, but before he could say another word, I pressed the playback button on my answering machine.

The first dozen messages were, as I had guessed, from Lauren Castle. In each message, Lauren berated me, calling me "irresponsible" and "childish." In a few of the messages, she claimed that my behavior bordered on criminal intent. What followed were a few desperate messages from M. Cat begging me to make Lauren stop calling him, that he was going out of his mind. "Dude," he said in one message, "this is, like, *your* problem? Not *mine?*"

All of these were left before I had dispatched M. Cat to find Vanessa, so I busied myself making coffee and brushing my teeth while more rebukes came in from Lauren. In one, she said, "Do you have any idea of the damage I could do to you, you shithead? I'm the head of publicity for a major New York publisher! That may not mean much to you out there in Ohio or Iowa or whatever the hell cowpoke state you live in, but it means something where I live, goddamn it. It means something in New York *fucking* City!" In her next message, she started pleading with me. "*Please,*" she began. "*Please* call me back. Vanessa Roberts's book is poised to be number one on *The New York Times* best-seller list. We just went into a second six-digit print-run. If she stops touring, she'll lose all this momentum. Bookstores will start sending back all those copies. I don't *even* want to think about that. Have you ever seen a warehouse full of a book that tanked? I have, and it's not pretty. I started out working in a warehouse—yeah, that's right: *me, in a warehouse!*—when sales for Jay McInerney's *Story of My Life* went south. We must have gotten a hundred thousand of those books back. Maybe two hundred thousand. Do you know what a hundred thousand books look like? Picture it, would you? You can't, can you? Well, then, can you imagine the psychological effect that that many returns has on—" The answering machine cut her off. The next message began, "Fuck it. What do you care? You're just a writer wannabe, right? You're just a slacker hanging out in a college town at his local coffee shop, wearing a beret—Am I right? Are you wearing a beret right now?—writing the Great American Novel on legal pads. Is this a bull's-eye or what? You probably smoke clove cigarettes and drink Jameson's but don't eat meat. You know what? You're pathetic. You're a living, walking cliché, and I bet deep down you know it too. Don't you?"

S. S. had wandered over to where I stood by the coffeemaker.

"Want a cup?" I asked.

"Who *is* this awful woman?" he asked.

"Oh, her? She's just a publicist," I said. "But I don't take it personally. They're all like that."

"Really? They don't treat *me* that way," he said.

"Of course they wouldn't. But media escorts? We're at the bottom of the food chain. Oh, wait: Here comes another one," I said, tipping my head toward the answering machine.

"I'm booking a flight there even as I speak," she said. "Travelocity, baby. Travel-fucking-ocity."

The answering machine gave one final, long beep—the equivalent of an electronic sigh. There were no more messages.

"Did she just say she was coming here?" I asked.

"She did indeed," S. S. said. "But have you peeked outside yet?"

I walked to the living room's bay window, pulled back the curtain, and peered out into the blinding whiteness. A man wearing a snowsuit was using a shovel to dig his car out. Two kids on plastic sleds slid down East Burlington, where, on a normal day, they would have been run over by a Heartland Express semi. Even the tops of stoplights were piled high with snow, like frosting on a cupcake. Each time I breathed, steam covered the window, and I finally had to reach up and wipe it away with my forearm, just to see out.

"She won't make it," S. S. said. "Not today." He sighed and said, "Oh well."

"Shit," I said and, coffee cup in hand, left my apartment and walked across the hall, pounding on M. Cat's door. I pounded several times, but there was still no answer. Back inside my own apartment, I explained the situation to S. S.—the disappearance of Vanessa, followed by my foolhardy decision to ask M. Cat to go looking for her—but in the midst of my story, I remembered that I was talking to a man who had himself effectively disappeared not for a day or a week or a month but for several years.

When I finished talking, S. S. shrugged and said, "She'll turn up. I wouldn't worry."

J. S. HAD TAUGHT in the University of California system for twenty years before his novel *Winter's Ghosts* hit the *Times* best-seller list, and then, like that, he simply disappeared. Sometimes I wondered if it was the teaching, rather than success, that had driven him into hiding. During my two years in the Workshop, I taught introductory fiction writing courses and entertained the idea, after reading a stack of my students' stories, of shooting myself in front of my class. If ever there was a course designed to drive a person away from teaching, it was short story workshop. My students, by and large, took the course to scratch a creative itch, but few of them had read anything other than what they'd been assigned in school, and most of them had resented the little they'd been made to read. If they had read anything on their own, it was usually a novel featuring vampires, or it was John Grisham's latest, or maybe it was a novelization of *Star Trek*. The worst were the J. R. R. Tolkien fans who saw themselves as the "serious readers" of the class.

In the stories that were turned in for the workshop I taught, main characters often died at the end, or else they revealed to the reader long-held secrets on which the entire plot of the story pivoted. Punctuation was random; students were unable to remain inside only one character's head; correct spelling eluded them. Despite their inability to master the basics, my students felt compelled to argue the most elementary points with me.

"I don't like concrete details. If something has too many concrete details, it doesn't leave enough for the reader's imagination," one girl pronounced. Or, "I *like* it when we don't know the narrator's name. It makes him seem more, I don't know, *universal*." Or, "I don't know why all stories have to have a conflict. It makes the story seem formulaic." Or, "What's wrong with clichés? I mean, we all know what the clichés mean, so why not use them?" Or, "I don't see why we can't use stereotypes. Like, stereotypes are stereotypes for a reason. People like that really do *exist*!"

The semester was flush with dead grandmother stories ("When I saw her powdered face in the casket, a single tear rolled down my cheek. 'Grandma!' I yelled. '*Don't leave us!*'"), stories about the big football game ("It was the fourth quarter, fourth down with twenty yards to go and only thirty seconds on the clock—it was now or never, baby!"), or stories that ended with the narrator's death ("The last thing I saw, as I stood on the tracks, was the front of the speeding locomotive with the maniacally laughing conductor inside . . . and then everything went BLACK . . . ").

Unstapled when I had asked otherwise, often missing pages, sometimes unfinished, the stories arrived week after week for those two years, and I dutifully read them, made comments in the margins, typed up critiques, and assigned grades. I had decided, midway through my first semester, that I would have preferred shoveling shit at a zoo or being a rodeo clown to reading short stories written by college undergraduates, and although I never had to make that choice, I saw several lean months after graduation and before landing the media escort job, and on more than one occasion, while doing data entry for a temp agency or taking typing-speed tests at the university, I'd had to sell my own plasma to make ends meet. The whole process of selling plasma took about an hour. There was always a movie playing (John Candy movies were particularly popular at the Plasma Center), so I would kick back in the heavy-duty recliner and watch *Uncle Buck* or *Spaceballs* as blood pumped out of my body. The blood would go into a spinning device that separated the plasma from the rest of the blood, and although the rest of the blood eventually got pumped back into me, the plasma container would continue to fill up. My container of plasma, after it had filled all the way up, looked curiously like a pitcher of Michelob. That first time, when the nurse came to unhook me, I motioned toward the container and said, "Cheers!" but all she did was pull the needle from my arm, make me hold a piece of cotton over the point of entry, and then place a Bugs Bunny Band-Aid over the cotton. Not once during my first plasma donating procedure, for which I was paid thirty dollars cash, did I regret that I hadn't pursued a career teaching creative writing, nor did I regret it during my subsequent visits to the center, visits so frequent that, many years later, I still had a white scar on the crook of my left arm.

S. S. Pitzer and I tromped down the stairs to the foyer, where four mailboxes hung on a wall, and then we walked outside together, but only after I'd leaned my shoulder into the door to push the snow on the front porch out of the way. The light was so blinding, I had to shut my eyes and then slowly open them again. I shaded my eyes with my palm, turned to S. S., and asked, "How did you do it?"

"Do what?"

"Teach creative writing for twenty years," I said.

"Oh," S. S. said. "Yes, well. *That*," he said. "The thing is, I quit reading their stories after five years."

"Really?"

We tromped down the porch steps, through the snow. I put on my ski mask.

"I always let the students talk about each other's stories—they always had plenty to say, of course—and I occasionally quoted Twain or Steinbeck or Flannery O'Connor when it seemed appropriate, but then I'd hand back each story with a giant 'A' at the end of it. Sometimes I wrote 'Well done!' above the grade."

"No one ever said anything?"

"Fifteen years without a complaint," he said. "It never crossed anyone's mind that I *wasn't* reading the stories. In fact, the year before I left town, I won the university's Gold Medal Teaching Award, given only to their very best. Sir!" he called out to the man still excavating his car with a snow shovel. "Care for a hand?"

The man, pinch-faced from the wind, paused what he was doing and said, "Thank you, but I think I've got 'er!"

S. S. saluted him, and the two of us walked on.

"And where are we heading?" S. S. asked me.

"I don't know," I said. "Back downtown? I need to look around for Vanessa, I guess."

"You think she's in a snowdrift, perhaps?" S. S. asked. He smiled and raised his eyebrows at me, amused by my lack of a plan.

"And my neighbor," I said. "M. Cat. He's missing, too."

"Everyone's fine," he said. "Trust me. The number of people who honestly disappear—and by 'disappear,' I mean people who have no choice in the matter—is statistically insignificant. Everyone said that *I* had disappeared. I didn't, you know. I simply drove away. *I* always knew where I was at." He stopped walking to look at me, and although he couldn't possibly have read my expressions through the ski mask, he said, "You worry too much. Look at this," he said, waving his arm at the snow, the kind of grand gesture an old-time actor would make by way of introducing his audience to the play they're about to see. "Isn't this wonderful? Doesn't it remind you of childhood?"

Across the street, at one of the unofficial frat houses, a guy wearing only too-short sweatpants stepped barefoot onto the snow-covered porch, walked over to the railing, and spewed a gallon of vomit. He remained bent over, forearms resting on the rail, panting, as steam rose from a snow-draped shrub.

"No," I said. "It doesn't really remind me of childhood."

"Too bad," S. S. said.

The college boy saw us, wiped his mouth onto his shoulder, then walked back to the front door gingerly on the balls of his feet, as though crossing a bed of hot coals. The letters across the ass of his sweatpants spelled *juicy*.

"Ah, youth," S. S. said. "Let's get some coffee. And a danish."

"Sure," I said. "Should we drive?"

"No, no. Let's walk." S. S. periodically swooped down, shoveled up a palmful of snow, packed it into a ball, and winged it at a stop sign. The first three times, he missed, but on the fourth time, he hit it head-on, causing it to clang while the snow that had been perched delicately atop the sign's narrow width came fluttering down. S. S. raised both arms into the air and said, "Yes!"

I couldn't help imagining how this street must have looked fifty years ago. Faculty used to live in these Victorians, their children playing together in the front yards, and on a morning such as this one, there probably would have been several snowmen in various stages of construction. This, of course, was long before those same children, now grown up and living in a new subdivision, partitioned their old childhood homes into multifamily apartments and then divvied them up again, a dozen years later, into even smaller apartments; before the houses were sold off, one by one, to property management companies; before students saw going away to college as solely an opportunity to party for four or five or six straight years; before the original porch railings had rotted away and new ones were hammered into place out of untreated two-by-fours, but only after the city had issued several citations for housing code violations. I used to imagine what Iowa City had been like back when Flannery O'Connor was a student in the Workshop, or when the Workshop's classrooms were held in army-issue Quonset huts, but at some point I quit superimposing the past over the present and began seeing the present for the way things were now.

S. S. reached up and slapped the stop-sign he'd pegged with the snowball. When he lowered his arm, he examined his hand and said, "Hm."

"What?" I asked.

"I believe I've sliced open my hand. Is there a hospital around here, by chance?"

"By the Foxhead," I said.

"Would it be faster to walk or drive?" he asked calmly as blood poured freely from his palm.

"Six of one, half a dozen of the other."

"Let's walk then," he said. "It's such a nice day."

S. S. BLED ALL the way to Mercy Hospital, leaving a convenient trail for hound dogs and crime scene investigators.

"You doing okay there?" I asked.

"Fine, perfectly fine," S. S. said. "The Ancient Greeks used to think that veins were filled with air until the physician Galen discovered that it was blood that filled them. After that, he started performing blood-lettings. He calculated how much blood should be removed based on how old the patient was, their constitution, what season it was, the weather, and where they were. Do you know the origin of the word *plethora*? It originally meant excess blood. Symptoms were thought to be headache, fever, and apoplexy." He looked over at me and smiled. "Perhaps I'll tell the doctor I'm suffering from plethora and foolishly took matters into my own hands."

"They'll lock you up," I said.

"You're right," he said and laughed. "They would, wouldn't they?"

We walked into the emergency wing of the hospital and walked up to the information desk. Hospitals made me skittish these days. Self-employed, almost penniless, I hadn't had health insurance since I was a student. I coasted from day to day on the thin hope that I was still relatively young. I didn't tempt the Gods of Calamity and Misfortune by skiing or rappelling or skydiving. I lived, as much as anyone could, a cautious existence. But I feared that I had been tagged the second I walked through the hospital's automatic doors as one of the uninsured, as though a chip, implanted at birth, could be activated or deactivated, depending upon my insurance status, and right now my deactivated chip was setting off red flags in offices throughout this building.

At the information desk, S. S. silently raised his hand and showed the receptionist the deep cut.

"You didn't hit a major artery," she said emotionlessly. "You'll live."

"Oh, good," S. S. said, acting genuinely grateful.

"Fill this out," she said, handing him a clipboard, "and then bring it up when you're done. Can you still write?"

"I haven't tried in years," he said, peeking over at me and raising his eyebrows. "But I'll give it a whirl."

We walked to the waiting area, where, curiously, only a few others sat: a man holding his kneecap; a child stretched out over several chairs and resting his head in his mother's lap; and a man wearing a suit and sitting in a wheelchair, watching *The People's Court*. In Minneapolis, where I grew up, there would be dozens of people in the emergency room, several of them in dire need of attention. Though the area would be filled mostly with men who'd suffered relatively minor on-the-job injuries, there would likely be someone who'd been shot through the leg or the arm, a flesh wound, and who probably didn't have insurance, which meant that they would have to wait longer than the rest of us, keeping pressure on the bleeding hole with a rag the whole time. The emergency room, bright and loud, had fascinated me back then: gurneys pushed in and out, sometimes occupied, sometimes empty; curtains for examination rooms parted just enough to reveal someone wearing a thin hospital gown, their arm hooked to an IV, a small pouch of liquid dangling from a hook overhead; the impatient fathers yelling at receptionists; the ever-present policemen speed-walking through the emergency room.

Once, when I was ten years old, I watched a doctor part the curtains of an examination area, and I saw a brown-haired girl about my age standing in her cotton gown next to her mother, and when the girl turned around, I saw that the gown she had on was open in the back, and I saw, without any obstruction, the nape of her neck, the length of her spine, most of her butt, and the backs of her skinny, tanned legs. I fell in love with her right then and there. How could I not have? Since it was years before I saw a real, live, naked girl again, I thought of that brown-haired girl often—almost every minute of every day for the first few weeks after my big toe, which I had gruesomely stubbed while wearing flip-flops, had been sewn back up. By the time I had reached my teens, I thought of her only once in a great while. Still, I never completely shook her, and there were times even now when I wondered if I had dreamed her. Why would a hospital, of all places, have provided such a perfect peeping opportunity for little boys to spy naked little girls? Why weren't gunshot victims tended to more quickly? Why were police always roaming the halls? But I swear, this is all true . . . and it was vivid to me once again at Mercy Hospital in Iowa City.

"Don't wait around," S. S. said, balancing the clipboard on his knee. "*You*, sir, have things to do, people to find."

"How about if I come back in an hour," I said.

"Make it two," he said. "You know how these things go. Oh, and in the event of my death, please notify the press. I'm sure my editor, if no one else, will want to retrieve my body." He winked at me.

"Will do," I said. I patted his knee and stood up.

I wandered over to the hospital's pharmacy to pick up some Tums for my sour stomach, but when I saw how much they cost, I put them back. I'd forgotten how broke I was; in fact, I had forgotten, until now, about the breast pump, which was reason enough to find Vanessa Roberts, who had fleeced me out of $214. I was about to leave when my eye caught sight of a novel on the revolving rack of paperbacks. The book was titled *Morning Dew*. Its author? Lucy Rogan, my romance writer. I opened the book and read the first sentence:

As Claire Darcy Wembley was about to mount Old Whiskers, her shiny black stallion, she caught sight of a man—a stranger, no less—so preternaturally handsome that her left foot missed the stirrup and she crumpled to the muddy ground below, causing her to sob uncontrollably, until the man, who introduced himself as Quentin Wembley (her second cousin, as it turned out), took hold of her filthy but dainty hands and, in one swift move, uncorked her from the soggy Earth.

"Good God," I whispered and flipped to the inside back cover, from which Lucy Rogan smiled out at me in a pose normally reserved for eighth-grade photos: arms folded over a split-rail fence, head tilted to the side, trees (possibly fake) standing majestically behind her. Her bio still said nothing about a husband, but there was a website, so I pulled a pen from my inside pocket and wrote it across my hand. I was about to return the book when Alice entered the pharmacy holding a brown paper bag.

My first thought was that she had come to get a prescription filled for the morning after pill, fearing I had impregnated her in the back seat of my Corolla, but then it occurred to me that she might have come to the hospital for a tetanus shot after slicing her foot on the cheese grater on my floorboard. When the pharmacist, a handsome man with prematurely white hair, stepped down from his elevated pharmacist's perch, walked over to Alice, took the bag from her, and kissed her on the cheek, I saw a bright and undeniable truth unfold before me—namely, that I knew nothing about Alice's life. For all I did know, she might have had children; she might have owned a hulking BMW SUV with plenty of legroom for getting laid; she might have taken up golf. Now that I thought of it, she had been trying to tell me something at Mickey's, but we conveniently let it slide. I had assumed because my own life had come to a halt that hers had as well. In CVS, and then later at the restaurant, I saw only a slightly older version of the person who had walked out of my life. The reason I had been unable to envision Alice in any context other than one that involved me was also why I had given up writing my novel: a failure of imagination. But what I wondered now was if my inability to write one more page of fiction—one more *word*—had, in turn, caused a complete meltdown of *all* my creative faculties, including the necessary ones for which basic survival was essential. If I couldn't have imagined that Alice, whom I hadn't seen in years, might possibly have gotten married in the interim, what the hell else wasn't I seeing?

Alice left the pharmacy, and I started to follow, but the pharmacist yelled out at me: "Hey! Did you pay for that book?"

I looked down. I was still holding Lucy Rogan's novel. I brought it up to the counter, dug out my few remaining bills, and handed them over.

I nodded toward the book and said, "Wife's in for . . . " *For what?* I wondered. I couldn't think; I didn't know. "A vasectomy," I offered, the only medical procedure that came to mind. When the pharmacist, whose photo on the wall identified him as Jerome Ruby, stopped what he was doing, unsure whether I was serious or not, I added, "A female vasectomy. *You* know." I snapped my fingers a few times, pretending to think, but nothing was coming.

"Tubal ligation?" he asked, narrowing his eyes.

"Bingo!" I said. "We already have five kids, so . . . Five seemed like a good place to stop. Do you have kids?"

"One," he said curtly. "Here's your change. Good day." He returned to his perch and began counting pills, peeking up at me over his half-glasses to see if I was still there, which I was.

I carried my book outside and into the snow-muffled morning, hoping to find Alice, but she was already gone. I looked for car exhaust rising into the air, like smoke signals from a teepee, thinking I might locate Alice that way, but the parking lot across from the hospital was as still as a graveyard.

"Dammit," I said. I walked toward the nearest corner, thinking maybe she had parked on a side-street, but in a split-second decision I veered to my right, up the stairs to the Foxhead, and walked inside. The only other people there were Neal, the bartender, and former weight lifter, now Foxhead regular, Larry McFeeley.

Neal pulled me a draw of Miller Lite without asking what I wanted. Larry looked over at me and nodded.

"Put it on your tab?" Neal asked.

"Please," I said.

Neal, aware of my precarious employment, let me run monthly tabs. What I loved about bars was the absence of self-righteousness. No one was going to ask me what the hell I was doing there on a weekday at noon. No one cared.

I carried my beer to the back booth, sat down, pulled Lucy Rogan's novel out of my pocket, and started reading more of it. The best I could tell, it was the story of forbidden love, the love of two cousins (*second* cousins, the narrator made clear again and again), and how they were going to overcome the stigma attached to such a love, not so much by society but by their own families, especially since Claire was poised to collect somewhere in the neighborhood of a hundred million dollars upon turning twenty-five. Would love conquer all? "Read on!" the book shouted to me at the end of each short chapter. And read on I did. I took breaks only to piss and order more beer. By the middle of the novel, the pages were turning themselves—or so it seemed. There were no real surprises, and all the characters were ones I'd seen before, mostly on soap operas that I used to watch with my mother when I was too sick to go to school, and yet, on a day as cold as this one, while slumped inside a smoky, sun-filled bar cocooned by snow, I couldn't have found a book more gripping than the one I was holding. I was so lost in the experience that I only dimly heard the door open and close, and I didn't even notice the two men walking toward me until they had stopped at the edge of my table and one of them cleared his throat. I looked up. It was Vince Belecheck and Tate Rinehart.

Tate, shivering, was still wearing only an old service station jacket. Vince, on the other hand, was dressed like a lumberjack in an insulated, red-and-black-plaid flannel shirt, a puffy down-filled vest, and a black knit cap with the Steelers logo. A gray fuzzy ball hung from the top of his cap. They were each holding a mixed drink.

"Hair of the dog," Vince said. "You mind?" he asked, but sat down across from me before I could answer, sliding over, and then patting the spot next to him, as one would for a dog. Tate obediently sat down. It was clear that Tate was suffering from a hangover of monumental proportions. His face was puffy, his stare like that of a dead fish packed in ice. Vince said, "Tied one on last night. Remember those two hotties?" He nudged Tate in the ribs, and Tate moaned. "You should have stuck around," Vince said. "On second thought, there *were* only two of them. Probably better you left when you did. They were poets, weren't they?" he asked Tate. Tate stared morosely into his drink, as if the cubes were slowly revealing the date of his death. "Anyway," Vince said, "poets are fucking crazy, man. Sex freaks. All you have to do is tell them you've read Sylvia Plath and what's-her-name. You know: the other one who killed herself. Oh, Christ, you know who I'm talking about. Oh, Jesus

Christ, what's her name? Fuck me," he said. "I think I wiped out almost all of my brain cells last night."

"Anne Sexton," I said.

Vince slapped the table with his palm. "Bingo!" he said. "How could I have forgotten that? Sex is in her name. *Sexton*. Christ. Wasn't she, like, doing her shrink? Anyway, I started talking about Plath and Sexton, and that was all it took. They were all over us. Like flies on shit." He thought about that and then said, "Maybe that's not the best simile. But you get the idea. So," he said. "What're you reading there?"

I shut the book. "Nothing," I said. Before I could slide it off the table, Vince reached out and grabbed it with one of his big paws.

"What's this?" he asked. "A *romance* novel? Jesus, Jack. Don't tell me you actually read that horseshit. Do you actually read this horseshit?"

I shook my head. "I know the author."

Vince let out a whoop. "You *know* someone who writes that shit? Tell us you're kidding. Are you listening to this, Tate? Jack here *knows* a romance writer."

Tate looked up and said, "I don't feel too good." He stood, lurched toward the bathroom directly behind us, and slammed the door shut.

For the next ten minutes, Vince and I sat in silence while we listened to Tate throw up in the toilet. At last, Vince said, "He and the chick he hooked up with were doing body shots. I didn't go down that road. I know my limits." He picked up Lucy's book, opened it to her photo, and said, "So. You nailing this broad or what?"

"No," I said. "I . . ."

Tate returned to our table.

"Feel better, sport?" Vince asked. "Sometimes getting it out of your system helps. Alcohol is poison, after all. Fucking arsenic." He picked up his drink and tossed it back until the ice piled up against his nose and steam came rolling like fog from the glass. He slammed the glass down and said, "What're you drinking, Jack? Beer? You want something harder?"

"I'm fine," I said.

"I need some water," Tate said.

"Yo, Neal!" Vince yelled, twisting around in the booth and motioning toward the bartender. "Can we get my boy here some water?"

The Foxhead didn't offer table service, but Neal, probably because business was slow, brought over three large glasses of water for us anyway.

"Thanks, Neal," I said, hoping a scrap of civility might differentiate me from the group.

Vince looked at me and said, "So, what's the game plan?"

"Game plan?" I asked.

"Yeah, you're Tate's media escort, right? You're the one who can charge all this shit back to the publisher, right? We didn't even think about that until it was time to settle up last night, and Tate and I were like *holy shit* when we saw the bill. No way was the publisher going to pay for *that* much booze. I think it was Tate who said we should have kept you around." Vince picked up his water, took a sip, and said, "Ugh. Christ. I thought this was beer. You ever do that, pick up something without looking at it and think it's something else you're about to drink? The worst is picking up a glass you think's full of Coke when it's really full of milk. That happened to me when I was a kid, and I almost blew chunks across the room. What about those people who are blindfolded and told they're eating, I don't know, a dog turd when they're really eating filet mignon, but just the *idea* that they might be eating a dog turd is enough to make them throw up."

"Guys, please," Tate said.

"But now that I'm sitting here thinking about it," Vince went on, "I'm wondering who the fuck would do that to someone—blindfold some poor son of a bitch and wave a sizzling piece of filet in front of them and say it's dog crap?"

"Please," Tate whispered. "Can we change the subject?"

"Sure," Vince said. "But I'm trying to remember now where I heard that damned story. Was it a scientific experiment, or was it torture? I can't remember. You know what we should do tonight, Tate? We should blindfold some chicks and try this out. Those poet chicks would have gone for it." He leaned forward and said, "Those chicks, Jack." He wagged his big head and said, "When we got back to our place, they started making out. I never saw anything like that. I mean, I've seen it in pornos, but not in the flesh like that. They were out of control."

"I'm glad you had a good time," I said flatly.

Vince sat up, narrowing his eyes at me, and then he grinned and said, "Awwwwww. You're jealous, aren't you?"

"I'm not jealous," I said. "Really, I'm glad you had a good time."

"Shit, man. There's no need to be jealous," Vince said. "All you have to do is publish a book. That's what gives you the mojo, pal. I mean, Tate here is a good-looking guy in that artsy-fartsy New York kind of way, but it's not like either of us is a fucking Adonis. No, man, it's the book that does it."

"I'll keep that in mind," I said.

"Oh ho! Now you're *sulking*," Vince said. "Look at you."

"I'm not sulking," I said. "All I said was, 'I'll keep it in mind.'"

"Yeah, but, you said it like I should be sorry I'm a published writer and you're not. Listen, don't bullshit me. I'm a student of human behavior. That's what the best fiction writers are. Isn't that right, Tate? Good writers are like psychologists. Or is it anthropologists? Anyway, everything I write is really about why people are the way they are. You can't bullshit us, man." Vince looked over at Tate and said, "I need out. I suddenly need to take a world-class dump. But you know what? I wonder if the opposite is true. I wonder if you hold a piece of shit under someone's nose and tell them it's a filet, if they'll eat it."

Tate ran to the bathroom again and started to vomit. Vince used the women's bathroom next door. I pocketed Lucy Rogan's novel and, while the two men were indisposed, quickly stood up. On the floor, slumped against the booth, was Tate's canvas messenger bag. I picked it up and slipped it over my shoulder.

"Don't let them put anything on my tab," I said to Neal on my way toward the exit.

"Not a chance," Neal said.

Larry McFeeley said, "Leaving so soon?"

"Busy day," I said and patted him on the back.

"You know what people don't realize about weight lifting?" Larry said.

I stopped walking and looked at him. He was already half in the bag, the poor bastard. "What's that?" I asked.

"Most of it's mental," he said, tapping the side of his head with his forefinger.

I nodded; I wasn't sure what to say. I wasn't sure what he *wanted* me to say.

"Have a good one now," Larry said, returning to his drink.

"You, too, friend," I said.

WITH TATE'S MESSENGER bag strapped over my shoulder, I tromped back to the hospital. I wasn't entirely sure why I had taken it. I'd never stolen anything before in my life, unless the ending of my optometrist short story counted, but every writer goes through an imitative phase, and there's a world of difference between theft and mimicry. That, at least, is what I had been telling myself for the past fourteen years.

When I walked through the hospital's automatic doors, I expected S. S. to be waiting for me with his hand bandaged, and I expected him to tip his head toward the messenger bag and say, "I see you have a new accoutrement!" But S. S. wasn't anywhere in sight.

"Excuse me," I said to the receptionist, the same woman who had informed S. S. that he wasn't going to die. "I'm supposed to pick up S. S. Pitzer. He's the one who needed his hand stitched up. Can you tell me how much longer he'll be?"

The receptionist typed a few words, then looked up and asked, "And what's your relation to Mr. Pitzer?"

"I . . ." I felt compelled to tell her the truth—that I didn't really know him at all, that I had met him only one other time, that he had arrived in town under mysterious circumstances and I had given him my sofa for the night. "We're friends," I finally said. "I brought him in. Remember?"

"Sorry," she said. "I can give information to family members only."

When I turned to leave, she said, "Pssssssst."

"Yeah?" I whispered.

She wrote something on a Post-it note and then handed it to me. I read the note.

"He *left*?" I asked.

"Shhhhhhhhh," she said. Whispering, she added, "I'm not supposed to say anything. It's just that . . ."

"What?"

"You looked so sad."

Why the hell did everyone think I looked sad?

"Did you see him leave?" I whispered.

The receptionist nodded.

"Did they stitch up his hand?"

"It was taped," she said. "I really shouldn't be telling you any of this."

"Okay," I said. "All right." I forced a smile, trying not to look so sad, but feeling sadder than I had in a long, long time. In fact, I almost felt like crying. I pulled the messenger bag strap higher up onto my shoulder, turned, and walked over to a bank of connected chairs and plopped down. Bracing myself for the cold, I pulled on my ski mask and gloves, but instead of standing up and leaving, I remained glued to the chair, immobile, staring blankly ahead through the mask's two holes.

It was likely—probable—that I would never get hired again as a media escort. New York publishing is like a small town where everyone knows everyone else, and I was certain that word of me losing an author, especially one as prominent as Vanessa Roberts, would travel fast, whispered inside buildings all along Avenue of the Americas and then spreading like a virus to the boutique literary agencies on both the Upper East and Upper West Sides, and then down to the lofts of SoHo that housed the few remaining independent publishers whose publicists I charged only half of what I charged a Random House or a Simon & Schuster. The fact was I'd already burned some bridges. A few years ago, when an imprint of a publishing behemoth didn't cut me a check within sixty days of my services, I sent them a subsequent bill with a $20 late fee. When I *still* wasn't getting paid, I wrote to say that I was going to take them to small claims court. That's when the head of publicity, Ross Traveaux, got involved. A check was promptly cut for the original fee, but then Ross himself sent me a personal check for the twenty dollars, along with a note: "We will no longer need your services."

The little shit, I thought. *The little ass-wipe.* What Ross Traveaux had failed to realize—what *most* publicists in New York failed to realize—was that the money I made as a media escort was what kept me afloat from month to month. *Not* receiving payment might result in a warning from the electric company or a disconnected phone. I also knew that they themselves—the behemoth publishing houses—played hardball with the independent bookstores, making it harder and harder for them to survive with so many chain stores opening up only a block or two away. It was all so dismal. And then throw into the mix a shit-heel like Ross Traveaux whose position as head of publicity for said behemoth publisher gave him all the power someone like him needed to feel that he was smarter than he really was.

For days I fumed, fantasizing about a trip to New York in which I waited outside his building with a . . . what? A cream pie to slam into his face? A flaming bag of shit to throw at him? A concealed lead pipe? I would never have gone to New York to confront him, of course, but every time I thought of him over the next year, I felt that there were unresolved issues between us, and I wanted him to understand, without any ambiguity, that being lucky in life was not the same thing as being intelligent, and that one day the boom would lower for him, if not professionally then personally—and then what? Who would be there to pick him up and dust him off?

And then one night, after a few too many drinks, I Googled him. The first entry that appeared was his obituary, a short piece in *The New York Times* about how he had gone to Spain to help promote the Spanish translation of the house's number-one-best-selling book, and while in Pamplona, watching the famous running of the bulls, a group of teenage boys, fueled by their hatred of America, pushed Ross out into the street, where he was gored by a bull and then crushed to death by the stampede that followed. He was only thirty-eight.

"Jesus," I said, reading and re-reading the article. I should have felt some glimmer of retribution, but in truth I felt bad for the guy. I could easily have imagined myself dying absurdly as the victim of a random and unprovoked event. "Poor guy," I said.

The blogs, however, weren't nearly as generous. They'd had their own dealings with Ross Traveaux, and more than a few bloggers Photoshopped Ross getting gored up the ass by pasting his head onto a naked and bent-over male and then adding an angry bull ramming him from behind.

After Ross's untimely death, I had hoped to start getting work again from said behemoth publisher, but apparently he had put me on some kind of interoffice blacklist, and the few emails I sent to publicists offering my services went unanswered. Whatever sympathy I might have had for him evaporated along with whatever extra income I could have been earning if Ross hadn't gone out of his way to screw me over. But in the end, who among the two of us had come out ahead? Ross Traveaux was dead. I, at least, was still alive.

But now, sitting in the hospital, overheated in my ski mask, I wondered if maybe I should have been a little more patient while waiting for the money they owed me. Maybe I shouldn't have thrown the tiny pebble of small-claims court at the hulking, multiheaded monster that I knew could eat me for breakfast and then shit me out before the lunch whistle blew.

Through the hospital's glass doors, I saw Vince and Tate walk by, probably looking for me. Vince stopped once, putting his hand up to his brow scout-style, as if peering into a dense forest, but then they walked on, Tate with his head down, Vince gesturing wildly. I was about to stand up to see where they were going when M. Cat appeared from behind me like a scene from a dream, walking toward the pharmacy and wearing a pair of oven mitts. Did he work in the hospital kitchen? Was there something about M. Cat that I didn't know? He was crying, I noticed. His eyes were red and he kept sniffling. That's when I realized that the tips of his ears were taped up, too, making him positively Spock-like in appearance. On closer inspection, I saw that he wasn't wearing oven mitts, after all. Both of his hands were wrapped in gauze and taped around the seams, like the hands of a burn victim.

I tried catching up to him. I said, "Hey, buddy," but when he turned around and saw me—a man wearing a ski mask rapidly approaching— he raised his arms into the air and said, "My ATM card is in my wallet. The PIN is 7625. Just don't hurt me, okay?"

I reached up and pulled off my mask. "It's *me*," I said, and M. Cat lowered his arms.

At the sight of me, M. Cat broke down altogether, weeping and holding both hands out for me to look at. "I got frostbite, dude."

"You're shitting me," I said.

"*Look!*" he yelled. "*Look!*" He shook his bandaged hands at me. The receptionist shushed him, and M. Cat wiped his wet face with his forearm. "How am I supposed to open doors? How am I supposed to take a *piss*? I'm going to need your help."

"My help doing what?" I asked. "Helping you take a piss?"

"Maybe," he said.

"Look," I said. "I don't know. I . . ."

"This is all your fault, you know," M. Cat said, leaning toward me. "You're the one who sent me looking for her."

This I couldn't deny: I had.

"Jesus," I said. "I'm sorry, man. Here. Let's take a seat, okay? I want you to tell me what happened. Could you do that?"

M. Cat sniffled a few times. When he first tried to speak, he sputtered and buried his face in the crook of his arm, but then he regained his composure and told me the story.

"After you called me," he said, "I decided to drive to all the hotels and motels around here, asking if anyone had seen Vanessa. I made it out to the Quality Inn and the Travelodge without any trouble, but once I got onto I-80 and started heading to Coralville, the storm really picked up. It was a fucking whiteout, man. I couldn't see a thing. I kept seeing these big-ass rigs and SUVs off in the ditch, and I started becoming a wreck, so I pulled out my one-hitter and . . ."

I held up my hand. "Whoa! Wait a second. Let me get this straight. You pulled out your one-hitter while you were driving through a blizzard?"

"For my nerves, brother," M. Cat said. "You don't know what it was like." I stared at him until he shrugged and said, "What?"

"I'm just saying, couldn't you have waited? You're driving through a fucking blizzard!"

"Until you've walked a mile in my shoes," M. Cat said, "I don't think you can judge me." He reached up to scratch his head but stopped when he saw his puffy white hand. "I've got an itch," he said.

"So, what happened?" I asked.

"After you scratch my head," he said. "It's driving me crazy."

"You want me to scratch your head?"

"Please," he said. I reached up, planted my nails into his scalp, and started to go to work, but M. Cat said, "Ow! Easy, easy. And a little to your left. No, wait: *my* left."

"How's that feel?" I asked, and he smiled for the first time, reminding me of how my childhood dog, ZaSu Pitts, would open her mouth when I scratched her, smiling up at me with her black lips.

"Oh, oh," he said. "That's good. No, wait. A little higher up. Yes, there, right there. Ohhhhhhhh."

"Okay," I said, removing my hand. "Enough. Now tell me what happened."

"Sure," he said, and he told me how everything had been fine until he lit the one-hitter, and then he thought he saw something run across the highway—a deer?—and he slammed on the brakes. It was this— his sudden attempt at stopping—that sent the car into a wild tailspin. Assuming a semi-trailer was going to hit him as he spun, M. Cat made peace with God. But, as it turned out, no one was behind him. The car spun off into the ditch, and in a matter of a few minutes, it was entirely covered with snow.

"What I didn't realize," he said, "was that I'd missed the Coralville exit by about five miles. I don't know how the hell that happened."

"You were lighting a one-hitter," I reminded him.

"Whatever," he said. "The point is, I wasn't anywhere near an exit, and when I climbed out of the car, no one could see me. And I was afraid of getting hit if I stayed too close to the highway, so I started walking what I thought was parallel to the road but far enough away not to get killed by an out-of-control car, but since I had to keep my head down, I was just walking across some fucking cornfield, dude. It was endless.

And I was getting colder. And I kept tripping and falling. Finally, I gave up and stood there."

"For how long?" I asked.

"I don't know. Four hours? Five hours? I had no idea where my car was. But then the snow finally stopped coming down, and I saw a light in the distance. A farmhouse. It was there the whole time about three hundred yards away."

"Shit," I said.

"No shit," M. Cat said. "You're telling *me*. So I walked over there, and it was this old couple, Amish-looking but not Amish. I asked them."

"If they were Amish?" I asked. "You asked them?"

"Yeah. But they weren't. He had one of those beards without the mustache. Not a good look, dude. Unless you're Amish. Anyway, once the roads were plowed, they drove me here. Oh yeah—get this. He's working on a novel. Seriously. So I gave him your name and address. Thought you could help him out."

"You didn't," I said.

"This dude . . . he saved my *life*," M. Cat said.

"All right. Okay."

"Now look at me," M. Cat said. "I'm screwed. With a capital S." He sighed; his eyes teared up. He turned to me and said, "I need to pee, bro."

Staring down into my lap, I nodded, not realizing at first the full import of what he'd said, but when M. Cat didn't move, I looked back up at him and shook my head. "You'll need to find someone else to help you. Sorry."

"You got me into this," he said.

"I just can't," I said. "You don't understand. I can't even pee if I'm in a restroom and someone else is waiting outside."

"That's a problem," M. Cat said. "But that's *your* problem, not mine. I can pee anywhere. Look, bro. Just unzip me once we get inside." When I didn't say anything, he looked pleadingly into my eyes and said, "Dude, my back teeth are swimming. I need your help, brother."

He stood and motioned for me to follow him. I didn't see any other option in sight, so I followed him to the men's room, right up to the urinal. Before he knew what I was doing, I reached down and unzipped him as fast as I could.

"There," I said.

He pawed at his crotch for a few seconds with his bandaged hands. "This ain't workin'," he said finally. "I need you to pull me out."

"No," I said. "Absolutely not."

"*Dude*," he said. "This isn't sexual. It's urological. It's *medical*. Don't think of it as holding my cock, *hombre*. Think of it as helping out someone less able than yourself."

The first rule of fiction writing is to burrow yourself into the consciousness of the narrator in order to view the world from his or her perspective, so that's what I did—I put myself in M. Cat's shoes, and I saw instantly how helpless and vulnerable he must have felt, how difficult it must have been to ask me for help.

"Okay," I said. "Okay, okay." I took a deep breath. "Stand up against the urinal," I said. "Let me get behind you."

M. Cat obeyed. I reached around and parted his fly. I started to pull the band of his underwear down when a man wearing a suit walked in and saw us. He paused, narrowed his eyes at us, said, "Excuse me," and then apologized, but on his way out, he said, "You should lock the door, you know," and then, as the door shut behind him, he said, "For God's sake! This is a *hospital*."

"I can't do it," I said and let the elastic band snap back into place. "I'll go get someone."

"Don't leave me, man," M. Cat pleaded, but I was already out the door, rushing to find someone who could take care of him. At the sight of the first nurse, a woman in her late forties who looked as though she'd seen pretty much everything in the line of duty, I said, "There's a man in the lobby restroom who needs assistance."

"What kind of assistance?" she asked.

"I really don't know," I said, "but he was calling out for help. He looks like a burn victim," I added. "His hands are wrapped in gauze."

The nurse looked around her for someone better suited for entering the men's room, then checked her watched and sighed. "All right. I'll see what he needs," she said finally. As soon as I'd successfully handed over the baton of M. Cat's woes, I put my ski mask back on and left the hospital, heading quickly away. A stranger might have even mistaken me for a man with a clear destination.

WAS I A terrible person?

This was what I wondered as I tried running through the snow, distancing myself from M. Cat while Tate's messenger bag banged against my side. A few blocks from the bookstore I finally slowed down, my heart pounding so hard I could hear myself wheeze, an unsettling noise like the crumpling of tinfoil at the tail end of each breath. Once I reached the bookstore, I leaned back against it and placed my hands on my knees. A knock on the window caused me to stand up and turn around. One of the bookstore's employees—a spiky-haired woman, probably a recent Workshop grad—was standing in the window's display area. She pointed at the smudges I had left all over the window.

"Sorry!" I yelled, and she resumed building a pyramid out of a hundred shiny copies of Tate's latest novel. A giant photo of Tate rested on an easel with a blurb from *The Washington Post* superimposed across his forehead: "The face of fiction's future!" In the photo, he was wearing the very messenger bag that I was now wearing.

I headed into the bookstore, walked upstairs and into the café, and ordered a cinnamon roll and coffee. Before finding a table, I perused the wide selection of literary magazines—*The Rhode Island Review*, *North Carolina Quarterly*, *Kerouac's Eyes*, and *The Angry Scribbler*. There were hundreds of magazines out there where thousands of desperate writers sent their work, clamoring for enough pages for their precious short stories or poems, but even in Iowa City, as literate of a city as one is likely to find, the magazines sat gathering dust, slumped against one another like hobos in line at a soup kitchen. I always made a point to pull one out and look it over, but I never recognized anyone anymore, except for Stephen Dixon, whose work appeared in every third magazine on the shelf, and other than examining the quality of the paper, the readability of the font, or the texture of its cover, I never actually read any of the work itself. I might as well have been studying an arrowhead or a piece of primitive pottery.

I had just sat down and sunk my teeth into my cinnamon roll when Jerry Ripley came over and pulled up a chair. Jerry was the store's head book buyer and one of my favorite persons in town.

"What the hell happened?" he asked, smiling, clearly amused.

"What do you mean?" I asked, my mouth full of pastry.

"Vanessa 'The Outhouse' Roberts," he said. "She was a no-show. I've been calling the publicist all day today to find out what happened, but I keep getting her voice mail."

"Oh that," I said. "Yeah, well, the thing is . . . she ditched me. She checked out of her hotel."

Jerry laughed, slapped the table. "Classic. Classic. Have you read her book?"

I shook my head.

"If you want a good laugh," he said, "you really should read it."

"Is it good?" I asked.

"The opposite of good. Furthermore," he said, "I don't believe it."

"Which part?" I asked.

Jerry looked like he was about to drift away. He had a tendency to zone out in the middle of a conversation and stare up and over a person's shoulder for an indefinite period of time. Eventually, his eyes would come back into focus. He was a Vietnam vet and had seen real combat, and there were days I wasn't sure if he was having a flashback or merely bored out of his skull with whomever he was speaking. And today that person was me.

He looked down at my hands, which were cleaning each other off with a napkin, and then he looked up at me, as if I had only now materialized in front of him, and said, "None of it." He slapped the table two more times and, standing, said, "Gotta run. How's Tate Rinehart treating you?"

"Oh, you know," I said. "He's from New York."

"An ostentatious jackass then," Jerry said. Two women sipping coffee at the next table over looked up, but Jerry didn't pay them any mind. I braced myself, though, because I knew where this was going. Jerry said, "This one's going to be on the radio, so just make sure he knows that he can't say 'motherfucker.' Or 'fuck.' Or 'cocksucker,' for that matter."

"Okeydoke," I said, staring down at the sad puddle of frosting on my plate.

Jerry took pleasure in shocking his clientele, especially the blue hairs, as he called them, sometimes loud enough for them to hear. ("The blue hairs come in here sometimes looking for the latest Danielle Steele," he'd told me once, "and I always tell them, 'Go to K-mart! We don't sell that crap here!' Or they'll call up and ask if we have that book, and when I ask, 'What book?' they'll say, 'That book from the 1970s. You know, the one with the yellow cover,' and I'll say, 'Oh yeah. *That* book. Let me go check,' and then I hang up.") Whenever the blue hairs were present, Jerry felt compelled to remind me which words the authors were to avoid, telling me as though I hadn't heard this speech from him a hundred times before.

Alone again, I slurped up the remainder of my coffee. I realized, with a clarity that I hadn't had in over twenty-four hours, that I needed to return Tate's messenger bag. I would need to provide a good excuse for why I had taken it in the first place, of course. I could say that something urgent had come up and I needed to run, but that I didn't want to leave the bag lying there on the floor, where anyone might take it. Surely he could believe that. I could tell him that, although I'd had no idea what was inside, the last thing I wanted was to leave the new Tate Rinehart manuscript unattended. I would say, "Imagine how much angrier you would have been if I'd just left the bag on the floor and it had gotten stolen!"

While I sat there, inert, committing my lie to memory, one of the older women at the next table over made eye contact with me, pointed to the corner of her mouth, and then mimed a wiping motion. I eased my tongue out and poked around my mouth until I tasted frosting. I smiled at the woman, nodded, and picked up a napkin to wipe the rest away. It was the sort of gesture of kindness that, on a day such as this one, with the light in the room shifting to the whims of the sun and clouds, from blaring bright to eerily dark to bright again, almost brought me to tears.

"Thank you," I said.

The woman nodded, and then she and her friend stood up, failing to gather their plates and cups, ignoring the protocol of busing one's own table.

I picked up Tate's messenger bag, committed to finding him and Vince. I shook it a few times, wondering what it was he kept in there. "Oh Christ," I said, looking furtively around. I finally gave in to temptation and opened the damned thing, pulling out a fistful of pens and pencils. I reached in again and pulled out an old paperback copy of Jack London's short stories. I opened it up, and next to the title "To Build a

Fire," Tate had written, "Perhaps set this in Brooklyn? Contemporary times?" I pulled out another paperback, this one an old orange copy of H. G. Wells's novel *The Island of Dr. Moreau*. Inside the front cover, Tate had written, "What if the island was Manhattan? Perhaps set it in contemporary times?"

"Hm," I said.

There was one more mass market paperback in his bag. It was *The Adventures of Huckleberry Finn*. Tate's note for this one was, "Would the Hudson River work instead of the Mississippi? Maybe Jim is a gang member. Make it contemporary?"

That was it. No manuscripts. No page proofs. Just three old paperbacks and a handful of writing utensils. As I began returning the books to the bag, positioning them as they had been, I felt a slight lump against the canvas. I opened the bag wide and peered inside.

"Ah ha," I said and zipped open yet another all-but-hidden compartment. I reached inside and pulled out a small notepad. Half of the pages were filled with notes, but only the last half of the pad was filled up: The first half was blank. The pages were written in Tate's familiar crabbed penmanship, the same penmanship that had graced the moldering paperbacks, and yet there was something more desperate about the writing here, as though a man overcome by fever had begun transcribing the voices inside his head. I could read the individual words easily enough, but the sentences were so cryptic that I couldn't figure out what he was writing about—that is, until I saw my name on the second to the last page: "Sheahan Jack." And then I realized that he was writing his notes backward, the way a child would encrypt his diary in order to confuse a nosy adult who might stumble upon it.

"What the hell?" I said. I turned to the last page and, beginning with the last word, read Tate's notes. The gist of it was that he saw ample fodder for fiction in my circumstances—namely, someone who'd had great early success but then spiraled into oblivion, working a shit job and living a shit life. He was particularly fascinated by how, in my role as media escort, I had become a butler to the kind of person I had once aspired to be. He wrote about my situation as though there were a caste system in America. The more I read, the more I began to think that maybe he had a point. After all, some smart but broke-ass kid who went to a fourth-tier state university couldn't ever have afforded to take an entry-level publishing job in New York, even if the higher-ups actually offered the position to the poor bastard, which, of course, they wouldn't have, given their own Ivy League pedigrees. Oh, sure, there might have been one or two examples to the contrary, but it certainly wasn't the rule. So maybe Tate was right. I would forever be a butler to the Tates and Vinces of the world. But then I read Tate's last sentence, which, to the untrained eye, would have appeared as the opening to his notes: "Himself killing from him keeps what?" Translated, it read: "What keeps him from killing himself?"

The "him," of course, was me.

The pad was small enough to fit inside my coat pocket, which is where I stuffed it. A thought came to me: What if Vanessa Roberts really was suffering from postpartum psychosis? This thought quickly morphed into a mild panic attack. What if I had grossly miscalculated this one? I closed the messenger bag and carried it down to the information desk, where Jerry sat high up on a stool behind a bank of computers, overseeing the store as though he were commandeering a spacecraft.

"I need a favor," I said.

"Shoot."

"Can I borrow your car?"

Jerry hesitated before asking where I needed to go.

"Unfinished business," I said. "It's actually an emergency, but I can't go into it right now."

"The roads are terrible," Jerry said.

"I'll be careful," I said.

Jerry studied me. "Do you have insurance?"

"Yes," I said, "I do." I pulled out my insurance card to show it to him, and then, for good measure, I pulled out my driver's license and pointed to the expiration date. "Look," I said. "It's still valid."

"You're not on any drugs, are you?" Jerry asked, reaching into his pocket for his keys.

I shook my head.

"It's the red Buick right out front," he said. "But please be careful, please."

"Who do you think you are? Raymond Carver?" I asked, smiling, waiting for him to smile in return. When he didn't smile, I said, "You know—the title of Carver's first book? *Will You Please Be Quiet, Please?*"

"I get it," Jerry said flatly.

On my way to the front door, I picked up a copy of Vanessa's book and carried it outside. I didn't even bother looking to see if anyone was watching me.

After starting up the Buick, I turned toward the store and saw Jerry and two bookstore workers staring at me through the plate-glass window. I waved at them, but no one waved back. Pulling out of the parallel parking space, I almost hit a pickup with a snowplow attached to its nose. The driver laid on the horn and gave me the finger, and when my shrugs and mouthed apologies didn't mollify him, I returned his gesture. At this, the driver quickly backed up. I was under the delusion that he was going to let me out, but then he began plowing mounds of snow up against the car, trapping me in place. He kept backing up and piling up more snow, until, finally, I couldn't see out the window on my side of the car. By now, Jerry had come outside, pounding on the passenger-side door and yelling at me to make him stop.

"Do something!" he yelled.

I crawled over into the passenger seat and then opened the passenger-side door, practically falling out headfirst, propelled forward by the door swinging on its hinges. I clutched and grasped at the door to keep from landing on my face and, potentially, knocking my teeth out. Back on my feet, with the door shut, I said, "He's crazy! Just look at him!"

Snow was draped over the Buick's roof. The pickup's driver, not yet satiated, continued packing half the street's snow against Jerry's car.

Jerry momentarily slipped into his zone, staring beyond the snowplow, looking into God-only-knew-what—a land mine about to be stepped on, Vietcong snipers hiding in trees—but then he opened the bookstore's front door and yelled, "Call the police! Hurry."

"Hey, look. I'm sorry," I said, but Jerry wouldn't even make eye contact with me.

"Just give me the goddamned keys back," he said, but he had no sooner finished speaking when we both noticed the same thing: blue-gray smoke pouring from the exhaust pipe. The car was still running. I reached down and tried the passenger door. It was locked.

"You locked it?" he asked.

"I didn't mean to," I said.

He looked down at the bulge in my shirt. It was the copy of Vanessa Roberts's book that I was trying to keep from falling out and into the snow.

"Did you pay for that?" he asked.

"I'll take care of that right now," I said, and walked back into the store.

While I was paying for the book, using a credit card that was dangerously close to maxing out, a squad car showed up, but it was too late: The pickup's driver had completed his task and moved on. Even when they showed up within a reasonable amount of time, as they did today, the police in Iowa City had a tendency to miss whatever it was that they'd been summoned to witness. How many times had I called them in the dead of night to report frat boys walking across the tops of my neighbors' cars, or pissing from their front porches, or shooting Roman candles down the length of a street instead of into the air? The police showed up, if they showed up at all, hours later, shining flashlights into bushes, as if maybe the culprits were now hiding instead of passed out on their puke-stained sofas or curled up like snakes around the cool porcelain of their hissing toilets. Not that I envied the police. They were victims themselves, as would be any university town's police department, answering hundreds of calls each night, most of them as inane as my own, calls about grown men knocking around empty two-liter pop bottles with hockey sticks at three in the morning, or pranks involving frat boys running a half-dozen lawnmowers in front of a sorority house in the middle of the night.

"I wasn't going to steal this book," I said to the cashier. "I was going to bring it back. The thing is, she's in trouble. She needs my help."

"Don't we all," the cashier said without looking at me. She didn't offer me a bag, so I took the naked book back out into the cold. Jerry, talking to a cop who was using a long flat metal device to unlock his passenger-side door, didn't see me. I continued on down Dubuque Street, past store employees salting patches of sidewalk, and then I crossed over to the pedestrian mall, heading for the frosted-over automatic doors of the hotel breezeway and then into the hotel's lobby, where only yesterday I had dumped off Vanessa Roberts.

At the front desk, I explained that Vanessa Roberts had checked in and then, later the same day, checked out, and now I was wondering if she had checked back in. I opened the book and pointed to the author's photo as evidence. It was the first time I had actually looked at it. The photo, taken by Marlis Messenger, who took all the famous authors' photos, featured Vanessa lying across a Victorian fainting couch, the back of her hand resting on her forehead, like a silent movie star. Marlis Messenger's photos looked like nineteenth-century daguerreotypes, with her subjects' eyes burning bright, practically glowing, from otherwise drab or overcast backgrounds. Vince Belecheck's photos always featured him stone-faced in front of a construction site or standing on a steel beam with his hands on his hips or, in his latest, wearing a hard hat and about to climb a telephone pole. Back when I still thought that I might one day see a published book of my own, I had imagined getting my photo taken by Marlis. In such a photo, I would stand in a blighted cornfield with two hunting dogs while clutching a shotgun (never mind that I didn't hunt or own a weapon); in another, I would be sitting at my modest kitchen table with my ancient gas stove behind me, all four burners turned on high, and, off to the side, my yellow slicker hanging from a nail on an otherwise empty wall while I stared with great intensity into the camera's lens. But after years of receiving free books from publishers for the authors I escorted and studying their photos, I had decided that I would forgo a photo altogether; in fact, I would probably just publish the damned book under a pseudonym. There was nothing healthy, I had decided, about meeting one's reading public.

"No, sir," the man at the front desk said. "She has not checked back in." He studied my book a bit longer and then said, "I've heard of that book."

"*The Outhouse?*" I asked, showing him the front cover.

"Yeah," he said. "Isn't it about a brother and sister, uh, doing it?"

I nodded. That was, more or less, the gist of it.

"Sick," he said.

"And the book's not that good, either," I said. "Or so I've been told."

Behind me, I heard, "There you are, you s.o.b.!" It was Vince Belecheck. He draped his heavy arm aggressively over my shoulder. "I think you have something that belongs to my friend," he said.

I turned around, and there stood Tate, master of the coded prose, glaring at me with his spider-veined eyes.

"Oh, yeah," I said, slipping the messenger bag off my shoulder. "I had to be somewhere, and I didn't want to leave it on the floor of the Foxhead. I was just dropping it off for you here, in fact. Where it would be safe." I returned the bag to Tate, who shook it a few times, as if determining its weight.

Vince leaned into me. He said, "You should have waited for us."

"That's the thing," I said. "I couldn't. I had to go."

Tate opened the bag, casually checking the contents. He looked satisfied and was about to close it when he started feeling around in a kind of panic, unzipping the inside pocket where he'd been keeping his notes about me.

"Everything there?" Vince asked, squeezing me even tighter. "Missing anything?"

Tate looked up at me. His face was flushed. He knew that I knew what he had written about me. He also knew that I knew that he had been contemplating lifting my life for a book. But Tate knew, too, that he couldn't say anything. This was between him and me now.

He looked over at Vince and said, "Everything's here."

"Good!" Vince said, letting me go. "Tate here needs to check into the hotel. Don't you, Tate?" To me, he said, "I think one night at Chez Belecheck was all he could handle. Yo, Tate," he yelled. "Make sure you get two beds. Just in case we, you know, bag some more lonely poets tonight."

The entire hotel staff behind the counter looked up.

Vince noticed them but didn't care. He said, "I don't want to bela-bor my point about these poet chicks, but I'm telling you, Jack, you should carve out some time to memorize a few Seamus Heaney poems—they eat that Irish shit up—or maybe some, what's his name . . . oh, you know . . . his name sounds like 'cole slaw'?"

A woman behind the counter said, "Czeslaw Milosz." According to the tag pinned to her black jacket, her name was Rhonda.

Vince smiled at her. "Yeah, that's the guy. Hey, are you a poet?" he asked.

Rhonda nodded. I could see that she wanted to gouge his eyes out, but Vince seemed unable to read her.

"Let me guess," Vince said. "You're a big Heaney fan, aren't you? What about Plath and Sexton? Do you like them?"

"Actually," Rhonda said, "I prefer Adrienne Rich."

"Who?" Vince asked.

"And Lucille Clifton," Rhonda added.

Vince shrugged. "Never heard of them. Me? I write fiction. So does *this* fella." He pointed at Tate, then leaned over and cracked him on the back, causing Tate's signature on the check-in form to leave the page. "Maybe you've heard of our books," Vince said. "My most recent one is—"

"I don't care," Rhonda said.

"Beg your pardon?"

"I'm not interested."

"Oh. I see," Vince said. To the person helping Tate, Vince said, "Do you have a business card for the manager?"

"Just drop it," I said quietly.

"Drop it?" Vince yelled. "*Drop it?*"

"Let it go," I said.

Vince turned sharply toward me, his nose almost touching my nose, and said, "Stay out of this. This doesn't concern you."

"Fine," I muttered.

Tate wheeled around and said, "He's right, Vince. Just let it go."

Vince took a deep breath through his nose, clearing his congestion, and then wagged his head, flicking his eyes from me to Tate and then back to me. He put up both hands, as if at gunpoint, and started walking backward. "All right," he said. To Tate, he said, "See you tonight? At the reading? If you still want me to come?"

"Of course I want you there," Tate said.

After Vince had gone, I turned to leave, but Tate stopped me.

"We need to talk," he said.

I looked down at his messenger bag, now safely strapped over his shoulder. "Maybe later," I said. "I've got a few more pressing things right now."

Outside, I walked past Vince. He was smoking a cigarette at the curb, where guests usually unloaded their cars, but no one was parked there. By the time I reached the parking structure, Vince began calling my name. "Yo, Jack," he yelled. "Yo, Sheahan!" But I marched on. When I rounded the corner, I slipped on a patch of hard-packed snow and almost fell. Holding my arms out, as though walking across a tightrope, I regained my balance. The entire walk back to my apartment was treacherous, and by the time I reached my front steps, I was relieved that I hadn't cracked open my skull or slid in front of a car that wouldn't have been able to stop before running me over.

I walked up the steps softly in case M. Cat had returned home, which, by now, he must surely have done. I unlocked my door and opened it slowly. Even so, the door creaked on its hinges, and I heard, at the first squeak, someone inside my apartment moan. It was S. S., sound asleep on my couch. When I shut the door and locked it, S. S. turned over onto his side, his arm with the bandaged hand dangling off the sofa. On the coffee table lay my spare key, which I had given to M. Cat years ago in the event I ever locked myself out. I wasn't sure what disturbed me more—that S. S. had invited himself back inside my apartment while I was away, or that M. Cat had freely given up the key to the first person who'd asked him.

I walked to my bedroom, shut all the mini-blinds, and crawled into bed, even though the day was still young and Vanessa Roberts, whose book I now owned in duplicate, remained missing.

PART FOUR

The Writers' Workshop gave me the time to become a writer.
I learned to spend less time at Gabe & Walker's Bar and more time at my typewriter.
I learned the fanaticism of art. I learned how to see cornfields as nature.
I learned that all writers are madmen and madwomen and to be strenuously avoided at all cost.

—T. Coraghessan Boyle

THE FIRST TIME S. S. Pitzer came to town, Gordon Grimes was still alive and I was still engaged to Alice. By then, though, I wasn't seeing as much of Grimes as I used to, and I had quit playing poker with him altogether.

During my first year in the Workshop, a few of us would straggle from the Foxhead to Gordon's house, while his wife and child slept (or tried to sleep) upstairs. We crept into the house like burglars, keeping our voices to whispers and turning on only the necessary lights, but after his wife started to complain about these late-night intrusions, we moved the games from one student's apartment to another, eventually landing at my place since I owned a kitchen table large enough to accommodate all the willing participants. The table had belonged to my parents, but it had been given to me after my mother died and my father let the bank repossess the house. It was a long, solid table from the mid-1970s with six gloriously overstuffed chairs.

"The pot's light," Grimes would say. "Who didn't ante up?"

We played several variations of poker, all with a dollar ante and half the pot limit. Pennies stood in for dollar bills. In a single game, it was possible to lose hundreds of dollars, money that we were required to pay in full by the end of the week. I supposed there were ethical issues with the director of the Workshop and the occasional visiting writer playing high stakes poker (high stakes to me, at least) with students who were living on monthly stipends that barely covered rent and groceries, but these were choices we made as adults. No one was putting a gun to my head.

I lost far more money than I won, and when I went to bed, usually around the time that the sun was rising, I dreamed about playing poker—dreams in which I played endless games and lost each one. In some of these dreams, I would sit out a hand to take a bathroom break, only to discover that someone had been betting for me, playing out my hand, and pushing my money to the center of the table without my permission. Poker dreams: Few things in life were more debilitating. I would wake up feverish and exhausted, the sheets damp from my own sweat. That year, I lost hundreds of dollars to my classmates, to an editor visiting from one of the glossy magazines, to the writers-in-residence. I lost to everyone, except to Gordon Grimes. After one grueling week, in which we had played every day, from eleven at night until eight in the morning, Gordon Grimes lost over $2,000 to me.

"I'm in," he'd say each time he got up to go to the bathroom. And when it was clearly time to call it quits, when birds were landing on my window air-conditioning unit to look in at us and chirp loudly, when it was just the two of us left, playing head to head, Gordon would say, "One more hand, Jack. And then I'll go."

I knew that one more hand meant four or five more hands, maybe even another two hours of playing, as Gordon's tab doubled and then doubled again. It was the week that he owed me $2,400 that he called the editor at *The New Yorker* and told him about my short story, "The Self-Adhesive Postage Stamp." At his insistence, I sat in his office as he made the call. Slumped down in his chair, talking in that peculiar W. C. Fields-by-way-of-Manhattan dialect of his, Gordon said, "You've got to read this boy's work. It's like reading a young Salinger, or a young Cheever. You see the same spark there, the same raw talent." Gordon raised his eyebrows at me, as if to say, *They're interested.*

In the end, I decided not to collect the $2,400 from Gordon, and two weeks after Gordon made the phone call, my story was accepted by *The New Yorker*. Several months later, when he owed me nearly $3,000 after a particularly long streak of bad luck, a letter from Houghton Mifflin arrived informing me that Gordon Grimes had chosen my story, "The Self-Adhesive Postage Stamp," for inclusion in *The Best American Short Stories*, which he was guest-editing that year. I didn't mention the three grand to him, and he didn't offer to pay me.

I never told anyone about these arrangements, our unspoken quid pro quo, maybe because I'd hoped that Grimes's support of my work wasn't connected to the money he owed me, and I continued to fool myself for the next several years, convinced that one thing had nothing whatsoever to do with the other. I distanced myself from Gordon Grimes, and after receiving the letter from him about my story in *Best American*, I quit hosting poker games at my apartment. In time, I rarely saw Grimes at all, except on the pedestrian mall or in a restaurant, situations that called for little more than a "Hello, how are you doing?"

It was shortly after I'd earned my MFA that I met Alice. We both worked for a terrible company that scored standardized tests, and for two weeks we sat side by side, barely a word passed between us, reading semi-literate essays written by high school seniors.

"I can't take this anymore," I said one day and walked out of the building, handing my name tag to the receptionist on my way out. A few minutes later, Alice joined me outside.

"I was waiting for someone else to leave," she said. "I didn't think I could do it on my own."

"Well, good for us," I said. "We should celebrate."

We walked over to Carlos O'Kelly's and drank margaritas, and then, too drunk to drive, we took a cab back to my place, where I played old Motown songs too loud and encouraged Alice to dance on my coffee table. She was working on a master's degree in Chemistry, but her undergraduate degree had been English, and whenever she was drunk, she would recite the first thirty or so lines of the *Canterbury Tales* in Old English and then take a bow. Two years into our cohabitation, I began media escorting for the bookstore, and my second job was to pick up S. S. Pitzer and take him to a local bed-and-breakfast. The day before Pitzer was to arrive, Alice informed me that she was pregnant.

"No," I said.

"Oh, but yes," Alice said. "The big prego!"

"Really?" I asked.

"Absolutely," she said. "Without a doubt."

Too often, I had mused about the kind of advance I might get for my novel, *After the Fall*, especially given my *New Yorker* publication and subsequent appearance in *Best American Short Stories*, and I had led Alice to believe that it might be the kind of money to set us up in a meaningful way—a new house, perhaps, or a year or two without having to do any menial work. But I'd been working on the novel at a devastatingly slow pace. On a good day, I managed to write a sentence or two; most days, however, were spent laboring over the next word, or not doing anything at all. I took long walks, telling Alice that I needed fresh air in order to solve a problem with the book's plot, or that a trip to the used bookstore might inspire one of my characters to act in an unexpected way and take the novel in a much-needed new direction. What I didn't tell Alice were the dubious circumstances surrounding my publications, or my deeper suspicion that I had no talent at all. The book that I had been working on—the much-anticipated novel that Alice and

I had been banking on—was gasping for air, but I was the only one who heard its rasping breaths.

I reached out and felt Alice's belly with the tentativeness that one touches the burner on a stove.

"So," I said. "This is good? Isn't it?"

"What's wrong?" she asked.

"Nothing's wrong," I said. "Why?" But I wasn't convincing. I was almost never convincing.

S. S. was on tour for *Winter's Ghosts*. When I met him at the airport, he greeted me with a hug, as if we were old war buddies, and said, "So this is it! The fabled Iowa City I've heard so much about!"

"Actually," I said, "we're in Cedar Rapids."

"Ah ha!" S. S. cried out. "And what's Cedar Rapids' claim to fame?"

"I don't know," I said, "but there's a dog food factory on the north side of town. It smells pretty bad."

"Oh, but the resident dogs must be in heaven!" he said. The look he gave me was mischievous, and I probably should have walked away from him right then and there, but he had already won me over. The only person I knew who was as charming as S. S. was Gordon Grimes.

"Luggage?" I asked.

"Good lord, no," S. S. said. "I wouldn't think of it. A man who can't carry all his belongings in a carry-on is a man who has no business leaving his house."

I didn't think much of it at the time—S. S. staying in a bed-and-breakfast—but in all the years since, no other writer requested staying anywhere other than at the hotel that the publisher had booked for him. I didn't recognize the name of the street on the itinerary, and I drove circles around town searching for it, but eventually I found it. "Splendid!" S. S. said upon arrival. "And I thank you for the tour. It's everything I imagined. The old Victorians. The tin roofs. The blonde-haired co-eds. Beautiful. All of it!" Everything else went according to plan—checking him in, picking him up for dinner, taking him to the reading—everything, that is, until he asked me after his reading to join him for a drink. I'd given up drinking because drinking was what had led me to gambling, and gambling was what had ultimately led me to question my talent.

"Sure," I said, and we went to the Foxhead.

Gordon Grimes was already there, stuffed into one of the booths, surrounded by students I didn't recognize. When he saw me, he blanched ever so slightly but then recovered.

"Sheahan!" he said. "Come over here, you rascal. Let me introduce you around." He gave a few perfunctory introductions, but when he came to a student named Erskine Lee, he said, "Erskine just had a story in *The New Yorker*. Last week's issue, was it? Hell of a writer. *Hell* of a writer." He looked down at the unopened deck of Bicycle playing cards on the table and added, "Not a bad poker player, either, are you, you son of a bitch?" Erskine looked up at me sheepishly, and I turned away, toward S. S. I introduced S. S. to everyone. In typical workshop fashion, everyone pretended not to know who he was. I knew, however, that if I were to have left him alone for even a second, any one of them would have buttonholed him, working the poor man for a future connection, a blurb down the road, maybe even a letter of recommendation. Oh, I knew the game, and they weren't fooling anybody.

Gordon looked up at S. S. and said, "That novel of yours. *Dreams of Lucifer*? Fine work. Really fine."

S. S. reached up, touched the rim of his hat, and tipped his head. "An honor," he said, "coming from you." He then peeked up at Erskine and said, "I look forward to reading your story. The book tour has caused me to fall overwhelmingly behind in every regard, but I promise you it's next on my list. In fact, I'll write your name down. Erskine Lee, correct?" To the other students, he said, "A pleasure."

S. S. and I nabbed a booth opposite the pool table. I could feel all eyes on us, and, sure enough, a quick glance over at Gordon's table, and the eyes, which had been trained on us, slid away. *We weren't looking at you*, their posture said. *We don't care what you're talking about.* But they *had* been, and they *did*.

S. S. ordered vodka martinis for us, giving the money to me while he headed for the bathroom to relieve himself.

"There's a quote by Barry Hannah in there," he said upon returning. And then, a moment later, "I wonder if he knows." He looked down at his martini. "Did they not have slices of onion?" he asked, but his disappointment vanished as quickly as it came. "Ah, well. So be it."

Long after Gordon's crew had lit out for the territories, S. S. and I stumbled across the street to John's Grocery for a bottle of whiskey and then waited on the corner for the cab we had called to arrive.

"What if I told you that I'm working on a formula for invisibility?" he asked.

"I'd congratulate you," I said, laughing and clapping his back.

"No, no," he said. "I'm serious. Invisible. Here but not here. What a beautiful concept."

"Why invisible?" I asked, slurring.

He smiled, staring at the glowing beer sign in the Foxhead's window. "You live as long as I have, you realize that enough people have seen you."

I was about to ask him what the hell he was talking about, but our cab pulled up. By the time we settled into the backseat, I could no longer remember what it was he'd just said.

We stayed up that night playing old Tom Waits CDs while Alice slept, or tried to sleep, in our bedroom. That was when S. S. asked me to read him the first chapter of my novel. And that was when, after I had finished reading, he had proclaimed the novel's brilliance. Beaming, he said, "This is going to put you on the map in a big way."

S. S. spent that night on my couch. The next morning, I found the bottle of whiskey, empty, sitting next to my copy of Gordon Grimes's only book. S. S. must have been reading it before he passed out. We were both shaky, and more than once S. S. mentioned that he might be compelled to stick his head out a window and express himself, but I managed to get him back to the B&B to pick up his carry-on and then I drove him to the airport, where he signed my copy of *Winter's Ghosts*: "For Jack, to Whom the Gods of Literature Have Whispered. Your faithful reader and loyal friend, S. S. Pitzer."

For the next two months, all I could talk about was the novel— what I was going to do with it, the new directions the plot might take, which characters I could cut, which I should leave in . . . and then I began talking about agents and publishers, about advances, how the book should be promoted, what the print run should be. I wrote nothing, but I talked endlessly, as if talking were like stretching before a foot race. All I needed was the sound of the gunshot to prompt me to begin writing, and off I'd go! But the shot never came.

"Maybe I should change the title," I was saying to Alice at least once a day. "What do you think? I mean, *After the Fall* is the name of an Arthur Miller play. I don't know what to do."

"Whatever you think best," Alice would say. "I mean, it's your novel."

And then one day, Alice said, "Jack?"

I was sitting at my desk, staring down at where I had left off on the novel, thinking of the next possible word. The choices were daunting.

"Yes?" I asked, trying not to sound annoyed but unable to remove the edge from my voice. I smiled to mask my irritation, but the smile felt forced, unnatural.

"Something's wrong," she said.

"Wrong?" I asked.

"I'm bleeding," she said, and that was all it took, the mention of blood, and I rushed her to the hospital. All the way I berated myself for not doing something sooner. She had complained earlier that week about a pinching pain on her right side, but she had insisted she was okay, that she was probably just cramping, that it was normal. *Fuck*, I thought as I drove us the five short blocks. *Why didn't I insist that she go to the doctor?*

"You're crushing my hand," Alice said gently.

"What? Oh. Sorry." I didn't want to let go of her hand, but I did.

In the emergency room, she was immediately taken into an examination room. A nurse got to work on her right away, taking her blood pressure. "82 over 37," she whispered, writing it on the chart.

"82 over 37? That's not good, is it?" I asked. The nurse cut her eyes toward me and then down at Alice and then back up to me, as if to say, *Don't scare her, you frickin' numbskull.*

In the short time between Alice telling me that she was bleeding and the nurse glaring at me, I made every imaginable deal possible. I wasn't religious, so I wasn't sure with whom I was making the deals, but I made them nonetheless, including giving up writing and getting a real job if it meant saving the baby.

A doctor came in, taking Alice's hand and assuring her that she would be all right. She made no mention of the baby, however. That's when I knew that the deals I was making were futile. The baby would be lost.

Alice moved out two weeks later, leaving behind everything we'd purchased together, along with any photographs taken between the time we had begun dating and the day she'd left me. I eventually gathered up the photos and put them inside a shoe box, and then a year later, when it was clear that she wasn't coming back, I took the rest of the stuff, our joint purchases, to Goodwill, dropping them off in the giant dumpster for donations that sat in the building's parking lot. That night, before I went to bed, I put my long-dormant novel back inside the manuscript box and stowed it on a shelf, piling old phone books on top of it, and that's where it had sat, tucked safely away and all but forgotten, until yesterday.

After my nap, I found S. S. wide awake and reading Lucy Rogan's romance novel. S. S. said, "I hope you don't mind, but I asked your neighbor if he had a spare key. The poor fellow. He can't unzip his own pants. I had to undress him."

"You undressed M. Cat?"

S. S. nodded. "He decided it was best if he stayed nude all day. No buttons, no zippers."

"That's his solution?" I asked. "To walk around naked?"

"Frankly, I couldn't think of a better one," S. S. said. "I actually thought it was kind of ingenious, to tell you the truth." S. S. looked down at Lucy Rogan's novel, folded the corner of one of the pages, and shut it. He said, "It isn't bad. A few good passages scattered about. I especially like the way she uses the word *stiffly*. As in, 'He shook her hand *stiffly*.'"

"Where did you go?" I asked.

"Go?"

"I went back to the hospital," I said, "and you were gone."

"Oh, that. Yes, well, they finished up with me in no time. I didn't know what to do, so I wandered about. I figured we'd find each other again, sooner or later."

"And we did," I said.

"We did indeed," S. S. said. His eyes, with their sagging pouches of fat beneath them, weren't as bright as they'd been all those years ago, and lines extended downward from the corners of his mouth, making him look like he was perpetually frowning, even when he smiled. But he looked even worse for wear this afternoon, worse than he had this morning. I figured it was the pain in his hand, so I didn't ask.

"I have to go to a reading tonight," I said.

"I'll go with you," S. S. said. "If you don't mind the company of an invalid." He raised his hand, like a dog with an injured paw, to show me.

"Tate Rinehart's reading," I said.

S. S. grimaced. "Good God. What's the name of that book of his? *The Prince of SoHo?*"

"*The Duke of Battery Park*," I said.

"Oh, yes, that's right. And what's it about?"

"It's *The Prince and the Pauper*. Only set in New York. In contemporary times. I hadn't realized that, though, until today."

"Clever boy," S. S. said. "Why do people like us, you and I, bother making something up whole cloth? I mean, really, we'd save ourselves a good deal of time, don't you think?"

"I'm not a writer," I said. "Remember?"

"Nonsense. Someone with your talent? You're in a slump, that's all. I'm in a slump myself. I—"

"Enough," I said, much too sharply. "Please."

S. S. nodded. He picked up Lucy Rogan's romance and studied the cover. "Why don't I ever meet women who look like this?" he asked. When I didn't say anything, he set the book down and said, "Well. Shall we go?"

T HERE WAS A time, many years ago, when I enjoyed going to readings by fiction writers. I saw Kurt Vonnegut, with his incredibly long and expressive fingers, talk about how gloomy the world was and why he had decided to quit writing fiction. I saw Isaac Bashevis Singer near the end of his life, as thin as a stick, pausing for so long after each question put to him that one feared he might have dipped into a coma. When a student raised her hand and asked the great man to illuminate the purpose of literature, Singer stared out into the audience for an unbearably long time, as if he had not heard the question, but just as we were collectively about to give up hope on him, he raised a finger and said, "To educate and to entertain." I listened to Susan Sontag discuss the arbitrariness of decades as lines of demarcation. I watched Norman Mailer berate a young man in the audience who would not give up the microphone to the next person wanting to ask a question. I even saw John Irving theatrically take off his leather jacket before a reading and toss it aside, as though he were a Chippendale dancer. I saw all of these writers, and more. I saw giants.

But in the past dozen years as a media escort, I was forced to watch one mid-list writer after another sail through town, desperately hawking their wares. Oh, some were celebrities, albeit minor ones, their fame sometimes already on the wane by the time they landed in Cedar Rapids, but by and large, they lacked the panache of a Norman Mailer or Kurt Vonnegut, and they lacked the critical acumen of a Susan Sontag. They showed up in town wearing seersucker suits to promote books with titles like *Bob Walks to School*, or they introduced themselves as "miniaturists" and read from books that might as well have been titled *The Navel Gazer*. One poor author, in an attempt to bring something new to the table, played a flute at key intervals during his reading, only to be asked by a crazy man afterward if he knew how to play the theme to *Star Trek*. The crazy man's name was Ted, and he used to come to every reading and ask crazy questions, until the owner finally banned him from public events. A store employee was now responsible for watching the front door before readings to make sure Ted didn't come in.

What I had once loved—going to hear writers read from their new books—now depressed the shit out of me. But it wasn't only the authors who brought despair to my life. It was the audience, too. Too often, week after week, I saw the exact same people, most of whom never bought a book; they came only because it was something to do. And they always asked the same inane questions: "Do you have a writing routine?" Or, "Do you think, now that people spend so much time on the Internet, that pretty soon no one will be reading actual books anymore?" One man stood up during the Q&A and asked if anyone had an antacid. He was a homeless man who'd wandered in from the cold, and during the middle of the reading, his acid reflux had kicked in, causing him to burp loudly and pound his chest with the side of his fist. Bookstores were the new bus stations, a place where people with no discernible plan (or, in some instances, without a place to live) ended up to pass the time. The ways in which the fiction readings themselves could quickly sour were innumerable. What was worse than nobody showing up, which sometimes happened, was only one person showing up; the author, unsure of what to do, would awkwardly read to that one person. For this, publishers paid thousands of dollars, forking over money for airfare, meals, hotels, and incidentals. They paid for *me*, for Christ's sake.

What publishers fail to realize is that many writers are social outcasts, or introverted and pathologically shy, and that sending them on the road, shuttling them from city to city to meet with small and large groups who show up for reasons that usually have nothing to do with the author, is a unique kind of torture, not only for the author but often for the rest of us as well. It is the rare author who also possesses celebrity-caliber mojo. Regrettably, during all my years of media escorting, I never met the new Truman Capote or Flannery O'Connor or Tennessee Williams.

My job was to reassure the author that the event went well or to make excuses for the poor attendance. "I think the women's volleyball team is in the playoffs," I might have offered. Or: "Gallagher's doing stand-up at the student union right now, even as we speak." On one occasion, the store had failed to list the event on its calendar, and no one showed up—not even Crazy Ted, whom I probably would have invited in to fill a chair, had I seen him. The author was Maureen Schiffman, and she wept on the short walk back to the hotel. I offered to take her out for dinner and drinks, and though food and alcohol didn't entirely snuff out the sense of humiliation she had felt, it at least mollified her enough that she thanked me for salvaging what was quickly becoming the most depressing day of her professional writing life. That night I realized that I wasn't overpaid for my services, as I had always believed. I meant far more to these people than a taxi driver would ever have, and I was, in ways both small and large, earning every dollar of it.

When S. S. and I tromped into the bookstore, I spied Tate standing near the back wall, in front of the gay and lesbian section, holding a manuscript and studying it. No doubt he was going to read from a work-in-progress tonight. Most writers read from a tattered copy of their book, sometimes from a bound galley, but Tate was going all old school on us, breaking out new manuscript pages for this occasion. Since I hadn't run across them in his messenger bag, I could only assume he'd been keeping them folded and tucked inside his vintage service station jacket. When he caught sight of me, his lips tightened, like an aperture, and he quickly turned around, hunching his shoulders.

"Looks like a pleasant chap," S. S. said.

"You should meet Vince Belecheck," I said.

S. S. smiled. "Ah, yes. I remember reading a profile of him in *The Times*. 'Belecheck's School of Hard Knocks,' it was called?"

"He went to St. Albans," I said.

"*No!*"

"And then took a BA from George Washington University."

"*You lie!*" S. S. said, grinning.

"The guy's never lifted a hammer in his life," I said.

"Too bad," S. S. said, sighing. "I need to buy a miter saw and was hoping to ask him for a recommendation."

Jerry, the head book buyer, walked up to me and said, "I like you, Jack. But please don't ever ask to borrow my car again, okay?"

"No problem," I said.

Jerry looked over at S. S., nodded a curt hello, and started walking away, but then he turned around to take another look at S. S. For his part, S. S. lifted a forefinger to his brow and saluted Jerry.

"Come on," I said. S. S. and I climbed the stairs to the place where the readings were held, and I led us to two back-row seats.

As it turned out, there were more attendees for Tate's reading than for most, probably because he fit the bill so perfectly: a New York writer publishing in all the hot glossies and journals; recipient of awards that several members of the Workshop would have stabbed their own mothers through the heart to have won; often titillatingly portrayed as an anti-establishment writer, out of the loop, even though he had worked at one of the major publishing houses while honing his craft, such as it was.

After Jerry read a perfunctory introduction for Tate, Tate walked behind the podium and pushed his eyeglasses higher up the bridge of his nose. He cleared his throat a few times. He raised his right hand, as though at a Senate hearing, and said, "No, I won't answer any questions about Scarlett Johansson tonight!" I dimly remembered a rumor that Tate and Scarlett had briefly dated, but based on the silence in the room, I seemed to be the only person who'd heard this. Tate chuckled and said, "Oh, okay, if you insist. But only *after* the reading." And then Tate read from the manuscript instead of his new novel. With the exception of Vince Belecheck, who sat in the front row and nodded meaningfully at every other sentence, the rest of the audience sat as emotionless as zombies. As was my habit at readings, I didn't listen. S. S. leaned over and whispered, "It's like *Tess of the d'Urbervilles*, only set in Hell's Kitchen." "Hunh," I replied. The Q&A afterward was an uneventful series of questions: "How important is 'place' to your work?" "What advice do you have for an aspiring writer?" "How did you find your agent?" The only truly awkward moment came when Jerry announced, after the Q&A, that Tate Rinehart would not be signing copies of his rare first novel.

"Just the *first* novel," Tate clarified. "And *just* the first edition. I'll sign paperbacks and, of course, subsequent printings of the hardback. Naturally, I'll sign copies of any of my other books!" He laughed, trying to play down any impression that he might be a snob, but even as he stood there smiling, the audience began filing out. It was clear that no one had brought with them *any* novel of his to get signed, let alone a copy of Tate's rare Gutenberg, a novel so bad that I had actually ripped up my copy and fed the pages into a shredder back when I was temping for Rockwell International, a job at which I spent eight hours each day typing in mysterious codes and, for all I knew, launching missiles toward small, sparsely populated countries.

The handful of Workshop students in attendance, along with Vince and Tate, had initiated a movement to go to the Foxhead. I offered the Dynamic Duo a ride, but they insisted upon walking.

"You sure?" I asked.

Vince rolled his eyes at me and walked away. Tate shrugged and followed Vince.

Outside, as S. S. and I sat in the Corolla waiting for it to warm up, we watched Vince holding forth on some topic or another. Vince had taught in the Workshop, off and on over the years (always on an as-needed basis), and he carried himself as the old sage in front of current students. Vince and company took up the entire sidewalk, requiring normal people to walk out into the street, over mounds of snow, to get around them. Vince gestured passionately, hitting the side of one hand against the palm of his other, then raised both arms into the air and clenched his fists. At one point he crouched down and, pouting, peered up as though he were standing in front of an adult who was disciplining him. The students' laughter was too enthusiastic, and from this distance, unable to hear even a peep over the roaring of my muffler-shy car, I interpreted the fervor of their laughter as a complicated mixture of pity and envy. They wanted what Vince had, but they did not want to be him. It was also clear from my vantage that by playing the role of clown, Vince was trying to usurp whatever attention was being paid to Tate. And it worked well enough that one of the women broke from her clump and hooked arms with Vince, trying to entice him to skip with her. She tugged at his arm several times until he finally pulled her close, bent down, and whispered something into her ear. She leaned back in mock surprise, hit him with her gloved hand, but then pulled him up against her for the rest of the walk.

I jerked the car into drive and rumbled toward the Foxhead.

"Did you know," S. S. said, "that you have a cheese grater on your floorboard?"

"Yes," I said. "I do."

"You wouldn't be hiding a block of cheese in here, would you?"

"No," I said. "I'm not."

"I'm sorry to hear that," he said. "Tate's reading—it made me famished. Isn't that an odd reaction to a selection of self-conscious prose?"

"Would a slice of Paul Revere's pizza do the trick?"

S. S. cleared his throat. Reciting, he began, "'Listen, my children, and you shall hear . . . of the midnight ride of Paul Revere . . . on the eighteenth of April, in Seventy-Five . . . hardly a man is now alive . . . who remembers that famous day and year.'"

"Longfellow," I said.

"I had to memorize it as a child," S. S. said. "I hadn't thought of it in over forty years. Funny how the mind remembers some things but doesn't remember others." His voice caught, and he took a deep breath. I was about to ask him if he was okay, but he pointed out the window and said, "You weren't kidding. A pizza restaurant named Paul Revere's! I wonder if there's a pizza restaurant in England called John Locke's. Somehow I doubt it."

Inside, we ordered, and then, pizza in hand, stared out Paul Revere's large plate-glass window and silently chewed our food as Vince, Tate, and their band of merrymakers eventually arrived at the Foxhead on foot.

"'Himself killing from him keeps what?'" I said at last, crumpling my paper plate and tossing it into the trash.

"You're not speaking in tongues, are you?" S. S. asked. "I spent two years living in the South. Never again, I told myself."

"It's what Tate wrote about me in his notebook," I said. "Only he wrote it backward. Forward, it says, 'What keeps him from killing himself?'"

"And you read this," S. S. said.

"I took his messenger bag while he was busy throwing up."

"Ah. Always a good time to take what's not yours." He chewed the remainder of his pizza thoughtfully. He slid his paper plate into the garbage can, wiped the grease from his hands, and said, "Are you worried that you don't have an answer?"

"For what?"

"Tate's question, friend."

I thought about it. "Maybe," I said.

We crossed the empty and silent snow-packed street as the traffic light pointlessly turned from green to yellow to red. At the Foxhead, the celebrity writers and their fans took up the two tables nearest the entrance. When Vince saw us, he raised his arms and said, "Yo, yo! We're over here. What took you girls so long?"

S. S., nodding hello to everyone, grabbed hold of one of the student's hands and shook it vigorously, even though the poor kid had only been reaching across the aisle for a beer someone was trying to give him.

"We'll be over there," I announced, tipping my head toward the pool table. Vince, however, had already turned his attention away, sucked back into flirtatious conversation with the women on either side of him.

S. S. ordered our drinks. I carried them to the back booth, where only this morning I had been enjoying Lucy Rogan's novel.

"How's your hand?" I asked.

"Sh-sh," he said, smiling and rolling his eyes in such a way that I knew he wanted me to listen to the conversation between two women in the booth behind him. I recognized the women because they had intro-duced themselves to me a couple of weeks ago when I was escorting the self-proclaimed guru of creative nonfiction, Matthew Klotz. They had come up to me after the reading to ask how I knew him. When I explained to them the nature of our relationship, they quickly lost interest and wandered away, searching for someone with a more intimate connec-tion to the man. Their names were Sally and Helga, and they were MFA students in the Creative Nonfiction program at the University of Iowa, a degree-granting program separate from the Writers' Workshop, which explained why they were sitting all the way in the rear of the Foxhead and not on Vince's or Tate's lap. Helga, who wore her dark hair like a helmet, was in the middle of a story about, as best as I could tell, the night she learned that her maternal grandfather had been a Nazi soldier in Terezín, a concentration camp in what is now the Czech Republic.

"It was this transit camp for Jews," Helga said, "who were going to be taken to Auschwitz. The Nazis put something like fifty thousand Jews there. And, oh yeah, get this: Sigmund Freud's *sister* died there. And my grandfather, he was one of the soldiers who oversaw the Jews who were forced to turn Terezín into a concentration camp. It's all so—I don't know—awful. And I just found out about all of this. The last time I was home!"

Sally said, "You're so lucky, bitch."

"I know, I know," Helga said.

"You write that memoir and throw in all that Nazi stuff," said Sally, "and I bet you'll get a six-figure advance."

"You think?"

"Shit, yeah, girl. At *least*. And you know what else?"

"What?"

"You've got the perfect name to write a book like this. *Helga*."

"Tell me about it. I used to hate my name, but since I started the program, I'm starting to see how I can use it to my advantage. You know: marketing-wise."

"You might have to dye your hair blonde. You know, the whole Aryan thing, or people'll be like, 'That girl's *German*? No way. Uh-uh.'"

"My father's Jewish."

"Shut up!" Sally said. "Get the fuck outta here!"

"Is that good or bad?" Helga asked.

"Ka-*ching*? Did I say *mid* six-figures? You better not forget about me. I swear. If I had a book coming out, you know the first person I'd offer to blow?"

"No. Who?"

"Matt Lauer," Sally said. "Just so I can be on the *Today Show*."

"Okay," Helga said. "Here's a question. Would you blow Al Roker?"

"He's the black guy, right? The one who does the weather?"

"That's him."

"And if I blew him, I'd get to be on the *Today Show*?"

"That's the deal."

"Yeah," Sally said. "I'd blow him."

"What about Jay Leno?"

"In a heartbeat. Are you kidding?"

"What about Larry King?"

Sally said, "I'd get to be on his show?"

"Yeah. On the show. Promoting your book."

"For how long?"

"What?" Helga said. "To blow him?"

"No," Sally said. "How long would I be on the show? Ten minutes? Twenty? The whole show?"

"Let's say fifteen minutes," Helga said.

There was silence. Then, "Yeah, sure, I'd blow him." Sally looked up, and our eyes locked. "Hey, Helga," she said.

"What?"

"I think those two guys behind you are listening to us."

"*What?*"

"I think they're eavesdropping."

"Ew," Helga said. She slid out of her side of the booth and joined Sally.

"Pervert," Sally said directly to me, but I pretended I hadn't actually been listening in on them and began picking at an imaginary string of food between my teeth.

"Sick fuckers," Sally said, one last stab at getting our attention, and then they began whispering to each other.

S. S. lifted his drink and looked into it. "Whatever happened to that lovely woman you lived with?" he asked.

"Alice?" I said her name as though my life had been flush with women who'd lived with me. I shrugged. "She left me," I said. "A long time ago."

S. S. reached over and patted one of my hands. "So sorry," he said and straightened up. "Tate Rinehart," he said, quickly shifting subjects. "Let's dissect."

"I'd love to," I said. "Literally." Before we could say anything more, Vince Belecheck stumbled over to our table.

Pointing at me, he said, "You humiliated me this afternoon at the hotel, Jack. But you know what? To show that there's no hard feelings, I won't bring it up again. In fact—"

"Mr. Belecheck?" S. S. interrupted.

"Huh?"

"It's an honor to meet you," S. S. said.

Vince said, "You look familiar, old man. Do we know each other?"

"I'm afraid not," said S. S., "but I know *you*. Or, rather, I know your *work*."

"Really," Vince said. He tried concealing the fact that he was pleased by forcing a frown and nodding, but his eyes, which only moments ago were bleary from his binge, were bright and semi-alert now.

"When a character of yours is sawing a board," S. S. said, "I feel as though I'm right there, smelling the fresh-cut wood along with him."

Vince smiled. "Well, hey, that's what I'm going for. That's the writer's job. Isn't that right, Jack?" he said to me.

S. S. said, "And when that character of yours—oh, what was his name, the fellow who worked for the electric company?"

"Jefferson Milosovec," Vince said.

"Ah, yes. An interesting combination of ethnicities you have there."

"My characters represent the melting pot," Vince said.

"An ethnic stew," S. S. offered.

"Exactly." To me, Vince said, "Where did you find this guy? You should have brought him along with you last night."

"I arrived late," S. S. said. "And by bus."

"In the blizzard? By bus?" Vince said. "Holy shit, old man, you're hard-core."

"That I am," S. S. said. "But I have one question for you."

"Sure. Anything."

"Do you mind?"

"No. Shoot."

"Who did you blow?"

Vince cocked his head, like a dog hearing an approaching siren. "I'm sorry?"

"All your success. The feature in *The New York Times*. My curiosity is piqued. You must have blown somebody. We were just wondering who."

I watched S. S. carefully. He kept grinning, staring innocently up at Vince as though they were old friends, but he had readjusted his grip on the beer bottle's neck so that it would be easier to use as a weapon. Vince must have noticed, too, breaking away from the staring contest to look down at S. S.'s hand and then over at me. My first impulse was to shake my head and shrug, to distance myself from the moment, but I decided to hold my ground. This way, it would be two against one—at least until Vince gathered together his troops, who, at this very second, were enthralled by something Tate was saying to all of them.

It was Sally who finally broke the silence. "Dude," she said, laughing. "He's joking. The four of us, we were all just talking about who we'd blow to advance our careers. He's teasing you, is all. Everyone just . . . *chill*."

"He's been asking everyone who's walked by tonight," said Helga. "He even asked *me*."

Vince met my eyes. "And who did *you* say you'd blow?"

"No one," I said.

Vince said, "Probably because you have to write a book first, right?"

"Oh, but he has written a book," S. S. said. "And it's a rather brilliant one, too."

Vince, taking a few steps back, said, "Hey, look. I don't mind a joke every now and then. Just be careful where you tread."

"Always," S. S. said.

After Vince had returned to his table, Helga and Sally slid out of their booths, migrating to ours. Sally said to S. S., "I know who you are."

"Please join us then," S. S. said. "Please, please," he said, scooting over.

Sally slid in next to S. S., and Helga sat on my side. My impulse was to be pissed off at Sally and Helga for their earlier accusations, but it was all water under the bridge for S. S., whose graciousness was genuine.

"And from whence do you two lovely women hail?" S. S. asked after I'd brought back another round of drinks for us.

Both Sally and Helga answered the question (Sally was from Berkeley; Helga, Poughkeepsie), but Sally was much more interested in S. S. and, after going on at length about how much *Winter's Ghosts* had meant to her, wouldn't stop drilling him for information. Where had he been hiding all this time? Was he working on anything new? What was he doing in Iowa City? Could he, if it wasn't too much trouble, put her in contact with his agent?

This was the arc of most conversations between aspiring and established writers in Iowa City—a few compliments, a few pleasantries, and then a not-so-subtle request that would enable the aspiring writer to advance three steps beyond his or her classmates. This was the Iowa Writers' Workshop Board Game in action: We all start together at GO, but as soon as the semester commences, we either advance or back up, depending upon the roll of the dice. With S. S. here at the Foxhead, Sally seized an opportunity to advance, maybe even at the expense of Helga, who, only a few minutes ago, was rapidly charging ahead of Sally with her Nazi grandfather at her side and a potential mid-six-figure book idea. Though I couldn't say with any certainty, I suspected, by the way Sally was leaning into S. S. and the fact that I couldn't see her hands, that she was rubbing his crotch right about now.

S. S. said, "My agent would love to hear from you, I'm sure. I'll call him first thing in the morning."

Helga turned to me and said, "S. S. said you've written a brilliant novel. When's it going to be published?"

"S. S. may have spoken too soon," I said. "It's actually not done yet."

"Oh," Helga said. She slumped in the booth, as if disappointment had a direct impact on her posture.

I hated to disappoint—the gene *not* to disappoint was wired into my DNA, probably inexplicably fused to the gene that was bound and determined *to* disappoint—so I said, "I had a story in *The New Yorker*. And then it got picked up by *Best American*."

"Really?" Helga said, straightening up again.

"What's this about *The New Yorker*?" Sally asked. "Do you know somebody at *The New Yorker*?"

"Not anymore," I said.

"But he had a story published there," Helga said. She was leaning into me now; I was her new best friend.

"I just wrote an essay that would be *perfect* for them," Sally said. "Or do you think it would be better for *Harper's*, Helga?"

"It's definitely a *New Yorker* piece," Helga said. To me, Helga whispered, "Who's your agent?"

Who's your agent? This was the city's mantra. Everywhere you went, you could hear someone ask, "Who's your agent?" Most of the time, you expected it, like thunder following lightning; you knew it was coming. But other times, you had no sooner walked into a bar or restaurant than you heard it in the distance, coming from a corner booth or behind the kitchen's double doors: *Who's your agent?* Getting an agent was the unpublished writer's holy grail, the difference between holding one's laser-printed manuscript and holding one's very own bound book. Certain agents took on mythical proportions in Iowa City, as storied as Sasquatch or the Loch Ness monster, and whenever somebody from the Workshop actually signed with one of the big ones, an almost visible aura surrounded him, like a person who's been brought back to life after being pronounced dead. *Who's your agent?* Everyone wanted to know. There were times, I swear, you could hear the question through the wind, or during a hurricane, or in the middle of a blizzard. You heard it in your sleep, as though someone were standing below your window, asking it of nighttime revelers who stumbled by, trying to find their home.

When I was in the Workshop, I had a meeting with Knox Hanson, one of the agents who'd passed through town trolling for clients. Knox was a wiry guy, younger than I expected given his roster of writers, and he was burning with more energy than anyone I'd ever known. We met in a room that had in it only two chairs: one for him, one for me.

"Hey, how are you? Sit, sit, sit! So, you're in the Workshop! You know what that says to me right there? It says that whether I take you on or not, you'll be just fine. I mean, the odds of getting accepted here are, what, a thousand to one?"

"I think it's about one in twenty-five," I said.

"What? Get the fuck outta here! It's more competitive than that. Trust me, I wouldn't be out here if it was only one in twenty-five. But listen: I don't care what the actual acceptance rate is—I can check on that later—what I want to know is what you're working on. What are you writing? Short stories? A novel?"

"I just had a short story in *The New Yorker*," I told him.

"You don't say!" Even though we were sitting only two feet from each other, Knox stood up to shake my hand. I wasn't sure whether to remain sitting or to stand, so I stayed put, but it was so awkward that I realized afterward I was supposed to have stood up so that he could have clapped my back or hugged me. When he sat back down, he said, "Tell me you're not going to make a *habit* out of writing short stories, are you? I mean, *The New Yorker* pub is great. That'll be our calling card when we approach publishers." Knox smiled at me. The switch from "you" to "we" was not lost on me. I smiled back.

"I've just started writing a novel," I said.

"Bingo! Now we're talking. Okay, here's what I want you to do. Ready? Name two established writers who epitomize your writing. If I were to say . . . what's your name?"

"Jack Sheahan."

"Blah. Won't work. Do you have a middle name?"

"Yeah, but . . ."

"Come on, come on. Lay it on me."

"Hercules."

"Hercules? You're fucking kidding me."

"You see, I told you. My parents, they—"

"What do you mean? I *love* it. Now *that's* a name people won't forget. Jack *Hercules* Sheahan."

"I don't know," I said.

"*What* don't you know? Listen. Are you an agent? Do you make as much money as I do? Here's the deal. *My* name is tied to my *clients'* names. If they suck, I suck. Simple as that. I wouldn't steer you wrong on something like this. Jack Hercules Sheahan sells itself. You gotta trust me on this one."

"Okay," I said, already caving in. "All right."

"Great. Now if I were to say, Jack Hercules Sheahan's writing is like X meets X, who would those two Xs be?"

I tried to think, but my mind went blank.

"Don't think about it," Knox said. "Go by your gut. The two writers whose names first come to mind. X and X. Okay, hit me with them."

"Raymond Carver," I said, "and Stephen King?"

"Wow," he said. "Wow. That's genius. Fucking genius! So, what I'm hearing you say is that you're writing a minimalist horror novel. Is that what I'm hearing? Well, I can already see the book review headline for this one: 'What We Talk About When We Talk About Cutting Off Your Head.'"

"I guess I was thinking more along the lines of a highly commercial domestic novel."

"Oh," Knox said. "Oh. Okay. That's different. Not quite as exciting, mind you, but I can work with that. Tell you what. Send me a copy of that *New Yorker* story, okay? I'm pretty certain that I'm going to sign you. I sign only one or two writers each time I come out here, but I like you. I think you've got what I'm looking for. But I never sign anyone without reading their work first, so send me that story, okay? Actually, that's not true. I've signed *plenty* of writers without reading their work. Can I confide in you? You start out in a business like this with ideals, with principals, but one by one they fall to the wayside, and pretty soon you find yourself doing pretty much everything you started out saying you would *never* do. Promise me something, Jack. Can you promise me something?"

"What?"

"Don't ever think about writing another short story. From here on out, it's just novels. Can you promise me that?"

"I'm not sure . . . ," I began, but Knox held up his hand.

"Ah-ah-ah," he said. "Promise?"

"Okay, I promise."

"And one more thing," he said.

I nodded.

"Don't talk to another agent. If I find out you're playing the field, I'll turn my back on you. That's how I am. I'm as loyal as a service dog, but I can be a pit bull if I'm betrayed. I've been known to foam at the mouth and bite a writer or two on the ass. Not literally, of course. Figuratively."

We shook hands. The next day, I packaged up my story and sent it to him. I waited for a month, two months, three months. After four months, I stopped by Gordon Grimes's office to ask him what I should do.

Gordon, slouched as usual, wearing a Members Only jacket and smoking despite the university-wide no smoking policy, said, "You may want to think about getting a different agent."

"Why's that?"

"What I'm about to tell you is *entre nous*," he said. As I stared blankly at him, he said, "*Entre nous*," again, and then, "Between us?"

"Oh. Sure," I said. "Between us."

"The thing is," Gordon said, "Knox is in rehab. Apparently, he had one hell of an addiction to crack. Lost all his clients."

"You're kidding," I said. "He said he was going to sign me." There was a slight whine in my voice that embarrassed me, and I noticed Gordon cringe ever so slightly.

"Hey, kiddo," he said. "*C'est la vie*. But trust me on this. You don't want to be represented by someone addicted to drugs you can buy on the street for pocket change. *Capisce*?"

"I don't have an agent," I told Helga.

"Oh," she said, wilting again.

S. S., listening in on our conversation, despite whatever was going on under the table, said, "Oh, but he'll have his pick! Jack has written that rare book, my friends. A book that is devoid of thoughts about the marketplace or the advance he'll get. His first priorities—his *only* priorities—are language and story. Choosing the right words. Capturing the right gestures. Making every scene both surprising yet inevitable. Imagine standing not on a hill but on a very long and subtle incline, and now imagine rolling a ball down that incline so that it rolls slowly at first, gracefully, all the while, almost imperceptibly, picking up speed. And yet, by the time the ball reaches the nadir of that incline, it is soaring. Even so, the roll is still smooth, still steady, still beautiful. Most novels these days are like boulders pushed off a mountaintop: Once the plot starts bouncing, there's no telling where it's going or who'll get killed before the story's over. Not so with Jack's novel. When he puts the final touches on it, *then* he'll look for an agent. But *only* then. Am I right, Jack?"

I nodded. I tilted my head to the side, as if to say, *Yeah, that's about it in a nutshell.*

I could tell that Sally and Helga were losing interest. Sally had already achieved her goal—S. S. was going to call his agent tomorrow and put in a good word for her—but I had nothing to offer either of them, except, according to S. S., the aesthetic pleasures of a brilliant novel, which, of course, were worth nothing. What I found particularly amusing was that neither Sally nor Helga remembered me from the night I had escorted the guru of creative nonfiction, Matthew Klotz. I knew their kind well—rarely meeting your eyes because they're too busy looking over your shoulder to see if someone more important has walked through the front door.

The most egregious examples of this occurred at conferences and conventions. One year at BookExpo, I had run into an old Iowa classmate of mine, Carlos Ramirez, whose third novel—touted as "a cross between *The Great Gatsby* and *Frankenstein*"—was about to be published by Viking. When he saw me, he let out a loud whoop, pitched proportionately higher and with far more enthusiasm than our friendship justified, but he had no sooner finished hugging me and asking what the hell I'd been up to when, peering over my shoulder, he began scanning the rest of the room, barely listening to what I was telling him. In the middle of something I was saying about still living in Iowa City, Carlos said, "Whoa, check it out. I think that's Norman Mailer over there. Is that Norman Mailer? Christ, someone's in my way. Would you fucking move, you moron? Oh, shit . . . do you think that guy just heard me? Oh, Christ, he *did* hear me. I hope he's not an editor. No, wait, he didn't. Good. Whew. You know what, though? That's not Mailer. I don't know who the hell that is. Does he look familiar to you? Yo, check out who's behind him, though. It's Jonathan Franzen. I think. It is, isn't it?"

"I should go, man," I said. "Good seeing you, though."

Carlos said, "Good seeing you, too, *hombre*," and locked me in a bear hug.

I took a good look now at S. S. and Sally, who were talking shop, and Helga, who was keeping an eye on the front door. I nudged Helga. "I'm sorry," I said, "but I need to go."

"What about our friend Tate?" S. S. asked. "Isn't he the very reason we're here?"

"He'll be fine," I said. "What about you? What do you want to do?"

S. S. frowned exaggeratedly at me, the Kabuki of contemplation. After Helga sat down on the other side of the booth next to Sally, S. S. leaned back like an aging king and, eyebrows raised, asked, "Would you think it rude if I remained here?"

"Not at all," I said. "I'll leave the door unlocked for you."

To Sally and Helga, he said, "I had to borrow a spare key yesterday from the naked man who lives next door."

"A naked man? This sounds good," Sally said.

Helga leaned across Sally, touched S. S.'s hand, and said, "You can't stop there."

S. S., smiling up at me, began telling them the story of the naked man, as though it were a fairy tale: "His name is Paul Thornley, but nobody calls him that anymore. Those who know him, know him only as M. Cat. In fact, they would be surprised to learn that Cat is not his real last name, or that M. does not stand for Michael or Mason." Sally and Helga were enthralled.

Instead of leaving through the front door, where I would have had to pass Vince and company, I exited through the back door, nearly slipping on a patch of ice with my first step. The near-fall alerted me to the fact that I was drunker than I had realized. Not that this realization kept me from driving. I wasn't seeing double, after all. And I didn't *feel* drunk.

I drove to Jerome Ruby's house and parked across the street. Jerome Ruby was the Mercy Hospital pharmacist who had kissed Alice this morning, and I had taken the liberty of looking him up in the phone book and then MapQuesting his drug-dispensing ass. He lived in a Queen Anne Victorian with all the trimmings: a wraparound porch, delicate spindle-work porch supports, an ornamented gable. Even in Iowa City, you had to pay through the nose for a house like this.

My car was so loud, I quickly killed the engine, but after only a few minutes of sitting there and staring at the house, my teeth began clacking together. I wasn't sure what I expected to find. There were lights on in a few of the rooms, but the curtains were shut, and although I couldn't smell any burning wood, a steady stream of smoke rose up out of the fireplace—probably just heat rising up out of the house and meeting the cold, like puffs of visible air coming from a warm mouth on a winter day.

I'd thought coming here might answer some questions, but seeing the house only made my stomach knot up, and I felt like opening the car door and barfing all over the street.

"Son of a bitch," I said.

I started the car, revved it a few times, and tried to pull out of the parking spot, but I must have backed onto a patch of ice: I couldn't gain any traction at all. Each time I punched the gas pedal, the car wiggled out of my control, and I risked rocketing forward into the car parked in front of me should one of my tires have unexpectedly grabbed onto something other than ice.

"Fuck," I said, hitting the steering wheel. "Fuck, fuck."

The front door of the Queen Anne opened. A man and a woman stepped out.

"Oh, shit," I said, and tried gunning it, but my tires merely spun in place.

The man—Jerome Ruby, I saw now—crossed the street, while the woman, who may or may not have been Alice, stood on the sidewalk, watching.

Jerome knocked on my window. I unrolled it. "Hi there! I'm just a little stuck," I said.

"Here," he said. "I'll get behind and push."

"Are you sure?" I asked. "I can keep trying to work it free."

"Don't be silly," he said. He started to walk away but then stopped and said, "Hey, don't I know you?"

"I don't think so," I said.

"Don't you work at Mercy?"

"Nope," I said, smiling.

He leaned forward and sniffed a few times. "Have you been drinking?"

"I just gave a ride to a friend of mine who was hammered. He called me from a bar," I said.

Jerome nodded. I glanced over at the woman, hoping to get a better look, but she had pulled up the hood of her long coat. Further obscuring my view was the hood's fake-fur trim, which circled her face like a Christmas wreath.

"Does your friend live around here?" Jerome asked.

"What? Oh, no. He lives over on Jefferson. I had to pull over to answer my cell phone."

Jerome looked around for a cell phone, so I gave my chest two quick pats, hoping to convey that my phone was now safely tucked away.

Jerome said, "I know I know you," as he walked around to the back of the car to push. "Okay," he yelled. "Hit the gas."

As ordered, I pushed the pedal, but still I went nowhere.

"Whoa!" Jerome yelled. "Try it slower this time."

I did, but nothing happened.

"Okay, okay, okay." Jerome walked back around to my window. That's when I noticed yet another woman; she was walking down the sidewalk, toward the woman with the hood. They hugged when they met, and then the hooded woman pointed at Jerome, who waved back.

"Hey, there!" Jerome yelled at the new arrival. "Tommy's inside, waiting for you. I'm just trying to get this guy unstuck."

The new arrival looked over at me now and said, "Jack? Is that you?" It was Alice.

"You know him?" Jerome asked.

"Jack!" Alice said, walking over. "What're you doing over here?"

Who the fuck is Tommy? I wondered. *And why is he inside waiting for Alice?*

"He pulled over to answer his cell phone," Jerome said, "and got stuck."

"Hi, Alice," I said, embarrassed at having been caught.

Alice said, "You finally got a cell phone, I see," but when I smiled and nodded, she could see that I was lying.

"Don't worry about me," I told Jerome. "I'll get out of here, if it takes me all night." To Alice, I said, "Tommy's waiting for you. I'm fine. Really." Without warning, I choked up but then cleared my throat to smother the gaffe.

"Tommy and I aren't going anywhere," Alice said. "I'm sitting for them tonight. You remember my sister, don't you? Emily?"

The hooded woman, still standing on the sidewalk, said, "Is that you, Jack? I *thought* it looked like you, but how long has it been? It's

the car that made me think it might be you. I do remember that car!"
she yelled and laughed.

"I don't think you ever met Jerome, though. He and Emily met,"
Alice paused, "after us."

"Hey, Jerome," I said, reaching out of my car to shake his hand. He
took hold of my hand, squeezing it harder than necessary.

"You guys really should get going," Alice said to Jerome. "You're
going to be late for the movie."

Jerome nodded.

Alice said, "Let me say goodbye to Emily, Jack. Hang on, okay?"

After Alice had crossed the street, safely out of earshot, Jerome said,
"I remember you now. This morning. The pharmacy."

"What? Oh, yeah! Yeah, yeah! Jesus, I'm sorry about that. My head
was really up my ass this morning. A friend of mine had sliced open
his hand and . . ." And then I remembered that this wasn't the story I
had told him. "And then my wife . . ." I began, but Jerome held up his
hand.

"Can I borrow your cell phone?" he asked.

"Battery's dead," I replied too quickly.

"I don't know what the hell you're doing here tonight," Jerome said
through gritted teeth, "but I want you to move along right now, you
hear? On foot, if need be."

"No problem," I said. "I can do that."

"Tell Alice you need to leave," he said.

"Alice!" I called out. "I need to leave!"

Alice said, "Can't you hold on a second?"

"No!" I yelled, probably too loud for the occasion. "I have to get
going!"

Jerome gave me one final stern look, then tightened his coat, turned,
and said, "Ready, honey?"

"Good to see you again, Jack," said Emily.

"C'mon," Jerome barked at his wife. "We need to hurry."

I got out of my Corolla and began walking. I weaved between two parked cars, tromped through calf-high snow, and then slipped on a patch of ice along the sidewalk, momentarily losing my footing. It astonished me that anyone over the age of sixty-five actually remained in Iowa. It seemed inevitable that if you lived here long enough, you'd eventually slip on ice and break your hip, or maybe pop your skull against the concrete, giving yourself a concussion, or tumble down your iced-over front porch steps, fracturing your leg in fifteen places. You could get snow tires, Timberland boots, and earmuffs, but you still couldn't stop the onslaught of elements: wind, snow, ice, sleet, freezing rain, tornadoes, floods, droughts. I saw winds so strong, a freight train crossing the Iowa River had been blown so that it hung upside-down, inexplicably clinging to the tracks. One year, the workers at a tiny stand-alone Dairy Queen next to the river climbed down into a storm shelter when news reached them of an approaching tornado. When they came up afterward, there was nothing left above them. The entire building had been ripped from the ground and blown away. I remember drought summers when my own sweat poured freely from my forehead, dripping onto the pages of my manuscript as I read it over, smearing words and bubbling the paper. Entire fields of corn shriveled and died. One year, as floodwaters rose, a fifth-grade boy who lived forty miles away, closer to the Mississippi River, was swept down a drainage pipe. My first winter here, while I was walking to a bar called Gabe's on a particularly cold day, a prairie wind came roaring through town, instantly dropping the temperature by almost twenty degrees. I wasn't sure whether to turn around and head home or try to make it to the bar. I was closer to my apartment than I was to Gabe's. Foolishly, I chose the bar, walking with my head down the whole way. Once inside, I had thought that I was fine, but my ears began to throb and then heat up and then, finally, burn. It was probably only frostnip, but even now, many years later, if my ears aren't covered when it's cold outside, the rims will start to throb and ache, a subtle reminder of how the choices you make can save your life or kill you.

So why did I stay? I honestly didn't know. Familiarity, perhaps. Maybe nostalgia. Most likely, though, the reason was inertia. The very thought of packing up, moving, and starting all over again didn't so much fill me with dread as exhaustion. My sense of adventure was limited to ordering Thai food "spicy hot" rather than merely "hot," and even then, I would weigh the short-term benefits against the long-term pain I might experience. All too often, at the very last second, I asked for "medium hot," moving down a notch instead of up, opting for what I knew to be safe.

My few good friends from the Workshop had all left town years ago. One published a well-reviewed novel that sold only five hundred copies in hardback and never made it to paper. Another went back to school to get a degree in psychology and now worked for the state of Arizona; I still didn't know exactly what it was he did. My closest friend from back then earned a PhD in English, took a job at a good university in the Southeast, and now drank himself to sleep each night. When I talked to him over the phone, which was no more than twice a year, he ranted the entire time about how lazy his students were and how much he wanted to beat up certain colleagues. "This asshole who teaches Faulkner?" he said. "One of these days, when he least expects it, I'm going to reach over and gouge his eyes out. I'm just going to reach out and sink my fingers into that bastard's eye sockets. Tell me *that* wouldn't send a message that he shouldn't have been such a pain in my balls!" The last time we spoke, he'd said, "You're lucky, and you don't even realize it. You're your own boss. How many people can say that? Huh?" And then, after an uncomfortably long silence, I heard him snoring.

The people I knew these days were barely more than acquaintances, like the bartenders at George's and the Foxhead, or those bars' regulars, men like former weight lifter Larry McFeeley, or Sand Man, who, thirty years after his pool-playing heyday, could still beat any punk at the table. I knew Jerry the book buyer, of course, but I had no idea what part of town he lived in or what he did in his spare time. I knew he was married, but I wasn't even sure if he had any kids. I occasionally spoke to the mailman, who parked his truck down at the end of my block to smoke and read other people's magazines. As for women, the one who probably knew me the most intimately at this point was Lupe, the waitress at El Ranchero, who remembered, among other things, to bring me a cup of shredded cheese with my fajitas. I saw her every Tuesday and Thursday during the tail end of her lunch rush, and I always left a 25 percent tip. On the rare day she wasn't there and I was placed in the hands of someone who didn't know the idiosyncrasies of my order, I felt temporarily adrift. Sometimes I would ask, "Where's Lupe?" but often the waiter or waitress didn't understand English, so the question would go unanswered.

Recently, in an attempt to meet new people over the Internet, I opened a MySpace account and sent "friend requests" to anyone still living in town who had attended the Workshop. The first message I received in return was from a twenty-eight-year-old poet named Gretchen, who wrote, "Thanks for requesting my friendship. Please state your name, country of origin, and the reason for your request. I have no idea who you are." At first, I interpreted the reply as simply a hostile "Who the fuck are *you*?" and I was tempted to write back, "Who the hell do you think *you* are?" But after reading it over again, I surmised it had more to do with the fact that I was a writer she hadn't heard of and, because I wasn't on her radar, wasn't worthy of her time: "Prove yourself, if you want to be my friend." Finally, I dismissed these theories and saw behind the words a soulless bureaucratic: "State your name, country of origin, and the reason for your request." She was living and breathing, presumably a human being, but she was as heartless as the computer on which she typed. Before anyone else could send a message to me, I canceled my account.

Himself killing from him keeps what? I was already a good four blocks from Jerome Ruby's house when I decided to turn around and head back.

When I arrived at the house, the lights, both inside and out, were all ablaze. I pictured the dial on their meter spinning like a circular buzz saw. I climbed the porch stairs and rang the bell.

Alice opened the door. A child ran laps behind her, a plastic hammer held with both hands over his head.

"Tommy!" Alice yelled at the child. "Honey," she said, softer. "Please quit running. We have a guest."

Tommy, who looked to be around three years old (but could have been anywhere between two and five, for all I knew about kids), lobbed the plastic hammer at nothing in particular. It spun through the air, end over end, like a tomahawk, then shattered a framed Norman Rockwell print of a pharmacist mixing up some medicine. In the painting, a child, covering his mouth, watches the pharmacist. Unlike Jerome, who wasn't much older than me and had a full head of hair, Rockwell's pharmacist was an old, bald man with a thick, old-timey mustache. It was exactly the sort of sentimental crap I expected from Jerome. The entire house was full of such nods to himself—antique apothecary jars, a battered leather doctor's satchel, an aluminum sign that read, in flaking paint, JEROME'S DRUGSTORE.

"Tommy!" Alice said. "Look at what you did, Tommy!"

Tommy, unrepentant, had already begun running again.

"Watch out for the glass," Alice said. "You're going to cut yourself."

"Maybe I came at a bad time," I said. When Alice didn't say anything, I called out, "Tommy!" I said it loud enough that he stopped running. "Hey, pal," I said. "Do you like your Aunt Alice?"

Tommy nodded.

"Then give her a break, okay? You're kind of pushing her buttons. Do you understand what I'm saying?"

Tommy was about to start running again, but I crouched down to his level and said, "*Hey!* Did you hear what I said?"

Alice was watching me, but I couldn't tell what she was thinking. Was she grateful for my help, or did she think I had overstepped my bounds? For a second, I started to believe I'd had some sway with the kid, but then he yelled, "I'm gonna tell my daddy on you!" and began crying—a cry so deep and horrible, you'd think I'd backed over him with my car.

I stood up. "Maybe I'd better go."

"Yes," Alice said. "You should." Her reply was more definitive than I anticipated.

I opened the door and stepped back into the cold.

"What were you doing here tonight?" Alice asked.

"Just now? I came back to see you."

"No," Alice said. "Why were you here in the first place?"

"Coincidence," I said. She regarded me with suspicion, so I shrugged and added, "It's a small town. What can I say?"

"It's not that small," she said. She sighed. "Good-bye, now."

"Good-bye, Alice," I said, and she shut the door.

I walked over to my car, got inside, and, miraculously, managed to pull out without a problem, as though there had never been anything keeping me there.

THERE HAD BEEN a time when I loved Iowa City—the patchouli-smelling girls, the carefree skateboarders, the night air filled with smoke from clove cigarettes—but my view of this city teeming with nothing but blithe spirits had recently mutated into a darker vision, that of a place populated with malingerers and hangers-on, where the only people who really made a killing were frat boy realtors who'd inherited swatches of land near I-80 on which they built repulsive shopping malls and fast-food chains to make even more money. Even though I knew that this change in my view was an extension of my own deep self-loathing, I suspected my analysis wasn't entirely off the mark.

Tonight, on my drive home, I passed a giant snowman in front of a sorority house. It had a carrot nose, eyes and mouth made out of charcoal, and tree-limb arms. It also had an enormous cucumber penis. Using charcoal briquettes, someone had spelled EAT ME across its chest. The tradition of the profane snowman began only a few years ago, signaling—what? A shift in morality? A slippage of interest in anything academic? A hatred for snowmen? I honestly didn't know, but I suspected it signaled *something*, and that whatever it portended couldn't be good.

Safely home, without getting pulled over for drunk driving, I crawled into bed and covered myself with as many blankets as I could. I awoke several hours later to the whine of my front door opening, followed by creaking floorboards and the door snapping shut. It was three thirty in the morning; my bedroom was pitch-black, except for the digital numbers on my alarm clock. I had been dreaming about Vanessa Roberts and her baby, and in the dream, the baby was mine, and Vanessa and I were lovers who'd had a falling out. I tried to remember more of the dream, but large chunks of it evaporated even as I sifted through it. My eyes adjusted just enough for me to see the outline of my vacuum cleaner, which looked, in the grainy blur of half-sleep, like a very small person standing in the corner of my room, watching over me. As a child, I took pleasure in scaring myself, imagining that my coat draped over a chair was really a werewolf hunched near the bed and about to pounce. A shadow across my ceiling, probably from the headlights of a car driving by the house, might have been a bat.

I took a quick, unexpected gasp of air. I wondered, usually when I was too asleep to research it, if I had developed sleep apnea and what, if anything, could be done about it. There were nights when I woke up from dreams of drowning, unable to suck in enough air, but these were typically nights when I'd had too much to drink. Was this how I was going to die—alone, and of some disorder that I was too lazy to Google? Whenever I considered the many ways I might die, I always ended up thinking about Tennessee Williams, who died choking on an eyedrop bottle cap in a hotel room in New York. He had a habit (a deadly one, it turned out) of holding the cap in his mouth while leaning way back to place the drops in each eye.

The floorboards creaked again. Each time a switch was flipped on, light streamed in under my door, but when the switch was off, the illuminated swatch returned to black. I started falling asleep again, but the ancient fan in the bathroom began to moan, keeping me from slipping completely under. A toilet flushed. The water faucet was turned on and off. It was as though the apartment had come alive, each part commiserating with the other: a light switch talking to a floorboard, the fan to the faucet.

My doorknob jiggled, turned. The door opened, and I woke up.

"S. S.?" I said. "You need something?"

The light came on, as startling as a handful of lime thrown into my eyes. I squinted and blinked, and when I saw that it wasn't S. S., I made a whimpering noise, sitting up quickly but scooting further away, pressing myself against the headboard.

"Jack Sheahan?"

"Lauren Castle?" I asked.

"Jesus Christ. I finally made it to this God-forsaken state," she said. "You have no idea what my day has been like. *No* idea!"

"What are you doing here?" I asked. I had expected her to be older, more frightening looking, along the lines of Joan Collins or Leona Helmsley, and though she had to have been at least in her early forties to have worked in the warehouse where Jay McInerney's third novel had been returned by the tens of thousands, she looked barely out of college. What made her seem older were her husky voice and her attitude. Otherwise, she could have been living down the street and posing with the X-rated snowman.

"What am I *doing* here? I'm here to find *Vanessa*," she said, looking at me as though I were the unreasonable one.

"No, no," I said. "*Here*. Inside my *apartment*. In my *bedroom*."

"Sheraton's sold out." She looked around my room. "So *this* is Iowa," she said. "Hunh."

I wanted to tell her that my bedroom wasn't really a fair representation of what the state had to offer, but Lauren had already walked away, back to my kitchen.

"Do you always leave your door unlocked?" she called out. "Is that how people out here live? Because, let me tell you something. If you left your door unlocked in Manhattan, you'd wake up the next morning missing a kidney. That's right. A *kidney*, Jack."

I pushed myself out of bed. I straightened up the covers. I cinched my sweatpants tighter.

I found Lauren in the kitchen, peering into my fridge.

"I'm starving," she said, slamming the door shut. "But not for anything in there. What's open all night around here?" she asked.

"The Quik Stop," I said. "You can get a microwavable burrito and a gallon of milk."

Lauren said, "Did you do something to her?"

"Who?"

"Vanessa."

"Did I *do* something to her? Like what?"

"She tries my patience sometimes," Lauren said. "I could certainly understand why someone might want to harm her."

"You're not serious," I said.

Lauren shrugged. "My plane was rerouted because of the blizzard, and then I had to rent a car in—what's it called? The Quad cities?" She shivered. "Terrible place," she said. "Awful airport. They were out of rentals, so I had to wait for something like five hours to get one. The food there was poisonous. Shriveled hot dogs probably sitting there since the 1990s." She sighed and shut her eyes, and for a couple of seconds, she seemed human, and I actually felt bad for her. But then she opened her eyes and said, "I'm not saying you killed her. Don't be ridiculous. What I'm wondering, though, is if you somehow drove her away from here. Maybe you got into a fight over the money for the breast pump? I'm just spitballing here. Work with me."

I'd almost forgotten about the breast pump. "Which reminds me," I said. "I'm billing you for that."

"Go ahead," Lauren said. "But we're not paying for it."

I walked to the door, opened it up, and said, "Goodnight, then."

Lauren stared out the door, incredulous. I expected her to cave in—it's what I would have done—but she took a deep breath and walked past me, out into the hallway. She turned to say something, but I shut the door and returned to bed.

PART FIVE

*Frank Conroy had said over and over that "the writing life is a hard life,"
and I'd resented him for it. Now, I owe him a debt of gratitude and think
I understand him. How difficult it must be to pass judgment on so much hope.*

—Fritz McDonald

N THE MORNING, while scrambling eggs in a skillet and cooking up two strips of blurry-looking bacon, I heard what sounded like whimpering outside my door, followed by scrabbling. Had a stray dog smelled the food and wandered up the stairs? I opened the door slowly, keeping my right leg raised, in case an animal tried forcing itself inside, but there was neither a dog nor a band of angry rodents out there: It was S. S. sleeping soundly, curled up on the small patch of floor between my door and M. Cat's.

I crouched down and nudged him.

"Hey, S. S.," I said. When all he did was moan, I nudged him again, harder. "S. S. Wake up. You shouldn't be out here." It was freezing cold in the hall, and because the front door downstairs never shut properly, loose snow frequently blew up the stairs whenever the wind came gusting down the street.

"Huh?" S. S. said. "What?" He opened his eyes. "Who did you say?"

"What?" I asked.

S. S. blinked a few times, looked around, then sat up. "Oh, oh," he said, "I was having a dream. A bad one."

"What're you doing out here?" I asked.

"The door was locked," S. S. said.

"You should have knocked," I said.

S. S., grunting as he stood, used my shoulder for support. "It was possible," he said, "that you were indisposed. It was not my intention to disturb you. I was going to knock on my old friend M. Cat's door, but I heard from inside what sounded like a bacchanal."

"In what regard?" I asked.

"As in commemorating Saturnalia," he said, stepping over the threshold into my apartment. When I looked blankly at him, he said, "The festival of Saturn? Celebrated in December in ancient Rome? Oh, *you* know—the time of unrestrained merrymaking?" I must have looked even more confused, because he leaned in close and whispered, "He was screwing somebody, son. And they were both—how shall I put this?— rather exuberant about it!"

"Oh," I said. I stared toward M. Cat's apartment. Screwing somebody? *Who*? With S. S. safely inside, I shut the door. "Did you have a good time last night?" I asked.

"Fleetingly," he said.

Again, I wasn't sure what he meant, but I let this one go. "Well, good," I said. "They seemed like nice women."

"Piranhas, the two of them," he said. "Do I have any flesh left?" He smiled at me.

"You hungry?"

"Ravished," he said. "Would that be bacon and eggs I smell?"

"Scrambled okay?"

"Perfect!"

"How's your hand?"

He raised the wounded mitt and said, "A dull throb is all. Nothing a few aspirin won't take care of."

I scooped out two dried clumps of egg and plopped them onto a plate. "I suppose I need to track down Tate today," I said, "and take him back to the airport." I scooped out the rest of the eggs and dumped them onto another plate. I gave each of us a sad-looking slice of bacon.

"No need," S. S. said. "He gave me a message for you last night. Apparently, the director of the Workshop wants to talk to him today about a visiting writer position."

"You're shitting me," I said.

S. S. took the plate of food and said, "No, sir, I am not."

"Jesus," I said. "Gordon would have seen through that little bastard."

"Ah, yes, Gordon Grimes," S. S. said. "A few weeks ago, I was in a motel in Tucson and couldn't sleep, so I turned on the TV, and guess what was on? The movie where aliens land in Gordon's backyard. Not Gordon's backyard, per se. Rather his *character's*. Or, more precisely, his character's *mother's* backyard."

"Gordon always saw through the fakers," I said. "He wasn't afraid to call a phony a phony when he saw one."

"The strangest of careers, though," S. S. said. "He wasn't one of the Little Rascals, too, was he?"

"What?"

"*The Little Rascals*," S. S. repeated. "You remember. Spanky? Darla? Alfalfa? Wheezer? Joe Cobb? He wasn't one of them, was he? Was there a rascal named Grimes?"

"No, I don't think so," I said.

S. S. saw Tate's notebook and slid it toward him. I said nothing as he flipped through the empty pages, but when he reached the end, where Tate took notes backward, he looked up at me and said, "He's not only a novelist, he's a cryptographer, too! Do the man's talents know no bounds?" He silently read the journal. Every few sentences, he glanced at me and narrowed his eyes, as if checking Tate's observations against his own. When he finished, he pushed the notebook aside.

"What?" I asked.

"I didn't say anything."

"You *looked* like you were going to say something," I said.

S. S. finished the food on his plate. He dabbed the corners of his mouth with a napkin. He said, "*You* should write it."

"What?"

"The story of your life."

"Oh," I said. "You mean how pathetic it is? What keeps me from killing myself?"

"Exactly," S. S. said. "Only more honest. And funnier. You think I'm kidding, but I'm not. Oh, I'm not saying your life is pathetic. But you've hit a few bumps in the road, and you're a decent fellow, and I bet you could pull off a pretty damned good memoir." I carried the plates to the sink. I was about to spray the skillet off when S. S. said, "Use cold water. Hot water cooks the egg onto the surface." S. S. reached up and scratched his earlobe with his forefinger. It was the most gentle yet idiosyncratic scratching that I had ever witnessed. He said, "I'm going to tell you something, but I don't want you to be mad at me."

I ignored S. S. and ran hot water over the pan anyway. When I finally turned back around, he said, "You're already mad."

"No, I'm not," I said. "I'm curious."

"Okay. Fair enough. *You* know I've been in a slump," he said. "I didn't believe in writer's block—that is, until I got it. I don't want to be melodramatic about this . . . but it descended like the plague." His voice took on the timbre of Laurence Olivier in *Hamlet*. "It laid waste to everything around me, especially the people I loved, so I quarantined myself by disappearing, hoping not to infect anyone else. If I were to die, I would die alone!" His eyes were about to boil over with tears. He blinked a few times and, with his shirtsleeve, wiped away the wetness. "I'm sorry, I'm sorry," he said. "It's a silly thing, really. The inability to think of the next word. There are men who dig ditches or pick up trash, and women who sit behind a sewing machine for eight long hours each day, every day, for their entire lives—and here I am, unable to think of the next word, after a career of thinking up nothing but words. I'm a lucky man, I tell you. The luckiest!" He sniffled. He took a deep breath and stared up at my ceiling, as if the worst of what he'd had to tell me was over. But then he said, "I had come here to rob you, sir."

"I'm sorry, but what did you say?"

"Your novel," S. S. said. "I was in Pasadena a few weeks ago, sitting by a pool in a squalid little Motel Six, you see, and out of the blue, with my eyes closed, I remembered the first sentence of your novel. I wondered what had ever happened to it. I went back to my room, got dressed, and drove to Barnes & Noble. I remembered your name and asked an employee, a short fellow with a large head, if there were any books by you. When he told me no, I drove to the public library and researched you on the Internet. Nothing. That's when I bought the bus ticket."

"So you were going to, what? Come in here and club me over the head?"

"Good God, no," S. S. said. "Do I look like a hooligan? No, no, I was simply going to take your novel back home with me and claim it was mine. And when I was sitting on your couch yesterday, reading it, I was already beginning to think of ways to finish it. In fact, I can tell you why you couldn't continue on. You made a wrong turn about ten pages before you stopped writing. You were heading down a path that had no exit. A dead end, my friend." It had been so long since I'd read the novel, I wasn't sure I could recall what part S. S. was talking about. S. S. said, "Hamlin Grobes should never have taken the job as a court stenographer, and you should never have brought that *femme fatale*, Melissa Welcher, into the story. She upsets the plot's balance, which, until then, was as seamless as *Gatsby* or *Bovary*."

"You're right," I said. "I put Grobes in a job that forced him to sit down and keep his mouth shut. I can't even remember now why I brought the girl into it."

"She probably reminded you of somebody," S. S. said. "In all likelihood, you didn't even realize it."

On the one hand, I wanted to ask him more of his thoughts on the novel; on the other hand, I wanted to kick him out of my apartment. Was the man standing before me insane, pathetic, or brilliant?

"In the end," S. S. said. "I just couldn't do it."

"Do what?" I asked. "Finish it?"

"No, no," he said. "I know exactly how to finish it. What I couldn't do was *steal* it."

I opened my mouth to speak, but before I could say anything, there was a knock at my door.

"We'll talk about this later," I warned, and S. S. said, "I hope we will."

The knocking came harder this time.

"I'm coming!" I yelled. "Just wait a goddamned second!"

I jerked open the door, and there stood Lauren Castle.

"Are you ready?" she asked.

"For what?" I wanted to know.

"We're going to look for Vanessa Roberts. Chop-chop," she said, motioning with her head toward my sweatpants.

"No, no," I said, thinking about the breast pump. "That's *your* problem. Not *mine*."

S. S. appeared behind me. "Come now, Jack. I may be able to help. After all, I've had a little experience with missing persons."

"And who are you?" Lauren asked.

I laughed. I shook my head. Why didn't it surprise me that the head of publicity for a major New York publisher couldn't recognize one of the great writers of her lifetime?

"What's so funny?" Lauren said sharply.

"I'm a friend, is all," S. S. said. "The name's Samuel."

"Well, Sammy," Lauren said. "I'll let you go along if you're going to be of some help, but I don't want you with us if the two of you are going to act like schoolgirls and giggle every time I say something."

"We have ourselves a deal," S. S. said.

"I need to take a shower," I said to Lauren. "Why don't you come inside and fix yourself a cup of coffee?"

Lauren entered the apartment cautiously, eyeing S. S. and then me.

"Here," S. S. said. "Allow me to take your coat."

She looked down at S. S.'s bandaged hand. She said, "What's the deal with all the injured hands around here?" She slipped off her coat and handed it to S. S., who carried it to the living room and draped it over the back of a chair, careful not to let any of it touch the floor.

"What do you mean?" I asked, but before she could answer, I remembered what S. S. had told me about M. Cat's bacchanal—the Saturnalia. "Wait a minute. Where did you spend the night?"

"You want to know something? No one locks their doors around here," she said by way of a reply. "The first door I tried after yours was unlocked, too."

"Was he still naked?" I asked.

"As naked as the day is long," she said.

"Coffee's over there," I said, pointing.

I stepped into the bathroom. I shut the door and turned on the bathroom fan. I didn't want to hear any more.

WE DROVE TOGETHER in Lauren's rental, S. S. riding shotgun at Lauren's insistence, even though I was the only one who knew the city. Apparently, they had hit it off while I showered and dressed. I'd stayed in the shower so long to avoid Lauren, the water had turned ice cold. Even now, my fingers were still pruney.

"Jack," S. S. said, twisting around to see me. "Tell us, would you, where you've looked for Vanessa?"

My heart clenched. Had I looked for her at all? I'd made a few sad stabs in that direction, but other than going to her hotel twice, I hadn't actually checked anywhere.

"Oh, you know," I said, "the main hotels in town and such."

In the rearview mirror, I saw Lauren's eyebrows rise above the top of her sunglasses. One look, and I knew what she was thinking: *Are you fucking kidding me?*

"It's been difficult," I said, "taking care of Tate and, well, *he* came to town unexpectedly." I pointed at S. S.

"Tate?" Lauren asked.

"Tate Rinehart," I clarified.

"He's in town?" Lauren asked.

"Indeed," S. S. said.

Lauren smiled for the first time. "I love his work."

S. S. nodded. "It's as though he's reinventing all the classics."

Lauren thought about this. "Turn a moldy old work of fiction into something shiny and new. A great hook."

"And that's a good thing?" I asked.

"What's wrong with that?" Lauren snapped back. I was the dog in the back seat that wouldn't stop scratching and whining. A few moments later, Lauren said, "Sam here tells me you're an amazing writer."

"Whatever," I said.

"He tells me you're working on a memoir," she said. "About your life as a media escort. About living on the margins. About writer's block. About the artist's life in the twenty-first century." Lauren said, "You could sell that book for six figures. Easily."

"Right," I said, staring blankly out the window. We passed the snowman in front of the sorority house. I was going to point it out, but when I saw that someone had cut the cucumber penis in half, a pain shot up from my groin into my bowels, and I remained silent.

"This is one of those books that'll get a front-page review in *The New York Times Book Review*." She seemed to think about this a moment before revising it. "Okay, maybe not a front-page review. Maybe one of those round-up reviews they do. Hey, you know what? *The Times* can kiss my lily-white ass. We're not even convinced they sell books, anyway. But you know who *does* sell books? *All Things Considered* sells books. *Talk of the Nation* sells books." She lifted her arm up, as though flashing me a gang symbol, and, nodding slowly and with deep purpose, said, "NPR, motherfucker."

"Very good shows," S. S. added.

"You should let us do it, too," she said.

"What?" I asked.

"The book, the book. I know the perfect editor for it."

"What if I haven't written it yet?" I asked.

"Doesn't matter," Lauren said. "It's the *idea* that matters. Hey, look, we all know that New York is in love with itself. So, what better than a book about the book business, but not by an editor or a publisher. No, this one would be told from the lowest rung of the business. The lowest of the low. The media escort!"

S. S. said, "It's like a book about the film business written by the boy who works in the mailroom at Paramount Pictures."

"Or the janitor who cleans the shitters," Lauren added. At the next stop sign, she said, "Where the hell are we going, anyway?"

"Jack," S. S. said. "Have you tried that old B&B I stayed in all those years ago?"

"No," I said. "I haven't."

"Shall we start there then?" S. S. asked. "It was such a wonderful place. French toast in the morning, sprinkled with powdered sugar, and maple syrup that could have come straight from a tree in their backyard."

Lauren reached over and slapped S. S.'s leg. "Quiet. You're making my stomach growl. I'm so hungry, I could eat a goddamned horse."

"They may well have it on the menu, my dear," said S. S. "They may well indeed."

T HE LAST TIME I saw Gordon Grimes was in the Foxhead. I'd had a particularly brutal morning, picking up a writer named Mwangaza Jones, who had brought her two children along with her, a five-year-old girl and a three-year-old boy. Mwangaza, an Oprah pick for her memoir *Every Drop of Blood Was Mine*, was on her cell phone from the moment I spotted her walking toward me until I dumped her off at the Sheraton. I'd had to carry the three-year-old, who had planted himself on the floor and wouldn't stand up. On the way to my car, I felt what at first I thought was a rush of warm air hitting my thigh, but when my jeans began sticking to my leg, I realized that the child had pissed himself and, ipso facto, pissed on me. I looked pleadingly over at Mwangaza, hoping to get her attention, but she was busy telling someone about the man who had been assigned to direct the adaptation of her memoir and how his requests for changes to her script were unacceptable. She paused from the conversation to ask where we were.

"Iowa?" I said, unsure how specific she'd wanted me to be.

"Hold on," she said into the phone. "I have a smart one on my hands today." To me, she said, "What *city?*"

"Cedar Rapids," I said, her child still clinging to me. I was about to mention the urine incident, but Mwangaza had returned to her phone call.

"I'm in Cedar Rapids, Iowa," she said. "I know, I know." She laughed at something her friend said. "You're telling me!" she replied.

I went back to my apartment and changed my pants, but I couldn't sit still. I paced. I yelled. I kicked one of my shoes across the room.

What I had wanted to do—what I should have done—was knock Mwangaza's cell phone away from her head and yell, *You're just a writer! That's all. A fucking writer!* But, of course, I didn't do anything. Like so many other moments of humiliation, I swallowed it.

Around one that afternoon, still fuming, I headed to the Foxhead. Alcohol being a salve for the deluded, the dreamers, and the demented, I decided to join my brethren, but when I opened up the door and said hello to Neal, there was, I discovered, only one other person in the entire bar. He was sitting in a booth with his back to me.

"It's Gordon," Neal whispered. He poured me a tall one and a short one, and I carried my drinks over to Gordon's table and stood beside him until he looked up and smiled. When I actually saw the shape Gordon was in, I may have winced or, at the very least, tightened my brow, but I told myself to act as though nothing was out of the ordinary.

"Jack!" he said. "Sit your ass down! Sit, sit!"

Always the student, I obeyed. Gordon's arms were covered in bruises, each one a different shade of purple or yellow. The palms of his hands were blotchy and red. His eyes were yellow where they should have been white. In front of him sat a glass of whiskey.

"Just came from Mercy," he said. At first, I had thought he was speaking metaphorically, but then I realized he meant Mercy Hospital next door. "I guess I'm dying," he said, smiling. He picked up his whiskey and took a drink. By the time he'd placed the glass back on the table, he was grimacing, as though someone were stabbing him with a screwdriver while whispering into his ear, "Act normal!"

"Cirrhosis," Gordon said. "You know, Billie Holiday died of cirrhosis. She was only forty-four. O. Henry died of cirrhosis, too." He looked wistfully around him. "A hack, though," he added. "O. Henry, that is. Not Ms. Holiday." He raised his glass and said, "To Lady Day," and took another painful swig.

"Surely there's something they can do," I said. "Treatments? We're not far from the Mayo Clinic."

He pulled a five dollar bill from the inside of his suit jacket. "Here," he said. "Put some music on. A bar's not a bar without music." He turned around. "Is it, Neal?" he called out.

"Is it *what*?"

"Just agree with me."

"You're absolutely right, Gordon," Neal said. "You're *always* right." To me, Neal said, "He tips better when I agree with him."

When I first started going to the Foxhead, they still had an old jukebox that played 45s, but, like every other bar in America, they eventually caved in and brought in a jukebox that played CDs. I knew that Gordon liked blues and jazz, but seeing him in the state he was in, covered in repulsive bruises and looking distinctly inhuman with his yellow eyes, I didn't concentrate a whole hell of a lot on the music that I was choosing. I merely punched in songs familiar to me at a glance, an amalgam from various periods of my life, including grade school and high school, without regard to the moment at hand. When a Whitesnake song came on, Gordon cocked his head at me and said, "What in fuck's sake is this?"

"I don't know," I said.

"Did you play this crap or didn't you?" Gordon asked.

I finished my drink, then reached over and put my hand on Gordon's shoulder. "I have to go. I'm escorting this real piece of work. Her son pissed on me," I said. "But you take care of yourself, you hear? I mean that. Don't let this being-sick-shit get the better of you." I tapped the rim of his glass with my finger and said, "And easy on *this* stuff."

The look Gordon gave me said, *Are you serious?* But then he smiled and said, "Pissed on you, eh?"

"Soaked my pants," I said.

"Well, don't let the little bastard get away with it."

"I won't."

"Next time you see the boy," Gordon said, "piss on *him*."

"I will."

He winked at me with a yellow eye.

I walked out of the Foxhead, leaving Gordon alone to continue his journey to death's door, accompanied by my poor selections of hair metal power ballads and techno mash-ups.

Three months later, Gordon's wife called me to ask if I would speak at his funeral, and, fool that I was, I ended up getting drunk at the Foxhead instead and, later, arrested for public intoxication. Vince Belecheck was tapped as Gordon's replacement to head the Writers' Workshop until a national search could be conducted. During his three-month stint, he was rumored to have slept with a half-dozen students and sired a child. The mother, a young Mormon poet whose first and only venture beyond the confines of Utah was her journey to Iowa, fled the Workshop and, to the best of anyone's knowledge, hadn't published so much as a single bad poem in an obscure magazine since her ill-fated tryst with Vince Belecheck. In all likelihood, she returned to the bosom of the Latter-Day Saints and now passed her days reading the prophet's book of scripture when she wasn't home-schooling little Zennith.

I never visited Gordon's grave. I didn't go to the Workshop's memorial for him a year later, either. To me, he was still sitting at the Foxhead, nursing his whiskey and listening to the crappy music I'd put on.

"Pull over here," I said now, pointing to the B&B.

Lauren parked without backing into the space. She pulled in nose-first, killing the engine with the car still angled out into the street.

"Ah, yes," S. S. said, staring out at the B&B. "I remember it as though it were yesterday."

"She'd better be here," Lauren said, opening her door. "I've already canceled readings in St. Louis and Memphis. I can't keep telling people she has the flu."

Together, we crossed the street, walked up the front steps, and entered the B&B with the gusto of a theater troupe. As S. S. and I stomped our feet, Lauren stepped toward the antique desk, behind which sat an ancient woman wearing a sweater and a stylish knit cap pulled to the tops of her earlobes. I could only imagine, from her perspective, that we looked like we were putting on a performance, what with the two men clomping behind the feisty yet vulnerable woman who, having stepped forward, opened her mouth as if to burst into song.

Lauren turned around quickly and yelled, "Quiet, boys!" as if this were all still part of an elaborate script. S. S., playing his role to perfection, turned to me and smiled, a smile that said, *Oh, but isn't she charming!* For my part, I rolled my eyes, as if to say, *Oh, S. S., you're such a pushover for that dame!*

We quit stomping—and as soon as Lauren began interrogating the old woman, who, until now, had been cheered to see us, the illusion that we were a band of traveling actors turned to dust. Lauren fired one question after another at the poor woman, sometimes following the woman's answer with, "Oh, *really*." I let it go on much too long. One of my fatal flaws was allowing people to do and say the most outrageous things without calling them to task, if only because I couldn't actually believe that they were really doing and saying the things they were. Later, of course, I would obsessively run through all the things I *should* have said, and I would keep revising those things until my retort became razor-sharp—the best possible response for that particular moment. Sadly, it would all remain inside my head.

But right here, right now, the words finally came to me, the best possible words, and I was about to speak them, but S. S. stepped forward and said, "Please forgive the tone, ma'am. We're all so worried, that's all. She has a child with her. A newborn. And we don't want to see any harm come to either mother *or* daughter. I'm sure you can understand." S. S. reached out and touched the old woman's hand. "It's easy to become just a little—you know—hysterical." He said the word *hysterical* under his breath, even though Lauren, about whom he was speaking, stood next to him, thumping her fingers along the edge of the antique desk.

"I understand," the woman said.

"It was my pleasure to have stayed here many years ago," S. S. said, smiling now and looking nostalgically about him. "In fact, I was just telling Ms. Lauren Castle and Mr. Jack Sheahan about the delectable French toast I was served!"

The old woman, clearly pleased, blushed. "We don't have any guests today," she said. "But if you're hungry, I guess I could . . ."

"We would pay handsomely," S. S. interrupted.

She led us into the dining room before leaving us alone. Lauren stood with her hands behind her back, examining the room's various paintings (most of them featured cows) as though she were at a Monet exhibit. S. S. rubbed his fingers over the dining room table's wooden surface then examined the tips of his fingers, like a homicide detective searching for the smallest of clues. For want of something to do, I opened the drawer of a bureau and looked around inside.

"What the hell are you doing?" Lauren asked.

S. S. wagged his head. "You really shouldn't, old boy," he said.

I shut the drawer. When they continued staring at me, I said, "What?"

S. S. pulled a flask from his coat pocket. "Care for a snort? Anyone?"

Lauren said, "What *time* is it?"

"I'm not driving," I said. "I'll take a snort." I took the flask and tipped it up quickly while keeping an eye on the kitchen door.

"Give that to me," Lauren said.

"But you *are* driving," I said.

S. S. nodded toward her. "Go on, Jack. Give it to her."

I handed it over. Lauren took a long, deep snort. Before giving it back to S. S., she turned it up one more time.

"You have no idea how much I needed that," she said.

"Did Tate say what time his meeting was with what's-her-name? The Workshop's director?"

"What's this?" Lauren asked, moving closer to us. The three of us now stood in a tight circle and, like a band of co-conspirators, stared at the floor between our feet while we plotted.

"Apparently," I said, "Tate Rinehart is being invited to teach in the Workshop. He's being wooed."

"He's meeting her at noon," S. S. said.

"Where's that flask?" Lauren asked.

S. S. unhesitatingly surrendered the flask. When she was done, she handed it to me. I took my share and gave it back to S. S. Lauren's eyes widened. She was staring at S. S.

"Hey. I know who you are," she said.

"Yes, you do," S. S. said. "I've been here all along."

"No," she said. "You're S. S. Pitzer."

S. S. cut his eyes toward me and said, "*Les jeux sont fait.*" He placed his two fists together and stretched out his arms, as if he were expecting to be cuffed. "Well played, my dear," he said. "Well played."

In a gesture of unexpected tenderness, Lauren took hold of his wrists. I imagined her telling him how much his books had meant to her, how they had seen her through dark times, how they had saved her life. She said, "Are you working on a new novel? Because we'd love to publish it."

"Actually," he said, "I'm two hundred and fifty-three pages into a new work."

"Two hundred and fifty-three?" she said, smiling. "Could you be more precise?" She let go of his wrists and laughed. "What's its title? You can tell me *that* much, can't you?"

"It's called *After the Fall*."

Son of a bitch, I thought.

"One condition," S. S. said, and he put his arm around my shoulders. "You must send us on the road together. We'll promote both our books at the same time."

"I love it!" Lauren said.

"And you'll be our publicist," S. S. said.

"Of course I would," Lauren said.

By the time breakfast was served, S. S. and Lauren were giddy with their plan. Whenever the old woman left the room, they passed the flask back and forth until they'd polished it off.

"Are we close to a liquor store, Jack?" S. S. asked.

"Not far," I said, pushing food around my plate.

S. S., eating breakfast for the second time that morning, said, "Why so glum?"

"Writers!" Lauren said before I could answer. "Always so damned glum!" She was drunk. Her eyes were losing focus. "Gloomy Gus," she said and pointed a fork at me. "Maybe that can be your pen name."

"Maybe," I said.

"Did the French invent French toast?" she asked. "If they did, we should call those little bastards and thank them. I mean, this is great fucking food. You know?"

"Oh yes," S. S. said. "I *do* know. I *do*."

Lauren took stock of her surroundings. "Iz not so bad here," she slurred. "Iowa," she said by way of clarification.

"Iz not, indeed," S. S. said. He winked at me.

In the end, S. S. and I had to carry Lauren back to the car, all the while thanking our host.

"Wonderful food!" S. S. continued calling out from the sidewalk, holding Lauren's ankles. "Did you pick the oranges yourself?" Lauren was muttering something, but the booze she'd consumed, combined with lack of sleep, had finally caught up with her, and all I could make out were the words "press kit" and "asshole."

"She reminds me of an old girlfriend," S. S. said. The back door of the rental was now open, and we were trying to figure out which way to shove her in—head or feet first.

"How so?" I asked.

S. S. said, "In that she was awfully unpleasant until she got lit. Let's put your end in first and then push. What do you say?"

"Sounds good." I gently set her head down, and then S. S. and I shoved her hard across the seat, until we heard a thump. It was the sound of Lauren's skull slamming against the other door.

"Is she all right?" S. S. asked.

"She's fine," I said. "I'm sure her skull is twice as thick as yours or mine."

"I heard that," Lauren said, followed by, "Ouch. My head."

"We *meant* for you to hear that," I said. "In point of fact, it's a compliment."

"I lied," Lauren said.

"Really?" S. S. asked. "How so?"

"I haven't read a word Tate Rinehart's published. Not a goddamned word." She started to say something else, but I shut the door.

"Good-bye, good-bye!" S. S. yelled toward the B&B before he climbed into the passenger seat, waving one last time and smiling as though seeing off a lover on a Europe-bound ship, even though the old woman had already gone back inside and all the curtains were shut.

27

WITH AN ARM draped around each of our necks, Lauren Castle played the clichéd role of the drunken sailor to perfection as we lugged her up the stairs.

"Jesus," I said, "she weighs more than she looks."

"We're coming in," S. S. announced loudly after knocking on M. Cat's door. Without waiting for a proper invitation, S. S. turned the knob and entered.

M. Cat stood naked in front of his bay window, his bandaged hands on his hips. I had to look away. Even in gym locker rooms I looked away from naked men, because if I didn't force myself, my eyes would, of their own accord, sneak a peek. It was not unlike driving by a bad car accident in that the mind tells you not to rubberneck while the eyes remain glued to the horrors along the highway's shoulder.

"Is she dead?" M. Cat asked.

"No," I said. "Just passed out."

"I lent my flask to her," S. S. said. "Poor woman."

"You got her *drunk*?" M. Cat asked. "She takes Lexapro. And then I gave her some antihistamines. You don't want to mix that shit with alcohol. I took the MCATs, dude. I know."

"You *failed* the MCATs," I said. "Remember?"

"Why do you always have to be so harsh, man?" M. Cat asked.

I shrugged.

"Why won't you look at me?" M. Cat asked. "You can't, can you? Not after what you did to me back at the hospital. That wasn't cool."

"You're *naked*," I said. "That's why I can't look at you."

"But this is how I came into the world, *amigo*," M. Cat said.

S. S. said, "A wee bit smaller, I would imagine."

"But naked," M. Cat said. "And you know what? This is how I'm going to stay, I've decided. If society can't deal with that, that's their problem, not mine."

"Good for you!" S. S. said.

"We're all just primates, anyway, right?"

"Monkeys in pants," S. S. concurred.

"Exactly!" M. Cat said. "Hey, can someone help me out with this one-hitter over here? It's way past time for me to get blazed."

"Only if you share," S. S. said.

"Now, *that's* what I'm talking about," M. Cat said.

S. S. packed the one-hitter, lit it, took the first hit, and held it up to M. Cat's lips. I wasn't looking at them, but I saw their funhouse reflections everywhere—in the toaster, in the microwave's plastic window, in the blown-glass double-bubble bong. They appeared as either elongated or blob-like, a quivering North Star moving between them. In one reflection, M. Cat's penis appeared to be as long as his torso; in another, his head was so large, he looked like a hydrocephalic man-child.

"Lexapro," I said. "That's for depression, right?"

Holding smoke in his lungs, M. Cat said in a high-pitched voice, "She's under a lot of stress, dude."

"Yeah, well," I said, "who isn't?"

M. Cat exhaled, and the entire room filled up with smoke. He said, "And now she's got a situation on her hands."

I nodded. I picked up the bong, examined it, and set it down. "What do you mean?" I asked.

"That chick I was looking for?" he said. "What's her name?"

"Vanessa?"

"Yeah. *That* chick. Well, she made up just about everything in her book. She doesn't even have a brother. There's no aunt or uncle. There's not even an *outhouse*! Is that fucked up or what?"

I turned to face M. Cat now. I stared into his eyes, trying to read if he was screwing with me, but he looked as innocent as a child.

"*New York Times* is gonna break the story on Sunday," M. Cat said. "A feature in their magazine."

"I think you're confused," I said. "They already did a profile on her. It ran last month."

"No, no," M. Cat said. "This profile—the one they're running *this* Sunday—it's all about the lies. Vanessa got wind of it and split." S. S. held the one-hitter up to M. Cat's lips. After M. Cat inhaled, he said in his squeaky voice, "Vanessa." He let go of the smoke and said, "She totally James Frey'ed everyone's ass."

The three of us regarded Lauren, who was curled up in a ball and sleeping soundly.

After S. S. and I left M. Cat with Lauren, I asked S. S. if he could give me a little time alone.

"Just a few minutes," I said.

"I'll be downstairs," S. S. said, "admiring the snow."

Inside my apartment, I pulled the most recent phone book off the stack and looked up Alice. It had been years since I'd looked up her number, and I wasn't sure why I was so surprised to find her listed, but there she was. I wasn't even sure why I wanted to call her. To apologize for the night before? To apologize for the sex in my car? To apologize for the cheese grater that sliced her toe?

I dialed. On the third ring, the answering machine picked up, but it wasn't Alice's voice I heard. It was a man's.

"You know what to do," the man said, and then the answering machine beeped.

I hung up. I studied the number and dialed again.

Three rings. Then: "You know what to—"

Before the man could say "do," the phone rattled, a squeal filled my ear, and Alice said, "Hello?"

I hung up. I was about to leave the apartment when my phone rang. I let the answering machine pick it up.

"Jack?" Alice said. "Did you just call me?" A pause. Then: "Jack? I've got caller I.D. Are you there?"

I left my apartment.

Outside, S. S. and I stood in the bitter cold and admired the snow together. For the moment, the only sounds were our breathing, S. S.'s louder than mine. Puffs of air rose above us like thought balloons in a comic strip. Then came a blast of wind, roaring off the plains. We squinted and tipped our heads to avoid the direct, icy onslaught.

When you live in the Midwest long enough, you become expert at predicting when it's going to snow. Today, the clouds were low-slung, bunched together, the slate-gray of old cats. My face had a thin sheen of precipitation on it. My ear, the one that had suffered all those years ago when I had foolishly continued my journey downtown instead of returning home, began to throb. All of these signs spelled *snow*. It hadn't started falling yet, but it would . . . and soon.

"Let's go for a ride," I said.

S. S. said, "You realize, of course, that this is what some people hear before they're taken somewhere and murdered." When I didn't answer, S. S. said, "Of course, sometimes it means nothing. Sometimes a ride is just that—a ride."

"It's just a ride," I said. "I promise."

The Corolla sounded worse than it had only a day earlier, as if another important piece of the exhaust system had fallen off. I suspected people could hear me several blocks away, the way you hear the groan of a fighter jet before you see it blazing across the sky. Every time I turned a corner, people stopped what they were doing to see what sort of monstrosity was rumbling toward them. I was clearly committing a faux pas, the automotive equivalent of farting in a crowded elevator.

"It's like we're at the head of an unpopular parade," S. S. said, waving to a family that had stopped walking to glare at us as we drove by.

I took us to the student union, which sat next to the river, and I parked at a meter reserved for guests of the hotel inside the union, a placed called the Iowa House. The Iowa House was part of Workshop lore, since many of the visiting faculty, who came to town for only a semester, took up residence there; but like some kind of haunted hotel, the Iowa House often had its way with the guests. It had been a glorified motel, a grim one at that, with small blue-carpeted rooms, green bedding, and walls that were either beige or dirty. TVs were bolted to dressers. Raymond Carver and John Cheever lived in the Iowa House when they were teaching in the Workshop in the spring of 1973. It was later reported that neither took the covers off their typewriters the entire time they were there. Instead, they drank—and heavily. Cheever, afraid someone was going to mug him, didn't like leaving his room. He and Carver made twice-weekly trips to the liquor store together, meeting in the Iowa House lobby and then driving to the store. A few years later, Frederick Exley checked into the Iowa House during his semester-long stint teaching in the Workshop. In *Pages from a Cold Island*—his sad, nearly unreadable follow-up to his glorious memoir *A Fan's Notes*—he wrote, "Before going to Iowa I'd promised myself never, *but never* drink in my room; that no matter the circumstances I'd force myself, for every single drink I had, to walk to one of the campus saloons and pay for it over the bar." The next scene in the book is one of drunken debauchery inside the Iowa House between Exley and a twenty-one-year-old groupie.

At the front desk, I asked if a Vanessa Roberts had checked in, but I was told no. S. S. profusely thanked the young woman, who was probably an undergraduate. She had cropped hair and, I noticed when turned around, a tiny tattoo of a blue star on the back of her neck.

Outside, I said, "You're drunk."

"Perhaps," he said.

I led S. S. down to the lip of the Iowa River. From where we stood, we could see the English Philosophy Building, where the Workshop had been housed for many years, including when I was a student. It was a dark-brick building with cave-like hallways and dim, flickering bulbs that made me think I was in an underground bunker, even when I was on the fourth floor, where the Workshop's main offices could be found. Before coming to EPB, as the building was more commonly known, the Workshop was housed in a series of Army barracks. From what I had read and been told, the barracks were broiling hot in the summer and freezing cold in the winter. In a word: miserable. And yet there were times, in the temperature-controlled rooms of EPB, that I longed for the primitive days of sheet metal and bad acoustics. It seemed a more appropriate place for writers to congregate. We were drunks and crazies, pissers and moaners. But my longing was both deeper and darker than a yearning for barracks. It was a desire to live in a time I couldn't possibly live in, a wish to meet people at a time in their lives that had already come and gone, a need to be a part of history in a way that I could no longer be. I suffered from what C. S. Lewis called *sehnsucht*, an inconsolable longing in my heart for

I knew not what. Sometimes, the *sehnsucht*'s grip was too strong, and it was all I could do not to curl up in bed and remain there for weeks on end.

I suspected that my predecessor, Max Kellogg, felt the same aching tugs at his heart the winter night that he drove through the guardrail and into the Iowa River with Joyce Carol Oates's itinerary and a copy of his own unfinished novel. I told S. S. the story of Max and then pointed to the spot near EPB where he had driven off the road.

S. S. shivered. "An awful way to go," he said. He looked around. "Is the liquor store near here?"

"No," I said.

S. S., appearing neither surprised nor angry, said, "Oh." He put his hands into his coat pocket and blew a visible puff of air toward the river.

"The anniversary of Max Kellogg's death is coming up," I said. "I just thought it would be nice to stop by here and pay my respects."

"A thoughtful gesture," S. S. said. "May I quote something in his honor?"

"That would be nice," I said.

S. S. cleared his throat. He raised his chin, peering out over the water. He said: "'Under thy shadow by the piers I waited / Only in darkness is thy shadow clear / The City's fiery parcels all undone / Already snow submerges an iron year . . . / O Sleepless as the river under thee / Vaulting the sea, the prairies' dreaming sod / Unto us lowliest sometime sweep, descend / And of the curveship lend a myth to God.'" His eyes teared up after he had finished. He wiped them with the side of his fist and said, "To your friend, Mr. Max Kellogg. From Mr. Hart Crane. May they both rest in peace."

I took S. S. by the crook of his arm and walked him up to my parked car.

"I *am* a little drunk," he said, simultaneously laughing and sniffling. "You know what they say about novelists, don't you?"

"No, what?"

"Why, they're nothing more than failed poets," he said.

"Do you believe that?"

"Sadly," S. S. said, nodding.

We said nothing else on the drive to the liquor store. I took us past the new Workshop building—a restored Victorian, complete with a brand-new library, and surrounded by a few acres of land. I suspected that once things got good, no one looked back on the crappier days with envy, so I seriously doubted any current students longed for the days (*my* days) when the Workshop was housed in the English Philosophy Building, let alone Army barracks.

Tate Rinehart was most likely inside right now, sitting before Gordon Grimes's replacement, a poet named Barbara Weatherby. Weatherby, a graduate of Radcliffe and Iowa (and one of my classmates), was a Yale Younger Poets winner and a finalist for the National Book Award. To the dismay of book critics, she wrote an inordinate number of free verse poems about lighthouses and squirrels. I should pause here to note that the professional worlds of fiction and poetry are light-years apart. Poets have it infinitely worse off than prose writers. No one wants to publish a poet's book, and if someone does, no one wants to read it; no one wants to give them a job; no one is going to option one of their poems for the movies; no one's going to choose their book for a national book club. It was a life full of grim prospects. According to a famous study that surveyed students at the Iowa Writers' Workshop over a fifteen-year period, poets had significantly higher rates of depression, schizophrenia, suicide attempts, and actual suicides than fiction writers. A successful poet, whose parents were wheat farmers, once told me that the only thing that would have been more devastating for his mother and father to hear was if he'd decided to become a professional mime. The fact was that poets had to do whatever was necessary to get a leg up. Normally, I wasn't surprised to hear about poets schmoozing their way into magazines and anthologies. This was part and parcel of a life dedicated to sestinas and iambic pentameter. But sometimes the stories were born of jealousy, and this was what I suspected when I began hearing how Barbara Weatherby had slept her way to the top—seducing her undergraduate creative writing professors; shacking up with one visiting writer after another while at Iowa; sitting on the lap of a decrepit, liver-spotted magazine editor at the hotel bar during the annual Associated Writing Programs conference. Over time, the stories grew stranger and more slanderous: poetry editors getting blown underneath tables at the Foxhead, a hand job given to a Nobel Laureate in the back of a limo while he was on his way to a reading at the 92nd Street Y. We were classmates, Barbara and I, and we had gone out on a few awkward dates those early weeks after we had arrived in town, but once the semester had begun in earnest, we gravitated toward people working in our respective genres. But even after we had parted ways, I still watched her from afar. She had green eyes and wide hips—a redhead whose freckles were more pronounced at the beginning of each school year after a summer spent in the sun. Her looks were those of a movie star, but they were distinctly more mid-century than contemporary. She could have been a young Rita Hayworth or even a Marilyn Monroe back when Marilyn, only a few years removed from foster homes and orphanages, was still a redhead named Norma Jeane. Students in the Workshop viewed success (*any* success) with suspicion and cynicism, but when that success was achieved by someone who was particularly attractive, the suspicion and cynicism increased exponentially. At Iowa conspiracy theories spread faster than chlamydia, and by the time Barbara Weatherby had been named Gordon Grimes's replacement as director, the theories had become a full-blown epidemic. There was no way—*no way!*—she could have landed that position on her own merits . . . or so the covetous convinced themselves.

"The Workshop," I said, pointing.

"Beautiful," S. S. replied, barely looking. "An institution, that place."

"Still thirsty?" I asked.

"A little parched, yes."

Playing Raymond Carver to S. S.'s Cheever, I pulled up in front of John's Grocery and let him out of the car so that I could search for a parking space. While backing into my old spot in front of Paul Revere's Pizza, I saw a familiar figure across the street. He was down on his knees in front of the Dutch Boy paint store but leaning ever so slightly forward, as if praying. When he opened his mouth, a stream of vomit came rushing out.

I rolled down the passenger-side window, considered yelling out, "Vince! Buddy!" but decided to lay on the horn instead. Down on all fours now, Vince glanced over at me, his expression that of a wet, lost dog with its tail slung low. I didn't let up on the horn. I wasn't exactly sure what had gotten into me, but I wanted to inflict more pain on the man.

A knock at my window caused me to jump. It was a manager from Paul Revere's Pizza.

"What the hell are you doing, man?" he asked. He was wearing a sauce-stained shirt with a name tag that said Mike.

I let up off the horn and rolled my window down.

Mike said, "Are you drunk?"

"Drunk?" I asked. "What time is it?" I laughed.

"Do you want me to call the police?" he said. "Is that it?"

"No, sir," I said. "I'm fine."

Mike looked over the hood of my car at Vince. "That your friend?"

"No, sir," I said. "I don't know him."

The workers inside Paul Revere's had walked up to the plate-glass window to watch us. They were an army of pizza makers, and I was speaking to their general.

"Everything's fine," I said. "I'll be leaving shortly."

Mike nodded, but I could tell he was skeptical. He walked back to his store but turned one last time to take in the scene.

Years ago, during my first year in the Workshop, I was arrested for public intoxication. It had been a weekday, and after drinking three pitchers of beer, I decided it was time to stumble home. My mistake was turning down an alley instead of walking the side streets. There, two cops sat in a squad car, waiting like spiders. Until then, I'd had no idea that such a law existed, or that someone who was walking home instead of driving could get arrested for having had too much to drink, and yet, there I sat in the backseat of the squad car after I'd been put through a battery of tests. My baseball cap was askew and driving me mad, but I was cuffed and couldn't move. I'd just finished reading Faulkner's novel *Sanctuary*, in which a character named Popeye calls over the sheriff moments before he's about to get hung for his crimes. "Psssst," he says. "Fix my hair, Jack." "Sure," the sheriff says, "I'll fix it for you." But then he springs the trap door, hanging Popeye.

I leaned forward and said, "Psssst. Fix my hat, Jack."

The cop in the passenger seat pivoted to regard me. I smiled at him. He reached out to fix my hat until the other cop, the one who was driving, said, "What the hell are you doing? Just leave him like that."

At the police station, the officer in charge of inventorying my belongings asked, "So, what do you do?" When I told him that I was in the Writers' Workshop, he nodded. "Uh-huh," he said. "We get a lot of those in here."

Now, sitting in my car in front of Paul Revere's Pizza, I realized how much trouble I could get into, and given that I needed my driver's license to earn my living, I concluded that I had caused enough trouble for one day.

I killed the engine. I walked over to John's. When I opened the door, a cowbell jingled. I checked the liquor section first, but S. S. wasn't there, so I walked up and down the aisles. No luck.

"Excuse me," I said to the cashier. I described S. S. in great detail, along with what he might have purchased. "Has he been in here?"

"He left five minutes ago," she said. She pointed to the back exit. "He went that way."

I ambled out the back exit, which opened onto their parking lot, but S. S. wasn't there. I circled John's twice but couldn't see him.

I'd hoped to find him back at the Corolla—perhaps, like actors in a vaudeville skit, we'd simply missed each other?—but he wasn't there, either. Vince, however, hadn't moved except to shut his eyes and curl up into a tight ball. It was possible, though I couldn't tell for sure, that he was sucking his thumb.

"Oh, for Christ's sake," I said. I hated myself for what I was about to do, but I couldn't simply leave him sleeping there in the snow. "Son of a bitch," I said, trudging across the street, stopping when my boots reached his head. "Hey, Vince!" I said. "Yo, Vince!" I tapped his cheek with the tip of my boot, and he moaned. His thumb was indeed in his mouth. "Come on," I said. "Let's get up. You can't sleep out here." I crouched down and gently slapped his face. "Wake up, Sunshine!" When that didn't work, I started piling snow onto his head.

"What the fuck?" he mumbled. When his head was almost covered, he reached up and slapped the snow away, opening his eyes. "Jack?" he asked. "Is that you?"

"Yeah, it's me," I said, already regretting that I had decided to help him.

"Who the hell was honking?"

"I don't know," I said. "A crazy person, probably."

"I'll bust his head," he said and made a soft fist while drool trickled out of his mouth.

"Yeah-yeah," I said. "But listen: You can't sleep out here, buddy. The police will come and haul you away."

"Police? Who called the police?"

"No one," I said. "Not that I know of. But they'll come by eventually and see you lying here, and they'll lock you up. So, why don't you come with me?"

"Where are we going?"

"You can rest up at my place, okay?"

Vince, looking as though he might barf again, nodded. Paul Revere's soldiers watched from their various pizza-making stations as I helped Vince across the street and then loaded him into my car. On a telephone pole hung a flyer:

> NAROPA READING AT THE MILL,
>
> COME HEAR REAL WRITERS—
>
> FOR A CHANGE.

The writing program at Naropa University was as maligned as, if not more than, Iowa's program but for a host of completely different reasons. Founded by Allen Ginsberg, the program was seen as flaky and silly, admitting groupies and wannabe hippies who paid little or no attention to craft. Instead of rigorous discussions on the sestina or point of view, they sat on dirty floors and banged tambourines—or so I'd heard. The reading was tonight at 8:00.

I tore the flier off the pole, folded it, and stuffed it into my back pocket.

"Roll down your window," I said after I had settled in. "If you feel the urge to throw up, don't do it in my car. Okay? Are we clear on that?"

Vince nodded. He rolled down the window with his eyes closed. As I pulled out of the parking space, I saw in the rearview mirror Paul Revere's manager step outside to write down my license plate number.

"Too much partying with the students last night?" I asked.

Vince said, "One of them slipped me a roofie."

"A *roofie*?" I said. "Are you *sure*? Do you know who?"

"I think it was this chick named Daphne. But maybe it was this dude named Grant."

At a stop sign, I turned to face Vince and said, "Did they *do* anything to you?"

"*Do*?" he asked.

"Did they do anything sexual to you against your will?"

"No, no," he said. "It wasn't like that. Daphne and Grant are engaged or some shit, and I was hitting on Daphne big-time. Have you seen her? Jesus Christ, I couldn't help myself. It was like I was possessed. So one of them—or maybe both of them, for all I know—slipped me a roofie. The next thing I knew, I was asleep in front of the paint store."

As I drove, I looked around for S. S., hoping to see him down a side street. "So, let me get this straight," I said. "This couple, Daphne and Grant, are engaged, but they keep a supply of roofies on hand."

"No, no," Vince said, opening his eyes. "The roofies were *mine*. They must have found them when they took my coat."

"Vince," I said. "What the fuck are you doing with roofies?"

Vince, blinking, straightened up now, clenching and unclenching his fists. "Look here," he said. "I've never used them on anyone, okay?

I'm a writer. Someone gave me a bottle of them once, so . . . fuck, I don't know what I was ever going to do with them. Nothing, probably. But I'm a writer, so I kept them. That's what writers do. Real writers at least. *Published* writers. They chalk what they do up to experience. *Everything* they do." He turned to face me. "I mean, who the fuck are you, anyway? You want to tell me you're a saint, is that it? You want to cast judgment on *me?*"

I stopped next to the city park.

"Get out," I said.

"What?"

"Get the fuck out of my car."

Vince said, "If I didn't feel like absolute shit right now, I'd offer to kick your ass."

"Tell you what," I said. "Let's keep that offer open."

"What offer?"

"The offer to kick my ass. I invite you to try," I said. "Now, get out of my car."

Vince swung open the door and, like someone fresh out of surgery, eased himself out of the car. Grimacing, he leaned down and said, "The only reason your story was in *The New Yorker* and *Best American* was because Gordon Grimes owed you money. Everyone knows that. No one thinks otherwise." He smiled and said, "Except maybe *you*." With the car door gaping open, Vince Belecheck walked slowly away, leaving behind him a trail of ghostly boot prints across a park of virgin snow.

I LEARNED TO TYPE on an old manual typewriter, a machine that was as heavy as an engine block. It had belonged to my mother, who'd dreamed of becoming a journalist. Her marriage to my father and then her pregnancy with me pretty much put an end to those and a host of other dreams. When I showed an interest in writing early on in grade school, my mother unearthed the cast-iron beast from the back of a closet, dusted it off, and bought a dozen new ribbons for me. I typed on it for nine years, until my high school graduation when my parents gave me a brand-new electric typewriter, this despite typewriters being only a few short years from being put on the endangered species list, joining record players and, a few years later, VCRs in landfills across the country.

These days, everyone writes on razor-thin laptops. (Hell, teenage girls in Japan *text message* entire novels.) Only the oldest of writers I escorted still faxed their editors from the hotel. The younger writers— and even some not so young—maintained lengthy blogs about their writing lives. If a writer didn't have a blog, he or she was being blogged about, often viciously, usually by wannabe writers who wielded their blogs like swords. Part of the appeal of being a writer was the anonymity, but the Internet had pretty much ruined that. Almost always when

I read blogs by young fiction writers whose work I admired, I ended up feeling embarrassed for the writer. Frequently, they revealed too much personal information, or they felt compelled to share all their opinions. There appeared to be no filter between what popped into their heads and what showed up on their blogs, and I wanted to beg them to reconsider being so public, but instead of dropping emails to them, I simply never read their books again.

A year ago, after a late night at the Foxhead, I made the mistake of pulling up a blog dedicated solely to rejections from literary magazines. The site was called "Rejections Are My Heartbreak and Misery," and each entry was about rigged contests or impersonal notes from agents who'd turned down the blogger's novel or the cruel wording of submission guidelines. One blog entry that I had drunkenly stumbled onto happened to be about MFA programs, a subject that brought the loons out of their closets by the dozens. Finally, they could rationalize their own lack of success by accusing publishers and writers of being part of a secret cabal, like Yale's Skull and Bones, that refused to let in anyone who didn't know the secret MFA handshake. The comments on the blog came pouring in, one after the other, the sentiment being that MFA'ers were coddled, that they didn't know the real world, that they were handed book contracts and cushy teaching appointments upon graduation, that they came from privileged backgrounds. The words "Ivory Tower" appeared again and again. Although I couldn't argue that my own publications *weren't* born of dubious circumstances, I foolishly decided to weigh in, letting everyone know that I had an MFA, from Iowa no less, and although most of my colleagues had come from backgrounds with money, I certainly hadn't. Furthermore, only a few of my classmates had received cushy teaching appointments after earning their diplomas; the vast majority pieced together work any way they could. Lastly, only a modest percentage of my classmates had published books after graduation, and of those who did, only two had managed to achieve the kind of reputation where someone, somewhere, might actually have heard of him or her.

"You're all so paranoid," I wrote. And then, for lack of a better closing, I wrote, "Good grief!"

I entered my comment, waited a few minutes, and refreshed the page. A man whose *nom de blog* was "Oscar Wilde and Crazy" responded to my comment with one word: "Bullshit."

I wrote back, "Bullshit?"

"I should kick your ass," Oscar Wilde and Crazy wrote. "You have an MFA from Iowa and you dare come here and chastise us? You're an asshole. Furthermore, I don't believe most of what you've written."

The anonymous blogger, who was known only as RAMHAM (the acronym for the blog's name), moderated the comments with such speed that it was only natural to assume that this person had nothing of import going on in his or her life.

"Now, now," RAMHAM wrote. "No name calling. Keep it civil."

"Are you kidding me?" I wrote back to Oscar. "Why the hell would I be making any of this up? Who the fuck are you?"

"I know your kind," Oscar wrote. "I live in Cedar Rapids. I see you Iowa snobs all the time. You think your shit doesn't stink. You walk around town like you own the goddamned place. You disgust me. I should drive down there and pummel you, just for fun, you pussy."

"Now, now," RAMHAM chimed back in. "Remember what I told you."

Even though it was true that many students in the Workshop did, in fact, think their shit didn't stink, and one did often get the sense that they walked the streets like kings and queens besieged by peasants, Oscar's attack was weirdly personal, and I'd had just enough to drink to call his bluff.

"All right, you son of a bitch," I wrote. "You know the Hawk-I truck stop in Coralville? Just off I-80? You want to meet me there in forty-five minutes? I'll be sitting in a booth—waiting!"

"Let's keep the discourse at a higher level, okay?" RAMHAM added. "No one likes being called a son of a bitch."

This time, after I sent my comment, there was no immediate reply from Oscar Wilde and Crazy. I refreshed my screen a dozen times before he finally logged in another message: "I'll be there," he wrote.

It was summer. The husks of dead locusts littered the sidewalks, and each time I took a step, they crunched under my feet. By the time I reached my car, the bottoms of my shoes were covered with dozens of translucent wings. I saw them all along the shoes' margins as I tried to insert my key into the door.

"Shit," I said when I dropped my keys for the second time. I shouldn't have been driving in the condition I was in, but what could I do? I had challenged a man to a fight, and I was going to show up as I'd promised! The fact that I had challenged this man over the comments section of a blog dedicated to rejections from literary magazines didn't matter.

I drove cautiously, fully aware that I was way over the legal limit. I drove past a cop parked with his headlights off in a grocery store parking lot. I drove past a state patrol car cunningly hidden up one of the I-80 exit ramps, waiting like a ninja in the dark. When I finally made it to the truck stop in Coralville, I did so without incident.

I knew it would be a while before Oscar Wilde and Crazy showed up, if he showed up at all. Cedar Rapids was a good thirty minutes away. It was possible he wouldn't come at all. The longer I sat at the booth sipping my Diet Coke, the sleepier I became. I took stock of each person entering, but it was obvious, from the moment they stepped foot inside, what their intentions were. Most were drunk college kids. Some were actual truck drivers. A security guard sat on a revolving stool and chatted up a waitress.

Eventually, I broke down and ordered pancakes, eggs, and bacon. The meal started to bring the absurdity of the night into sharp and disconcerting focus. What if the man did show up? Where would we fight? Near the gas pumps? In a ditch alongside the interstate? And what would we tell the security guard? *Don't mind us; we just have a difference of opinion about MFA programs.*

The waitress had already brought my bill. As I speared the last stack of syrup-soaked pancakes with my fork, an older man walked in wearing a gray cardigan sweater, a T-shirt, and old wool slacks. Even at three in the morning, it had to have been ninety degrees outside, and yet I swore I saw a shiver pass through the man as he stood there looking around. He wore wire-frame glasses and had the sort of unkempt graying mustache that collected food scraps. He also wore a baseball cap, the kind that people had custom-made with words along the hat's brim, composed of iron-on felt letters, usually to announce their name to the world. At first I thought the word the old man had chosen for his hat was OW!—a funny thing to see across someone's forehead, as though calling attention to a chronic headache—but then I saw the letters for what they really were: Oscar Wilde's initials. The exclamation point was there to emphasize his enthusiasm for the writer.

"Oh, no," I said.

As if to call me out into the open, he unbuttoned his cardigan and took it off. On his T-shirt was the famous Oscar Wilde quote, "An idea that is not dangerous is unworthy of being called an idea at all." He had to have been between sixty and seventy, almost as old as my father. Each time he blinked, his red-rimmed eyes looked as though they might fill with tears.

"Can I help you?" the security guard asked.

"Just waitin' for someone," Oscar Wilde and Crazy said.

"It's open seating this time of night," the guard said. "Have a seat, if you like."

The old man walked over to the counter and sat down. The one time we made eye contact, I quickly looked down at my bill and started fishing money out of my pocket.

What did this man think he was going to do? Did he really come down here to fight me? Was showing up a matter of pride for him, or was he indeed crazy?

I left money on the table. The waitress swooped in quickly to collect it, fearful, I'm sure, that I might have been trying to leave without paying—a problem of epidemic proportion in college towns.

On my way out, Oscar glared at me, so I nodded toward him. I was almost free, reaching for the door handle, when Oscar said, "You him?"

I stopped, took a breath. I turned around. "I'm sorry?"

"You him?" he asked.

I gave the security guard a look that said, *Is this guy nuts?* I shrugged. "Sorry," I said, shaking my head. "I'm not *him*."

I opened the door and stepped outside. The air was suffocating. Three bats circled one of the preposterously high lights that illuminated the parking lot. A hundred different genera of bugs crawled along the restaurant's windows, drawn to the brightness inside. I was shaking by the time I reached my car. I felt like vomiting. When I peered back at the restaurant, I saw that Oscar was still watching me, so I turned quickly away.

The next day there was a message from him on the blog: "Where were you, you asshole? I was there last night, but you weren't. As I suspected, you're a chickenshit mama's boy. Don't ever come to this site again, you hack with an MFA."

"Now, now," RAMHAM posted a few seconds later. "You know the rules."

I didn't ever return to the site. In fact, I quit reading any blog that had to do with writing.

I was certain, however, that the blogosphere would all be abuzz once the *Times* article ran about Vanessa's memoir being a sack of lies. Back at my apartment, I took one of my two copies of her book and plopped down on my couch to read it. S. S. wasn't there, and all was quiet in the apartment across the hall. This was the first time in over two days that I'd experienced what felt like honest-to-goodness downtime. And it felt great. It felt *right*, unlike the past forty-eight hours, during which my life seemed as though it had belonged to any stranger passing through town who made claim to it.

I opened Vanessa's book to page one.

The outhouse is usually a place for solitude, it began.

I clapped the book shut. The publicity materials actually had the gall to compare the book to Richard Wright's *Black Boy* and Elie Wiesel's *Night*, one memoir about racism in the South, the other about the Holocaust. Did publicists have no shame? Or were these the books that Vanessa herself had compared her own crap to when she pitched the book to her agent?

"Jesus," I said.

The outhouse is usually a place for solitude.

It was the sort of sentence that made one want to burn the book and then shower under scalding water. I opened it again, forcing myself beyond the first sentence, though it took several pages before I forgave Vanessa. Her prose was overwrought, with so many clauses piling on top of one another that the main clause often suffocated under the weight of its subordinates. The prose was probably supposed to be stream-of-consciousness, but it read like someone who was getting paid by the word, the way old pulp writers would add six adjectives when one good one would have done the trick. Even Lucy Rogan, with her adverb-burdened sentences, wrote prose that was more terse and precise.

A few things I learned from the first hundred pages of Vanessa's book: Her brother was named Jedediah after their grandfather, an Amish man who hailed from Shipshewana, Indiana. (We knew now that she made up having a brother, which naturally called into question the Amish grandfather as well as any familial connections to Shipshewana.) Where I kept expecting titillating scenes between herself and her brother, I received instead lengthy lectures on the Amish: their ethnicity (Swiss-German), their history, their religious practices, their separation from the outside world, their lifestyle and culture, their dress, their education, even their portrayal in popular entertainment, such as the Harrison Ford movie *Witness* and, more disturbingly, the Farrelly brothers' movie *Kingpin*.

I quickly flipped through the pages, hoping Jedediah might slip his hand under her bra, or she might unzip his fly. But no: We learned even more about the Amish. Amish foods, Amish ceremonies, Amish vehicles.

I leaned back and put my feet up onto my coffee table. I was about to forge ahead when I lowered the book and examined the space around my feet. It was empty.

"Why, you son of a bitch," I said, standing up and searching the apartment for my novel. I looked under the phone books; I checked the bathroom; I scanned the tops of bookcases.

It was gone.

I went out into the breezeway and pounded on M. Cat's door. At first I heard nothing, but during my second round of knocking, M. Cat yelled for me to open the door. A bed sheet was wrapped around him, as though he were getting ready to go to a toga party.

"What's *this*?" I asked, smiling, but before I could say another word, Lauren Castle came out from the bedroom, also swathed in a sheet. The look she gave me was that of a boss dealing with an incompetent employee.

"I hope you're here because you found Vanessa," Lauren said. "Otherwise . . ." She raised her eyebrows.

"Have either of you seen S. S.?" I asked.

Without another word, Lauren headed back toward M. Cat's bedroom. M. Cat said, "Dude, can this, like, wait?"

"So you haven't seen him," I said.

"Well, yeah, we saw him maybe twenty minutes ago," M. Cat said. "He gave me a message to give to you." M. Cat glanced toward the bedroom. He reached up with a bandaged hand, as if to say, *Hold on!*

"And?"

"And he told me to tell you that he was sorry but that it was all for the best, and that if you couldn't see that right now, you would eventually." M. Cat said, "Sorry, dude, but I need to go." With his foot, he shut the door.

I stood there until an overwhelming exhaustion blanketed me. Nothing seemed particularly real. My head felt as though it had been carefully packed in cotton. For a moment, I couldn't fathom why I had spent so much of my life in Iowa, of all places. The sensation was like waking from a bad dream, only to realize that things were worse in real life than they had been when sound asleep.

I drifted back into my apartment, locked the door, put up the security chain for the first time in years, and crawled into bed.

PART SIX

There isn't a great deal of difference between fact and fiction,
it's just how you choose to tell a story.

—James Frey

T HOUGH I LIKED most of my classmates at Iowa, there were still the
liars and the lunatics to contend with, like Tom O'Malley, who did
his undergrad at Bowdoin, one of the most expensive private col-
leges in the country, but was a kleptomaniac (he'd ask you for a quarter
for the parking meter and then slip the coin into his pocket, or he'd steal
the tips off the bar when no one was looking), or Christopher Le Grand,
whose father was a psychotherapist to Hollywood's A-listers but who,
one night at my apartment when I went to the bathroom, turned up all
the knobs of my gas stove, filling the apartment with poison. Chris and
I went to the Foxhead that night and drank hard, and then I slept the
next day until 5:00 PM. What finally forced me out of bed and into the
hallway was a burning desire to check my mail for the daily batch of
rejection slips, and it was only after groggily returning to my apartment
with *Missouri Review* and *Shenandoah* rejections in hand that I heard
the hissing stove and saw what Christopher had done.

In truth, I could deal with the Toms and the Christophers of the
Workshop better than I could deal with the whiners, the ones who couldn't
take criticism. Each of us had been the star writer at our undergraduate college, but now we were just one of many. Some of my classmates couldn't
stomach this sad reality, and none took it worse than Brian Albrecht.

Brian was a forty-something student who dressed like a janitor and wore a three-foot wallet chain that scraped the floor when he sat down, and on the first day of Peter Stark's workshop, Brian volunteered to turn in the first eighty pages of his novel for the following week's workshop. Stark was a famous magazine editor, notorious for sending cutting rejections to writers like John Updike and Eudora Welty, and this was the first time he'd stepped foot in a classroom as teacher.

That next week, we students talked diligently about Brian's novel as though we were discussing *The Grapes of Wrath*. Stark sat at the head of the table, remaining silent but smiling as we prattled on. When we were done, Brian Albrecht, pleased with our comments, turned to Stark and said, "Well?"

Stark said, "Starting on page sixty-three, you've got two good pages, but the rest of it is maudlin and melodramatic. I'd take a good look at those two pages but throw the rest of it away."

Brian, who was sitting next to Stark at the long conference table, said nothing. When Stark asked for volunteers for the following week, Brian's arm shot up.

Stark, grinning, probably trying not to laugh, said, "Are you sure?"

Brian nodded. When he sat up straighter, his chain dragged across the tile, clanging against the chair's legs.

The next week, the scene repeated itself almost verbatim. We, Brian's classmates, diligently praised the subsequent seventy pages of his novel while raising the occasional question about character motivation or plot convenience; Stark remained silent, but the look on his face was that of a man who was thinking of a funny incident from his past.

When we were finally done patting Brian on the back for a novel that, in all honesty, was horseshit, Stark said, "I want to congratulate Brian. I mean, after last week and all, I certainly wouldn't have turned in another installment. But I'm glad you did."

Brian was grinning now, waiting for vindication.

"Remember how last week I said there were two pages worth saving?" Stark said. "Well, I've reconsidered that. I think you should throw *all* of it away."

Brian, who was still seated directly to Stark's right, sat up and said, "What's your problem, man?"

"No problem," Stark said. "This just isn't working. Last week I was *trying* to find something good to say, which is why I cited those two pages, but *this* week I realized that I'd done a disservice. Just throw it in the trash, Brian. All of it."

Brian stood up, fists clenched. "Come on," he said.

"What?" Stark asked, smiling but looking around the table at all of us now. We remained frozen in place, waiting to see how this was going to play out.

"Come on, you son of a bitch," Brian said.

"Brian," Stark said calmly. "Sit down. No one's fighting anyone. Go on now," he said in the reassuring voice of a hostage negotiator. "Just sit down so that I can continue. Okay?"

Brian finally sat down, slumping so far in his chair that his wallet chain coiled up beside him like a snake.

Stark stared at Brian for a minute, then reached over and squeezed his shoulder.

Brian didn't workshop another word but continued to show up, even though he said nothing. As for Stark, he left Iowa at the end of the semester with the reputation of having been the worst teacher the Workshop had ever seen—an unfair but predictable assessment.

Witnessing so many other writers pout taught me one thing: Never sulk. Or, rather, never sulk in public. Public sulking wasn't pleasant to watch. Most of the time, after a particularly brutal workshop that left the writer under scrutiny sulking and defensive, I would walk away embarrassed for him. Brian Albrecht's semester-long silent treatment, even during discussions of his classmates' stories, sent a clear message that he thought he was better than all of us: Since his own work wasn't greeted with the fanatical enthusiasm that he felt it deserved, he wouldn't waste his time reading and responding to our crap. By semester's end, I wanted to strangle him with his own wallet chain.

I had been dreaming about the Stark-Albrecht workshop when a ringing phone woke me. I had no idea what time it was, or even what day. For that matter, I wasn't even sure at what point in my life I had woken. I could have been back in the Workshop, Gordon Grimes could still have been alive, and I might have had a new short story due this week.

"Jack?" the voice said. "Jack, is that you?"

"Who is this?" I asked, blinking, reaching for the light switch. It was extraordinarily dark in my room, but I was still wearing my shoes.

"It's S. S., Jack," he said.

"Oh yeah," I said, and the day came back into sharp focus: the B&B, the drinking, the Iowa River, Paul Revere's Pizza, roofies, my novel. The key to making the most out of a dull life was to pack it all into about six or seven hours.

"Please don't sound so disappointed," S. S. said. "You're breaking an old man's heart."

"You stole my novel," I said, flipping on the light.

"That I can't deny," S. S. said. "But I want to convince you that I'm doing this more for you than for me."

"You're in denial then," I said. "You're doing this for yourself."

"Perhaps," S. S. said. "But this novel . . . it's killing you, my friend. It's given you terminal writer's block. You're suffering. By cutting this tumor of a book out of your life, I'm saving you."

"Very poetic," I said. "Good use of the extended metaphor. Very nice."

"Thank you," S. S. said. "But do listen to me—"

"No, you listen to *me*. I'm going to find you, you son of a bitch."

Someone knocked on my door.

"I need to go," I said.

"I beg of you," S. S. began, "there's something I need to tell you first," but I hung up.

The knock came again. I knew it wasn't M. Cat; his hands were bandaged. I doubted it was Lauren Castle; the knocks weren't hard enough. Vanessa, perhaps? But how would she have known where I lived? Vince Belecheck would have kicked open the door with his work boots, whereas Tate Rinehart, knowing what I now knew about his journal, wouldn't have dared track me down.

I eased open the door. A woman stood in the hallway, holding a small suitcase and smiling up at me.

"Jack Sheahan?" she said.

I looked at my watch and saw that it was six thirty.

"Do you know what time of the morning it is, lady?" I asked.

She examined her watch. "It's six thirty," she said, "in the evening."

"Oh," I said, and there was something about the way this woman looked at me, a commingling of hope and pity, that brought who she was into sharp focus.

"Lucy?" I asked. "Lucy Rogan?"

She was shorter than I had remembered, and she had a gray swath of hair that looked more purposeful than the ravages of age, but I could see it now in her eyes, this same woman who had sat in my car and made herself so vulnerable to me all those years ago.

She nodded. "May I?" she asked and stepped over the threshold into my apartment.

"Sure, sure," I said, moving out of her way. I glanced at my coffee table to see if Lucy's novel was still there—I didn't want her to know that I had been reading it—but, along with my own novel, it too was gone.

"Have a seat," I said, motioning toward the couch. "Can I get you something to drink? Diet Coke? Diet Cherry 7-Up? Mug Root Beer? Sprite Zero?"

"Do you have water?" she asked.

"Bottle?" I asked.

"Tap's fine," she said. "With an ice cube?"

I opened the freezer, making sure I could fulfill her request. There was only one tray of cubes that hadn't yet given up the ghost.

"One tap water with a single cube coming up!" I called out.

When I brought it to her, I could tell that she was reading the spines of the books in my bookcase, but unlike most people I knew, who would shout out an author's name with glee ("Dan McCall! Oh, my God. I thought I was the only person who read Dan McCall," or "I can't believe you own Rick Demarinis's first novel! I've never even seen a copy of it"), Lucy regarded my collection with suspicion.

"A lot of interesting books," she said.

I nodded. I sat in a chair across from her. I said, "Wow, it's good to see you again."

Lucy smiled but said nothing.

I said, "It's been, what, five years? Six?"

"I'm sorry," Lucy said, setting her water down on Vanessa's book, something a book collector, fearful of ruining the book's dust jacket, would never have done. "Do we know each other?"

I stared at the ever-growing ring of condensation on Vanessa's book. *Did we know each other?*

"Have we met before?" Lucy asked.

"I don't understand," I said. "I thought you came here because . . ." I stopped. I realized just how creepy what I was about to say would sound, that she had come here because she had been thinking of me the way I had been thinking of her. "So, *why* are you here again?" I asked.

"I was hired," Lucy said, "by a writer named S. S. Pitzer to come here and help you. He said you'd be expecting me."

"To help me what?"

"He told me you're starting a new book and need help getting going on it."

"You're kidding," I said. "And, what, you flew in this morning?"

"Oh, no," she said. "I live in Cedar Rapids."

"You *moved* here?"

"About three years ago," she said.

"Let me get this straight. S. S. *hired* you?" I asked.

"I'm a writing coach on the side," she said. "He must have seen my website."

I reached down, removed Lucy's drinking glass from the book, and then picked up the book and wiped it on my pants leg, setting it on top of a stack of books by writers I had escorted last month, writers who, given these last few days, I barely remembered now. And if I could barely remember the authors I'd escorted, how could I have expected Lucy to remember me? It was foolish to think she would. She had published dozens of novels, and for each one, she had been sent to a dozen cities. In the past five years alone, she had probably met over a hundred author escorts.

"I'm sorry," I said, walking to the kitchen and delivering Lucy's glass to the sink. "This has all been one big mistake." I spoke loudly so that she could hear me, explaining that S. S. didn't know what the hell he was talking about, that if anyone needed a writing coach, it was S. S. Did she even know who S. S. Pitzer was? Hadn't she heard of *Winter's Ghosts* and the story of its author who had disappeared after the book had become a wild success?

When I walked back into the living room and saw that Lucy was crying, I felt about as low as I'd ever felt. What had gotten into me? Why was I taking this out on her, of all people?

"I'm sorry," I said. "Hey, look, I'm sorry."

"I can't do this anymore," she said.

"Hold on," I said, and I grabbed a few napkins off the kitchen table and brought them to her. She wiped her eyes and blew her nose. "Do what?" I asked.

"*This*," she said, motioning to me, her suitcase, the window. "I've been living here for three years, trying to find my place, and I foolishly thought helping people with their own writing would give my life some meaning out here."

Listening to Lucy reminded me of the time she had spent in my car, telling me all about her failing marriage. She had wept openly then as she did now, and I had admired her willingness to be vulnerable around a perfect stranger. Because that stranger happened to be me, I had felt special. *Chosen*.

"Your books are best sellers," I said. "You don't need the money. Why would you do this?"

"It's not about the money," she said. "It's about belonging. I'm all alone here," she said, her eyes starting to water again. "I don't know anyone. No one."

I pulled up my chair and touched her shoulder. "It's okay," I said. "Everything's going to be okay."

Lucy breathed congestedly through her nose, snorted a mildly derisive laugh, and said, "That's what I keep telling myself."

"Let's think about this for a second," I said. "What was so special about your first trip here?"

"I don't know anymore," she said. "If I knew, maybe things would be different."

"Look," I said. "I *do* need help. I *want* your help."

Lucy stared at me through blurred eyes.

I said, "I've got writer's block like you wouldn't believe." I sounded like a man with a bad bout of constipation.

She dabbed her nose with the tissue. She said, "When I spoke to S. S., he told me that you had thrown your novel away. You shouldn't have done that. I mean, you *should* probably start something new. This old book is probably the reason you can't move on. But you never know when you'll go back to it."

"I didn't throw it away. It was stolen," I said.

"I don't understand."

"S. S. stole it," I said. "He took it."

"Why would he do that?" Lucy asked.

"It's hard to explain," I said. And I was about to attempt an explanation, but my door swung open and Lauren Castle burst in as though she and I were old roommates.

"I did it," Lauren said. "I fucking did it."

I motioned to Lucy. "Lauren; Lucy. Lucy; Lauren."

"What did you do?" Lucy asked, interested.

"I talked our publisher into giving M. Cat a five-figure deal for his book."

"What book?" I asked.

"*The Naked Man.*"

"What's it about?" Lucy asked.

"It's about Jack's neighbor," Lauren said, "spending an entire month completely naked, and how society can't deal with it."

"He hasn't left the house yet," I said. "How do you know society can't deal with it?"

"Jack," Lauren said. "Don't you know *anything*? We sold it on the basis of a proposal. Well, in this case, a pitch; we didn't even have time to actually type something up. You think what's-her-name, that *Eat Love Fuck* chick, actually wrote her book first and *then* sold it? Think again, my friend. Think again."

"*Eat Pray Love?*" I said.

"Whatever," Lauren said. "The point is, I talked my own publisher into giving M. Cat a massive amount of money—what Publisher's Marketplace would call a 'significant deal'—which proves what I've suspected all along."

"And what's that?" I asked.

"That I'm wasting my talents being a publicist. I should be an agent. I should be out there landing six- and seven-figure deals instead of busting my ass promoting whatever crap the publisher hands to me." She looked over at Lucy, as if seeing her for the first time, and said, "What do you do, Lisa?"

"Lucy," Lucy corrected gently. "I'm a writer."

"Really?" Lauren said. "Do you need an agent?"

"Her books are on *The New York Times* best-seller list," I said. "I think she's doing fine."

"Let her speak for herself, Jack." To Lucy, she said, "*Are* you doing fine? Are you in need of new representation?"

Before Lucy could answer, M. Cat walked into my apartment. He was still naked, so I looked away.

"Oh, sorry," M. Cat said. "I didn't realize you had company. Yo, Jack, when you get a chance, could you stop by my apartment? I need some writing advice."

"Don't leave," Lauren said. "Stay. This is the whole point of your book, isn't it? To see how people will react? So. What do you think, Lucy? Is this shocking? Are you offended?"

"Would both of you get the hell out of my apartment?" I said. "Please?"

On her way out, Lauren said, "Have you found Vanessa yet?"

"No. Not yet."

"Well, keep looking. My publisher's going to be very unhappy if I don't find her, and I don't want to burn that bridge."

Once they were gone, I shut the door and locked it.

Lucy said, "Were those oven mitts on his hands?"

"Bandages," I said.

Lucy took a deep breath, held it, then let it go.

"Do you ever get writer's block?" I asked.

Lucy shook her head, the way a child might: tight-lipped, holding back a smile, eager to answer the question. It was one of the reasons I had become so infatuated with her the first time I met her—her innocence. "I published three books last year," she said. "I'm working on my thirty-sixth right now."

"Jesus H. Christ," I said. "That's amazing!"

"I've got an outline for my thirty-seventh, and some preliminary notes for numbers thirty-eight, thirty-nine, and forty."

"I'm jealous," I said.

"I should probably go back to Cedar Rapids now," she said.

I nodded toward the suitcase. "What's in there?"

"A change of clothes," she said. "My toothbrush. The usual."

"You were going to stay?"

"In the Sheraton, yes," she said. "I took the bus down. I don't drive."

"You don't drive? How did that happen?"

"I really should go," she said. "I don't want to miss the next bus."

"I thought you were going to help me," I said.

Lucy stood and picked up her suitcase. "You're just being polite."

"No, no," I said. "I'm serious. I need your help."

"Really?"

"I do," I said. "You have no idea."

"Okay," she said. "Then I've got an assignment for you. S. S. tells me you're writing a memoir?"

I nodded.

"I want you to tell me who you are. Can you do that?"

"Who I am? Isn't that a little too . . . *existential?*"

"No, no," she said. "I don't mean like that. I mean, who *are* you? What do you *do?*"

"Oh," I said. "You mean like, 'I'm a—'"

"Shhhhh!" Lucy said. "Don't say it. Write it."

I nodded. I waited for more. When Lucy offered nothing, I said, "That's it?"

"You'll see." She carried her suitcase to the door.

"Here, let me drive you to the hotel," I said.

Lucy shook her head. "You've got an assignment," she said. "I want you to get to work on it right away."

Was she kidding?

Lucy Rogan stepped out into the hall and said, "We should get together tomorrow morning. First thing."

"I'll call you," I said.

As though we were concluding our first awkward date, Lucy nodded and said, "I'd like that."

CARRIED MY LAPTOP to the kitchen table, opened it up, blew dust off the keyboard, and typed

I was a media escort.

I stared at that sentence for a good long while, head in my hands, wondering where to go from there. It was a familiar feeling, this creeping dread, as the light from outside abruptly shifted, turning my apartment dark. I reached over and flipped on the kitchen light.

I was a media escort.

"Oh, Jesus Christ," I said, standing up so fast my chair fell backward. What the hell was I doing following the feel-good writing therapy that Lucy Rogan was selling? And what the hell did she know about writer's block, anyway? She'd already knocked out thirty-five novels, with another four in the pipeline. What she was offering me was pop psychology à la *Writer's Digest*: How to Write a Best-Selling Memoir in Thirty Days! Eager to please, I had taken the bait.

I shut my computer. I took a quick shower to rinse off my liquor-laced sweat and then I slipped on my old Iowa sweatshirt, one that Alice had bought for me and I still clung to, even though the fabric had begun to disintegrate and I could poke a finger through any number of holes. As I pulled on my socks, I started whistling. I never whistled—and yet here I was, whistling a tune I didn't even know, a mysterious, light-footed melody taking root inside my brain and blooming. Where did such things come from? How, for that matter, did I used to write short stories, or even as much of the novel as I had written—words building toward sentences, sentences shaping paragraphs? On days when things were going really well, the pages wrote themselves. I know it's a cliché, but there was no other way to explain it. You couldn't type fast enough to keep up with the images flashing in your head. You didn't even have to *think*. It was as though your hands were merely a conduit through which the story expressed itself. Before you came along, the story had been floating through the air, waiting for someone to catch it and transcribe it. I wondered if musicians felt similarly, that they themselves were merely the mediums for something that already existed.

It was possible that this phenomenon was the reason I had been drawn to writing in the first place. My third-grade teacher, Mrs. Varner, wanted each of us to write a short story, and while the rest of my classmates fumbled, unable to color in more than a sentence or two of their imaginary world, I wrote a full-fledged story called "The Crawl Fish." The catalyst for the story was based on my mishearing of the word *crawfish*, and it featured a fish that, too tired to walk upright, crawled everywhere. People would stop and say, "Look at that crawl fish," and the fish, for which I felt great sympathy, would say, "I'm just so tired. So tired!" I wrote four pages of the story without pausing, stopping only because Mrs. Varner wanted us to put down our pencils and, one at a time, read our stories aloud. Until that day I had been a mediocre student, struggling with multiplication and division, but as I read my story out loud and, looking up, saw Mrs. Varner smiling or, at the best parts, silently clapping the way she did whenever she was delighted by something we said or did, I sensed something in my life shift, though I wouldn't have been able to pinpoint it for years. More than anything else, what changed my life was the experience itself of stringing together words without consciously laboring over each one, as if I were a haunted little boy transcribing words of the dead. I wanted to experience it again, and again, and again. Sometimes it worked; other times, it didn't. My mother would say, "What in the world are you working on, Jack?" and I would shush her, afraid I might lose the next word, afraid that whatever it was that had taken hold of me would leave me for good if I didn't remain dedicated to it and it alone. Even as a child, I knew that this thing that other people saw as a talent might not stay with me forever.

I opened my door, but something stopped me. A sentence. I walked back to my kitchen table, popped open the laptop. I typed

That was how, twelve years after graduating from the Iowa Writers' Workshop, I was earning my keep.

I re-read what I'd written and then typed

I worked freelance, negotiating my fees with publicists at the major publishing houses, but I was occasionally thrown work by a woman named Barbara Rizzo, who had escorts waiting, like operatives, all across the country.

I continued typing, one sentence building upon the other, a miniature story about my job and one of the authors I had escorted, about the things that people do to each other, and about the inexplicable ways we feel afterward. An hour had passed, and I'd typed six double-spaced pages. I printed those pages, tucked them into my back pocket, and put on my coat. It was time to start looking for S. S.

L ESLIE BUTTONS HAD been the Workshop's coordinator for as long as anyone could remember. She'd lived through the reigns of four Workshop directors and had actually outlived Gordon Grimes, who had arrived deep into her watch. Though her position was technically an administrative one (some might even have said it was a glorified secretarial appointment), Leslie actually wielded more power than most agents in New York. She had worked with writers at all stages of their careers: Nobel Prize winners passing through Iowa City to give readings, Pulitzer Prize winners on the permanent faculty, novices who would go on to become literary celebrities beyond anyone's wildest expectations. She invited high-powered agents to scout talent; she received calls from publishers looking for her most gifted. Even under Gordon Grimes's directorship, it was well-believed that Leslie Buttons was actually the one behind the curtain, pulling the strings by way of appointing TAs, choosing visiting writers, and pushing certain manuscripts into the hands of those who could change a budding writer's fortunes. Rumor had it that she was even responsible for covering up lurid affairs between a certain award-winning poet and her students.

And so when I passed Mickey's and saw through the all-but-frosted-over plate-glass window Leslie Buttons having dinner with Tate Rinehart, I knew that it was a done deal: Tate had been invited to teach in the Workshop.

"Son of a bitch," I said. I knocked on the window. When Leslie and Tate turned toward me—Leslie smiling at the sight of me, Tate holding a burger up to his mouth—I gave Tate the finger. I slammed it against the window so hard, the restaurant's other customers turned to see what had just happened. And then I walked on.

Leslie knew me well, of course. When I was in the Workshop, my funding came from a special bequest that was earning interest. Instead of getting paid directly through Human Resources, the way nearly every university employee was paid, once a month I was given a check handwritten by Leslie Buttons from one of the Workshop's many special accounts. One weekend, after several days of bad luck at poker, I was called into Leslie Buttons's office. On her walls were old posters for readings by John Cheever, John Hawkes, Gail Godwin, Kurt Vonnegut, Margaret Atwood, and a dozen others, all of them signed to her, many of them thanking her profusely.

"I'm not giving you your check this month," she said to me. She was sitting on her floor, rummaging through a box. She pulled out a nameplate with John Irving's name on it. She held it up for me to see. "This used to be on his door," she said. "Should I keep it?"

"What do you mean, you're not giving me my check?"

She returned John Irving's nameplate to the box and pulled out a tiny ceramic pig. "Jane Smiley gave this to me," she said. She threw the pig into the trash can, placed the lid back onto the box, and said, "I hear you're gambling it all away."

"That's my choice," I said. "It's my money. I can do whatever the hell I want to do with it."

"The money we pay you with," Leslie said, "was given to us by a famous writer on her deathbed. I can't say who it was—that was part of her wish—but I thought you should know that."

"So?" I said. "I'm failing to see the point."

"The point," Leslie said, "is that you are wasting money that was given to us in good faith."

"Fine," I said. "Tell you what. Give my money to Vince Belecheck, okay? I'm sure he needs it to buy more fucking work boots!"

Even back then, everyone in the Workshop knew that Belecheck was a trust-fund baby who was merely playing a role from one of his own bad short stories. A week after I had stormed out of Leslie's office, she phoned me at home.

"Jack?" she said. "I'm calling to say that I've reconsidered. There's an envelope in your mailbox."

"I bounced two checks yesterday," I said, "and my rent is past due."

I waited for an apology, but none was forthcoming. She said, "You can pick it up anytime," and hung up.

Needless to say, it was highly unlikely, even if my career had taken off, that I would ever have been invited back to the Workshop for a semester to teach. I wasn't one of Leslie's little darlings, as Vince Belecheck had been. And now to see a fraud like Tate sitting across from her all these years later was too much.

"Jack!" a man behind me yelled out. "Jack. Wait up, you asshole!"

I turned quickly, as if expecting a fight, and saw Larry McFeeley, my ex-weight-lifting drinking buddy from the Foxhead, trudging through the snow toward me and grinning. In all these years, I'd never seen him anywhere other than the Foxhead.

"Larry. What the hell are you doing?" I yelled.

"I got kicked out of the Foxhead," he said when he reached me.

"You *what*?" This was akin to getting an eviction notice on a house you had paid off and owned.

"About two weeks ago I started taking steroids again and—"

"Whoa!" I said. "Wait right there. You started taking *steroids*? Are you *kidding* me?"

Larry shrugged. "I shit you not." He wiped a wet, meaty hand over his face and said, "Look. I smoke, I drink, I haven't taken a decent shit in over two years, my diet is horrible, I eat antacids like they're fucking Raisinets. I don't think taking steroids for a couple of months is going to kill me."

"But why?" I asked.

"I wanted to feel how I used to feel, you know, thirty years ago," he said. "Just for a short while. I wanted to feel strong again."

"What happened at the Foxhead? Did you get into a fight?"

"No, no," he said. "I made a bet with this college kid that I could lift the pool table up over my head."

"And?"

"And all I did was tip it over and break the damned thing."

"Who do you think you are?" I asked. "Chief Broom?" When Larry said nothing, I added, "*You* know. *One Flew over the Cuckoo's Nest*? That water fountain thingamabob? He lifts it over his head and throws it out a window? Does any of this ring a bell?"

"A water fountain?" Larry said. "Who the hell *couldn't* do that? This was a fucking pool table. Solid slate." He wagged his head, disappointed that I couldn't see the difference, and sighed. "So," he said, "what's going on with you?"

Without intending to, I unloaded it all on Larry—losing Vanessa, the breast pump, the arrival of S. S., the horrors of Lauren Castle, the theft of my novel—all of it, every last detail. I was succinct but thorough.

"Holy Christ," Larry said. "You need a drink. Where should we go?"

We?

"Actually, I'm looking for the guy who stole my novel."

"I'll help you," Larry offered.

"I'm just heading over to the Mill," I said, "for an artsy-fartsy reading. He might be there. But, really, you don't need to help. I appreciate it and all, but, really, I'll be fine." I started walking, hoping Larry would veer off toward the Brown Bottle or the Airliner, but he matched me step for step.

"Naw, this sounds about my speed tonight," he said.

I didn't say anything. I didn't want Larry McFeeley coming along, but what could I do? Before today, I'd barely exchanged more than a few words at a time with the man, and although those words had had a cumulative effect over the span of years that I'd been going to the Foxhead, I honestly knew very little about him.

"You went to the Workshop, right?" Larry asked.

"Once upon a time," I said.

"I write a little my own self," Larry said. "Poetry, mostly. Maybe they'll let me recite some of it tonight."

"I'm not sure it's that kind of reading," I said.

Larry said, "Well, if it happens, it happens. I'll talk to whoever's in charge."

"Sure," I said. "You could do that, I suppose. If you really want to."

"I don't have a degree in it," Larry said, "like you. I guess I'm of the belief that writing should come from the heart." When we passed an alley, Larry stopped walking and pulled out a vial of medicine. He held it up between two fingers, showed it to me, and then shook it. "Want a boost? I can shoot you in your calf, if that works for you." He started heading into the alley.

"You're going to shoot it out here?" I asked. "Like a junkie? They've got bathrooms at the Mill, you know."

265

Larry stared at the vial, holding it before him like a rare diamond, before reluctantly putting it away, and then the two of us trudged on to the restaurant.

NSIDE THE MILL, I looked for S. S., hoping to find him regaling a group of Naropa poets, but he was nowhere to be seen.

"Shit," I whispered.

After we secured a booth, Larry disappeared into the bathroom for a good ten minutes. I half-expected him to emerge with his shirt and pants ripped apart, looking like Lou Ferrigno in *The Incredible Hulk*, but as he waddled back to our table, I saw that he was still the same pot-bellied alcoholic I'd always known.

"First round's on me," he said and motioned for the waitress, ordering two shots and two drafts. I nodded. I should have told him that I was dead broke, but I was too humiliated to broach the subject. The drinks came, and Larry paid.

Vince Belecheck, walking into the back half of the Mill where the poetry reading was going to take place, slammed open the swinging double-doors like an old-time gunslinger. After a few minutes at the bar, he sauntered right up to our table and set down two shots and two beers, pushing one of each toward me.

"What's this?" I asked. "Reconciliation?"

"Free booze," Vince said. "Don't look a gift horse in the mouth."

"What the hell does that even mean?" Larry asked. "What's a gift horse, and why the hell shouldn't you look it in the mouth?"

Vince pulled up a chair and sat down uninvited. "Do we know each other, friend?" he asked Larry.

"You don't know *me*," Larry said. "But I've seen *you* around."

"So, Vince," I said. "Hoping to pick up a hot, young Amy Clampitt tonight?"

Vince wagged his head. "Nah. I'm meeting my fiancée here."

I had picked up my beer and was about to slurp the foam but paused at the word *fiancée*. Was he shitting me?

"Wait a minute," I said. "What about those poets you and Tate hooked up with? What about . . ."

Vince held up his palm. "Easy on the self-righteous indignation, Dr. Phil. We've been separated, okay? Is that good enough for you? But now we've decided to work things out." His eyes wandered over to a table of six young women. He blinked a few times, as if trying to make them disappear, then turned back to me and said, "Tate Rinehart," and huffed.

"What about him?" I asked.

"Want to know what that little fucker did to me?"

"He took your teaching spot for next year," I said.

"How the hell did you know that?" he asked.

I shrugged.

Vince rubbed his face hard. "I knew he was called in for an on-the-spot interview, but I figured they'd just hire us both. The two of us together? It'd be like having Led Zeppelin and Elvis on the same marquee."

"No doubt," I said. I did both shots in quick succession. "But here's what I'm wondering."

"Shoot."

"Why should I care?"

Vince cocked his head.

"About you," I added. "About your fate."

"Fuck you, then," Vince said. He picked up his drinks and carried them to a booth near the stage, settling in by himself.

"Do you know how much the human head weighs?" Larry asked.

"I have no idea."

"About twelve pounds. About the same weight as a bowling ball. That's about 8 percent of a person's total weight." He thought about it a moment. "Seven or eight. Less if it's a fat person's head. Feel my bicep," he said. "Go on. Give it a good squeeze." Larry struck a bodybuilder's pose with his one arm, even going so far as to tilt his head toward his fist. I looked around to see if anyone was watching, then reached over and squeezed it. To my surprise, the bicep was as solid as oak. It was as though his sagging stomach served as beard for the strongman he apparently still was. He motioned for the waitress. "This round's on me," he said, as if he hadn't yet paid for any drinks. I didn't argue.

Over the next hour, Larry took two more trips to the restroom. Whether to shoot more steroids into his thigh or take a piss, I didn't know. As the restaurant filled, I recognized some of the Workshop students, the ones I frequently saw at the Foxhead and George's, including a few who had been out with Vince and Tate last night. The vast majority of the people, however, were strangers. Whiskered and sunburned men roamed the restaurant like Bedouins, while mysterious-looking women clustered in groups, clutching poetry manuscripts to their wombs, or sat alone in booths, anxiously playing with their packs of cigarettes.

"Where the hell is he?" I asked.

"Who?"

"S. S.," I said. "The guy who stole my novel."

"If we find him," Larry said, "do you want me to pop his head?" He held his hands apart, as though holding an invisible basketball.

"No," I said. "That wouldn't be good."

The emcee finally climbed up onto the barely raised platform, motioning with his hands for the crowd to shush.

"My name is Billy Wexler," he said, "and I'm a student in the Jack Kerouac School of Disembodied Poetics!"

A good three-quarters of the audience stood and cheered. A few held their fists high and hammered the air while barking like a pack of sickly dogs: "Whuh-whuh! Whuh-whuh!"

When the crowd quieted down, Billy Wexler leaned close to the mike and said, "For the record, we at Naropa don't write poems about vacationing on Martha's Vineyard or our year abroad. We write about *important* things. Things that actually *matter!*"

More "whuh-whuhs" filled the room. The Workshop students visibly bristled.

Billy Wexler established the ground rules. Someone from the Jack Kerouac School of Disembodied Poetics would read first, followed by someone from the *famous* Iowa Writers' Workshop, if there were any volunteers. The word *famous*, I realized, was going to be the night's recurring insult.

First up was a guy who looked like he belonged in a Spin Doctors tribute band. His name was Dusty Rhodes.

"Go, Dusty!" someone yelled. "Show these fuckers what we got!"

Dusty pulled a few crumpled sheets from his back pocket. He unfolded them and smoothed them out, looked up, grinned and chuckled, shaking his head, and then looked back down at his poems.

The first poem was about a woman slicing open her wrists as semen leaked from her veins. The final line was, "Your seed penetrates my carpet as I once penetrated you."

"Whuh-whuh! Whuh-whuh!"

Larry McFeeley looked around, checking to see if anyone else was as disturbed as he was.

Dusty's second poem was about a brutal rape between an Army drill sergeant and a ten-year-old Vietnamese boy.

"Whuh-whuh! Whuh-whuh!"

Dusty lowered his head by way of taking a bow and, trying to hold back his grin but not succeeding, returned to his booth, where a Janis Joplin wannabe high-fived him.

Next up was Sioban Mo, a Workshop student I recognized from George's. Her hair was dyed brick red and chopped artfully in a post-punk 'do, and she wore skirts with thick leg warmers that had been popular in the 1980s. According to the introduction for her, she had published in *Poetry*, *Prairie Schooner*, *Tin House*, and about a half-dozen magazines that ended with the word *review*. I expected big things, maybe something along the lines of Sylvia Plath's "Daddy," a poem with some muscle and bite, but when she read the first line of the first poem— "O, you of the iambic pentameter police"—I flagged the waitress.

"Another round," I said. "Could you make the shots doubles?"

"I'll get this one," Larry said, and I offered my most serious nod of appreciation.

We drank steadily throughout the readings. During intermission, Larry said, "I need to talk to the head honcho. I don't want to seem like a megalomaniac or anything, but holy shit, I could write better poems with a Bic stuck up my ass."

Larry unsteadily launched himself out of the booth and stumbled toward the emcee. I looked around once more for S. S., but no luck. What I did spot, however, was a woman about to sit down across from Vince. Vince made eye contact with me, as if warning me not to come over.

I laughed. Of course I was going to go over. How could I pass up a chance to meet the woman who would consider marrying a fool like Vince Belecheck?

I weaved my way through the literati, knocking into people without meaning to and prompting more than one person to warn me to watch where the hell I was walking. Was I drunker than I thought?

"Vince!" I yelled, and several people turned in their booths to see who was screaming. "I've come to meet the future Mrs. Belecheck!" When I reached the booth, I pitched forward and gripped the edge of the table for balance, but then I saw that the woman with Vince was Alice—*my* Alice. I straightened up and said, "Oh. I'm sorry." I bent to wipe off my knees, as though I had fallen, but I hadn't. "I thought you were someone else," I said to Alice.

Glaring at me, Vince said, "Alice? Jack. Jack, this here is Alice." He cut his eyes up at me, another sharp warning not to mention these past few days, and added, "My *fiancée*."

"Alice?" I said.

"Hi, Jack," she said and looked down at her hands, which lay like two lifeless objects on the table.

Vince looked confused.

"I . . . ," I began, but I couldn't think of anything to say. I forced a smile and said, "I *really* need to take a leak." I rapped the table twice with my knuckles and headed for the restroom.

Standing inside a stall, I pissed long enough to read all the graffiti. When I was done, I pulled the Sharpie from my shirt pocket, uncapped it, and drew a dialog balloon starting at the tip of an enormous penis, as if the helmeted beast could talk. Inside the balloon, I wrote, "Has anyone seen my luggage?" It was the first time I'd ever written on a wall, and I was pleased with myself in the way that people who have had too much to drink are often pleased with themselves, but I couldn't stop my hands from shaking. I capped my pen and said, "Fuck." I flushed the toilet and said, "*Fuck.*"

I stepped out of the stall, pulled the folded manuscript from my back pocket, and looked it over. *I was a media escort*, it began. I tossed the pages in the trashcan.

Alice was waiting for me outside the restroom. She was wearing her coat and knit cap, and for an instant, I experienced the bright light of optimism. Was she going to suggest that the two of us run away together?

"Jack," she said and reached out, brushing a piece of lint off my shirt—the tell-tale sign that whatever had been between us was over. She was cleaning me up before sending me out into the world alone. "This old sweatshirt," she said. "You haven't thrown it away yet?"

I took a deep breath. I wanted to wish her well, but what came out was, "Vince Belecheck? Vince *fucking* Belecheck?"

She said, "I tried telling you. I did."

"Just one question. Can you answer me one question?" When Alice didn't say anything, I asked, "What's so special about Vince? That's all I want to know. What's so goddamned special about Vince Belecheck?"

She took a deep breath and held it, as if anticipating a blow, but what she said was undeniable. "He finishes what he starts," she said. "Look, I'm going to go now. I just explained to Vince about the two of us, and—"

"You mean you never told him about me?"

"It was so long ago," she said.

"It wasn't *that* long ago," I said. "We were engaged."

"We were young, Jack."

"We were going to have a baby," I said, but as soon as the words left my mouth, I knew I shouldn't have gone there.

Alice sighed. "I really need to go now," she said, and for once I didn't wheedle or cajole. I simply let her go.

W HEN I RETURNED to the main room, I found Larry sitting across
from Vince.

"We lost our table," Larry said. "One of us should have stayed
behind."

Vince, glaring into his drink, said, "Just sit the fuck down, Jack."

I was about to obey Vince when I spotted M. Cat and Lauren Castle.
M. Cat was wearing a ski cap with a giant white ball dangling from the
top like an ornament, a terry-cloth bathrobe, and mukluks. He looked like
a man who had wandered away from a psychiatric ward, whereas Lauren
Castle, holding him by the wrist, could have been the off-duty nurse who'd
found him. Upon spotting me, M. Cat smiled and waved with a bandaged
hand, then pointed me out to Lauren, who sneered. After they snaked
their way over to us, I perfunctorily took care of the introductions.

Larry moved over to Vince's side. M. Cat and Lauren sat across
from them. My options: sit on the side of a man I despised or sit on the
side of a man who might disrobe. I plopped down next to Lauren and
M. Cat.

Vince avoided looking at me. Instead, he trained a bead on M. Cat.
"Yo, Hef," he said. "There's a dress code here."

"Jot that down," Lauren said to M. Cat.

M. Cat showed her his wounded mitts and said, "I can't. I'll just have to remember it."

Before Lauren could berate M. Cat, Billy Wexler stepped back onto the platform to announce that intermission was over. The Naropa clan applauded and hooted. Billy, acting as though he'd just delivered Ronald Reagan's "Tear Down This Wall" speech, stared defiantly out into the audience.

And then the readings continued, volleying back and forth between us and them, or rather, since I wasn't a poet, between *them* and *them*. One Naropa poet finished by throwing the microphone stand down in such a way that it barely missed the head of an Iowa MFA student, a jug-eared fellow who sat with his back to the stage and was oblivious to the injuries he had narrowly avoided.

Close to midnight, Billy Wexler mounted the stage and said, "For our final reader of the night, I give to you a man from the community," Billy said, "a man *not* affiliated with the *famous* Iowa Writers' Workshop, a man who is an Iowa City *laborer*—Mr. Larry McFeeley."

With Larry belonging to neither camp, the applause was tentative, so I whistled and yelled, "Go Big Lare!"

Larry climbed up onto the stage and stared blankly ahead. He blinked a few times, squinting from the light bearing down on him. "I'm not a professional poet," he said. "I'm just a guy who loves words."

The cheers of encouragement from the Naropa students made me feel a warmness toward them that, until then, had been lacking. The Iowa students whispered to each other; a few of them got up to order more drinks.

Larry shut his eyes, as if the words were written on the insides of his lids, and, after clearing his throat, recited a poem, the first line of which was, "From the roof's still-icy peak, beside the steeple, his descent began."

Everyone, including Vince Belecheck, sat up to pay closer attention. The poem, on the one hand, was about a roofer who'd fallen off a church while on the job. On the other hand, it was about the fall of man. It was beautiful and haunting with a kind of James Dickey or Philip Levine grace, which was to say, poetic but accessible.

When he finished, the audience stood and cheered. A one-word chant grew in volume, the audience demanding, "More! More! More!"

Larry, grinning sheepishly, raised his hand and, after shushing us with his palm, agreed to recite another. Even cold-blooded Lauren who sat beside me like a lizard on a rock shivered in admiration when Larry's poem reached its zenith.

After reciting four poems, Larry returned to the table amid thunderous applause. Someone started chanting, "Lare-EE, Lare-EE," and before long, every patron in the restaurant seemed to be chanting it, too, until Larry stood and took a bow.

A group of Naropa and Iowa students crowded our table to ask Larry questions. Larry would shrug and say, "I don't know," or he'd offer up the moment of the poem's genesis. "It just came to me one morning," he said, "when I was hauling buckets of tar up onto the Hy-Vee on Waterfront Drive."

Vince, stuffed in the booth's corner, eyed Larry's fans with suspicion. "Hey, give me a little room," he said to Larry a couple of times.

After his boosters retreated, Larry took a deep breath and said, "Whew. I wasn't expecting that."

"Well," Lauren said, "you can expect more of that once I land you a big-ass book deal."

Larry wagged his head. "I don't know if I want to publish them," he said. "It's just a pastime for me."

"I wasn't talking about your poems," Lauren said. "Good God, nobody reads poetry. No, what I'm thinking for you is a memoir. The publishing world needs another *Iron John*."

"Well . . ." Larry began, but before Larry could spit out what he was going to say, Vince slammed down his glass and piped up: "He just said he doesn't want a book deal, lady. So give it a rest."

Larry's face tightened. He said, "You don't want to talk to her like that."

Vince, raising his eyebrows, said, "Hey, buddy. I was defending *you*. You told her you don't want a book deal, but she keeps pushing it."

"Your tone," Larry said. "It's unacceptable."

Vince said, "Oh! I see what's happening. You get a couple of fan-boys and suddenly you think you run the show? Is that it? You're the shit now? Is that how you see things?"

All the joy drained from Larry's eyes. He leaned toward Vince and said, "How much does your head weigh?"

"My what?"

"Your head. How much does it weigh?"

"Don't go there, Larry," I said, but it was too late: Larry took hold of Vince's head, as if it were a cantaloupe, and, rising ever so slightly from the bench, started pressing. As Larry clenched his teeth and gritted, Vince's eyes started to bulge. He tried reaching for Larry to make him stop, but Larry had the advantage of longer arms. Holding Vince's head as far away as he could, he squeezed so hard his own face turned red.

I knew I should have tried stopping Larry, but I was mesmerized by the sight of what was happening: Any second now, a man's head might explode. Finally, Billy Wexler and a few Naropa students rushed over and grabbed Larry, prying him off Vince.

"I'm okay," Larry said. "I'm fine." To Vince, he pointed and said, "*You* need to learn some manners." Larry put on his coat and deftly maneuvered through the patrons, weaving his way to the front door where he disappeared into the blur of snow.

For the rest of the night, Vince alternated between complaining about his head and complaining about Larry.

"That son of a bitch is gonna be sorry for this," he said. He reached up, touched his head, and said, "Ow! Something doesn't feel right."

Lauren leaned into M. Cat and said, "So? What are we waiting for?"

M. Cat, still wearing his terry-cloth robe, stared glumly ahead. He looked like a reprimanded child who had been warned not to cry.

"I can't do it," M. Cat finally said.

"You *can* and you *will*," Lauren said.

"I can't," M. Cat said. He sighed heavily. "I guess I'm not a writer, after all."

"Who said you were a writer?" Lauren asked. "Let me make something clear. You're *not* a writer. You're an *idea*. You're a *concept*."

"It's all right," I told M. Cat. "Don't do anything you don't want to do. Remember Polonius's advice to Laertes? 'To thine own self be true.'"

"Stay out of this," said Lauren. "You've caused enough problems these past few days."

"I'll be back," Vince said. "I need to pull those files we've been talking about."

Lauren, M. Cat, and I exchanged looks. *Files?* Vince stood and wandered the restaurant like a somnambulist, as if unsure where he was or how he'd arrived there, and after a while he walked out the front door. He'd left his coat behind, and although he was wearing his usual insulated overalls, it was too cold outside without the extra protection.

I stood and picked up Vince's coat.

"I better go look for the bastard," I said, but neither Lauren nor M. Cat looked up at me. They were both sulking, and I was of absolutely no consequence to either of them.

I put Vince's coat on over my coat, but before leaving the Mill, I veered off for the restroom one last time. I peeked into the stall. Someone had crossed out the words I'd written on the wall and replaced them with their own. The giant penis was now saying, "I'm a graduate of the famous Iowa Writers' Workshop."

My manuscript still lay in the trashcan, beneath a couple of crumpled paper towels. I fished out the pages, tucked them into Vince's pocket, and zipped the coat all the way up, bracing myself for the worst.

HE WEATHER WAS nastier than I had been expecting: the howling winds, the blasts of blinding snow, the ice creaking underneath my feet. The streetlights blinked yellow. The skin at the corners of my mouth felt as though it was cracking. My five o'clock shadow became stiff, lifeless bristles sticking out of my face's numb flesh. I looked around for Vince but didn't see him anywhere.

I saw from the corner of my eye, however, a shadowy figure lurking in an alley, and as I picked up speed, I heard, "Pssssssssssssst." When I didn't stop walking, the man said, "Hold on. Please."

I stopped and turned. It was S. S. In the illogical way that my life worked, the moment I stopped looking for one person and began searching for another, I found the person I had given up hope looking for. I cinched Vince's coat tighter.

"Jack!" he said after I had stopped walking. "Friend! I *thought* it was you. I've been looking all over, but to no avail."

"Where've you been looking? In alleys?"

"In alleys! In thoroughfares! Wherever the scent led me," he said cryptically, as though he were a man-beast and I just so happened to have caught him while he stood on two legs instead of sniffing down on all four. He unzipped his coat and pulled out a manuscript box. *My* manuscript box. "I can't do it," he said. "I can't just steal this from you. I was wrong to think I could."

"My novel," I said. I had every intention of taking it from him, but when S. S. actually extended it toward me, I stepped back, as if it were explosive.

"What's wrong?" he asked.

"I don't want it," I said.

"Don't be silly," S. S. said. "It's yours. You've toiled over it. For years!" he said, lifting the box up and shaking it at me.

The mere suggestion that I should take it back filled me with a lurching dread. What would that mean? That I would have to sit down and finish it? Even if I were to hide it, I would know it was still there, the way murderers who'd buried their victims' remains in forest preserves must sense their looming presence every time they drove by.

"Here," S. S. said. "Please."

"No!" I shouted. "I don't want it."

"Easy, now," S. S. said. "Take it easy."

"It's yours," I said, nodding toward the box. "I want you to have it."

"I swear on my dear mother's grave," S. S. said, raising his free hand, "that this is the most cherished gift I have ever received."

I was shivering—it was as though my body was having a physiological response to the death of my novel. "I'm freezing my ass off out here," I said. "How long have you been outside?"

"I've lost track of time," S. S. said. "A few hours? I should be careful, I suppose, or I'll end up like your poor neighbor, forced to spend my waning days in the buff."

"I'm heading home," I said. "Do you want to crash on my couch?"

"A couch," S. S. said. "I can't begin to tell you how delectable that sounds!"

We turned toward the alley's mouth when a squad car's lights began to swirl. There was no siren, so I had assumed that a police officer had arrived to deal with the streetlights that had gone on the blink, but when S. S. and I took another step, the cop's voice came over the PA: "You two. Hold it right there."

The cop was disturbingly young, practically a child. I saw this as he approached us in his too-stiff coat and plastic-wrapped hat.

"Where did you two come from?" he asked.

"I came from the Mill," I answered calmly.

"I came from the womb, my good man," S. S. said.

Even with sheets of snow slapping our heads, the cop didn't blink. His eyes were trained on S. S., as if he had come face to face with the man who had molested him in childhood but wasn't entirely sure now what to do with him.

"We're heading back to my place," I said. "This man is a visiting author and—"

"Quiet," the cop said. "I wasn't speaking to you." He took a step closer to S. S. and said, "Have you had a few tonight?"

"Why, sir, I've been drinking since early this morning," S. S. said. "Isn't that right, Jack?"

The cop looked at me now. "And you? Have you been drinking since this morning?"

"Don't lie, Jack," S. S. said.

"Yeah, sure, I had a few drinks this morning. But then I took a nap," I said. "And when I woke up, I wrote the opening of a new book. And *then* I started drinking again."

"You're both under arrest for public intoxication," the cop said. "You have the right to remain silent," he began.

When I looked over at S. S., his smile was gone, and I saw him for what he really was: a tired old man. The cop frisked S. S. and then frisked me.

"What's this?" he asked, reaching into Vince's coat pocket. He pulled out a pill bottle. He extracted a small flashlight from his holster and shined it on the bottle.

"Uh-huh. Do you want to tell me what you're doing with Flunitrazepam?" he asked.

"With *what*?" I asked.

"Roofies," he said. "You slip these into drinks when you're at the bar? Is that it?"

"This isn't even my coat," I said.

"Right," he said. "You think I haven't heard that before?" He shook the bottle, frowned, then twisted off the cap. "It's your lucky night, I guess."

"How so?"

"Bottle's empty," the cop said. "You must've already had your fun this month." He put the bottle and cap into his own pocket and said, "Don't think I'm not going to run a thorough search on you. It's scum like you who are ruining this city." He cuffed me, opened the back door of the squad car, and shoved me inside by pushing down on my head. A few moments later, S. S. was sitting next to me, also cuffed. When the cop opened his door and tossed my novel onto the passenger seat, I saw S. S. wince ever so slightly, as though the novel were a small pet being cruelly treated.

"It's okay," I said. "We'll be all right." And though S. S. nodded, he didn't remove his gaze from the manuscript box the whole way to the police department.

PART SEVEN

Success is not final, failure is not fatal: It is the courage to continue that counts.

—WINSTON CHURCHILL

A FTER S. S. and I were separated at the police station, I asked for my one phone call with every intention of calling someone, but when an officer led me to a pay phone at the end of the hall, I realized that there was no one I could call.

"Are you going to use that phone or not?"

I shook my head, returned the receiver to the hook, and was led to my cell, where, safely guarded from the chaos of my life, I fell into a sound sleep.

I didn't see S. S. again until the next morning when, wearing orange jumpsuits and white booties, we were handcuffed together and driven the few short blocks to the courthouse in an old Ford van for an 8:00 AM appearance before the judge.

Upon arrival, S. S. said, "Ah, yes. The Gulag of the Plains."

"Quiet!" a policeman barked.

One by one, after insinuating that a plea of innocence would only piss him off and result in at least a month of jail time, the judge asked us if we were guilty, and one by one, we entered our guilty plea. Afterward, we were processed (S. S. paid my fine as well as his own), taken back to the police station, given our belongings, and set free.

I waited in the police station lobby for S. S., and when he finally showed up, whiskery and clutching my novel, we walked outside together, where a taxi that S. S. had called was waiting for us. I climbed in and slid across the cold seat. S. S. eased himself inside, giving the cab driver my address.

"We'll take you home," S. S. said, "and then I'm off to your lovely airport."

At the word *lovely*, the cabbie glanced in the rearview mirror.

"I would be happy," S. S. said, "delighted, even, if you agreed to look at our novel once I'm finished writing it. If you don't like what I've done, you can take it back from me. What do you say, old companion?"

"No, no," I said. "The book's yours. Do with it as you see fit."

S. S. nodded. "Very well, then."

"I'm sorry about last night," I said. "You know, the two of us getting arrested and all."

"Oh, please," S. S. said. "It was cheaper than a night at the Sheraton. And nicer, really. Free transportation. Everyone was rather friendly, too."

I expected the cabdriver, after pulling up in front of my apartment, to kick us both out, but he didn't. After I had stepped into a knee-high snowdrift, S. S. rattled my novel at me and said, "We'll share the Pulitzer, you and I."

"Take care," I said.

"Always!" S. S. said, and I shut the door.

I looked up and saw M. Cat staring down at me from his bay window. The bandages were off his hands, and he was wearing an old cable-knit sweater with leaping deer across the front and tan corduroys. He waved at me, and I waved back.

In the narrow stairwell, I came face to face with Lauren Castle, who was carrying her suitcase.

"Back to New York?" I asked.

"Did I just miss that cab?" she said. "I was trying to get your attention from the window."

"I'm sorry," I said. "I didn't notice."

"Of course you didn't. Why am I not surprised?"

"Still going to become an agent?" I asked.

"My one client reneged on his contract," she said, rolling her eyes up toward M. Cat's apartment, "and my other potential client doesn't want to publish a book. I guess it's back to the Publicity Department for me."

"I may need an agent," I offered.

Lauren merely snorted and said, "What? For *your* book? I won't hold my breath. No offense."

"None taken," I said.

Inside my apartment, there were no blinking lights on my answering machine, no gas burners turned all the way up, no novel that needed to be finished. Other than being dead broke and potentially unemployed, I was in pretty good shape.

I showered, put on fresh clothes, and, with yesterday's pages in my back pocket, drove to the Sheraton to call Lucy for my next writing prompt. Amazingly, even though I had woken up this morning in a jail cell, I still managed to make my appointments, a testament to either the efficiency of the Iowa City Police Department or my will to continue on—I wasn't sure which. And yet there I stood in the hotel lobby. The elevator binged, two doors opened, and Tate Rinehart stepped out. I put the phone down.

"Tate," I said.

"Oh, hey, Jack," he said. He looked nervously around. "I should have called to tell you. I'm taking a cab back to the airport."

"A cab?" I said. I had completely forgotten that I was supposed to take him back to Cedar Rapids this morning.

"Actually," Tate said, "I'm heading over to the hospital first to see Vince, and *then* I'm going to the airport."

"The hospital? What's wrong with Vince?"

Something caught Tate's eye, and he squinted at me, sizing me up. I looked down and saw that I was wearing Vince's coat. Tate quickly regained his composure. He said, "Someone found him passed out on the river last night. Luckily he didn't break through."

"The guy does drink a lot," I conceded.

Tate pulled the strap of his messenger bag higher up onto his shoulder. "Apparently, he has a concussion," Tate said. "They were afraid there was internal bleeding in the brain, but they did a CAT scan and didn't find any. They did find a hairline fracture in his skull, though. Possibly two fractures."

I imagined Larry McFeeley's house surrounded by a SWAT team, urging him to come peacefully outside. "Does he know what happened?" I asked.

Tate shook his head. "Poor guy can't remember a thing."

"Jesus. That's too bad."

"I know." Tate sighed. We stared at each other for an uncomfortably long time. Then Tate opened his mouth, as if to speak, but then closed it.

"What?" I said.

"Nothing."

"No, go on. You were going to say something."

"It's just that—" He paused, thinking of the best way to convey whatever news ticked before his eyes. "I didn't take the job."

"Oh."

"I didn't think it was right," he said. "This is your city."

I was about to ask him what the hell he was talking about—after all, I didn't have any connection to the Workshop anymore—but another elevator opened, and Lucy Rogan stepped out into the lobby.

"There you are!" Lucy said. "You have something for me?"

"I do?"

The look she gave me was that of a stern but loving teacher waiting for her promising but lazy student to remember the last thing she had told him.

"Oh, yeah," I said. "Here." I handed over my assignment. "Sorry!"

I wanted to introduce Lucy to Tate Rinehart, but Tate had shuffled away, the frosted-over automatic doors sliding open, a taxi already waiting for him.

"Friend?" Lucy asked.

"No," I said. "Vanquished foe."

Lucy smiled. "Are you running him out of town?"

"On a rail," I said.

T HE COROLLA WAS nauseatingly loud, but Lucy said nothing. Instead of driving us back to my apartment, where we could continue chipping away at my writer's block, I asked Lucy if she minded taking a detour so that I could stop off at Oakland Cemetery on the north side of town.

"I need to visit a grave," I said.

Lucy nodded solemnly, then touched my hand for comfort.

The famous Black Angel resided in Oakland Cemetery. It was a bronze angel that stood eight feet tall. Over the many years it had been there, the metal had oxidized, turning the angel black. Unlike most graveyard angels that look up with open wings for ascension into heaven, the Black Angel peered down with its wings partially closed. For years, rumors about the Black Angel persisted—the reason why it had turned black and the powers it possessed—but the rumor that appealed to me the most was this one: If you rubbed the hand of the Black Angel, you yourself would die shortly thereafter. By and large, I wasn't a superstitious man, but there had been days, after my novel had stalled and I saw no chance of ever resuscitating it, when I had driven to Oakland Cemetery and rubbed the angel's hand, tempting the Gods of Superstition and Conjecture to reveal themselves to me.

"Look," I said today, pointing. "The Black Angel."

In the middle of telling Lucy the story of the statue, she pulled out a notepad and began scribbling furiously. I stopped talking.

"What are you doing?" I asked.

"I'll write a novel about it," she said. "Tell me more."

It was as simple as that for Lucy Rogan—a few interesting details, and a novel bloomed in its entirety. All that was required was for Lucy to sit down and transcribe it. How could I not admire that? She was Charles Atlas to my puny, sand-in-my-eyes self.

I parked by the more recent graves. Last night's snow had covered the markers, but I had been here so often since the death of my own novel that I could probably have found it with my eyes shut. I led Lucy down a few rows, paused to get my bearings, then down a few more. I crouched and began wiping away snow. I was off by two markers, which wasn't bad, really, given the expanse of blinding whiteness all around us.

Lucy stood beside me. She read the grave marker aloud: MAX KELLOGG. WRITER. "I'm afraid I haven't read any of his work," she said.

"You wouldn't have," I said. "He never published anything."

"Was he a friend of yours?" she asked. "A classmate?"

"I never knew him," I said. "I took his job after he died."

"What job?"

"Media escort," I said. I turned toward Lucy now. Her cheeks were red from the wind, her eyes glassy. "I was your media escort when you did your signing in Cedar Rapids."

Lucy blinked a few times before reaching up and dabbing the corners of her eyes with a pink-cashmere-gloved fist. She smiled at me, and I returned the smile. We walked silently back to the car. I opened Lucy's door for her, but we both paused at the clip-clop of a horse going by. It was an Amish man riding his buggy past the cemetery. Cars had lined up behind him, weaving into the opposite lane to see what was holding them up, impatient for the first chance to zip past. Lucy and I watched until the buggy, with a familiar orange triangle attached to it, rounded a bend, disappearing from our view.

"Shit," I said.

"What's wrong?"

"Nothing," I said. "Do you have a little free time this morning?"

"I've got nothing planned," Lucy said, "except our next lesson."

"Good. Do you want to go for a drive?"

Lucy smiled. "Why wouldn't I?" she asked.

A mile down the road, we passed a sign that read WATCH OUT: BUMP AHEAD, and I touched Lucy's knee and nodded toward the warning so that she could brace herself as I slowed my speed.

THIRTY MILES SOUTHWEST of Iowa City sat the town of Kalona, home to the largest Amish community west of the Mississippi. When we reached it, I pulled over, popped the trunk, and pulled out the publicity materials for Vanessa Roberts's book. Inside was a glossy five-by-seven photograph. I tucked it into my coat pocket and then drove from business to business, stopping to ask each proprietor if anyone had seen this woman. Like a detective in a dime-store novel, I flashed Vanessa's photo.

"Why do you think she's here?" Lucy asked.

"A hunch," I said. "Her entire book reads like a Wikipedia entry about the Amish."

"Is she Amish?" Lucy asked.

"I don't think so. No."

At a house that sold pies, I met an older Amish woman who wouldn't look me in the eye when I spoke to her, but when I showed her the publicity photo, she led me onto her front porch and pointed to a decrepit store down the highway that sold antiques.

"Thank you," I said.

Lucy bought an apple pie from the woman. When she turned to face me, I could see in Lucy's eyes another idea for a novel percolating.

The name of the store was Jakob's Antiques. It was housed in an old gas station that still had two ancient pumps outside, the kind topped with glass bulbs.

We walked inside the tiny store, and a bell dangling overhead announced our presence. Sunlight streamed through the otherwise dark room. The entire place was crammed full of stacked glassware and old, rusted tools in ancient wooden soda pop crates. A few broken toys, coated with dust, sat on shelves.

"Look," Lucy said and pointed to an old cast-iron typewriter. It was the exact same typewriter as my mother's, the kind I had first begun writing on. I hit a key with my forefinger. The corresponding typebar rose, smacked the roller, and fell back into line. I pushed the carriage release lever all the way to the right, and the bell dinged.

"Beautiful!" I said. "I want it." But then I remembered that I didn't have any money. "I'll come back and get it later."

"Why?" Lucy asked. "You should get it now. You can start writing your new book on it."

"I'm a little strapped right now," I said.

"I'll get it for you."

"No, no, I couldn't."

"Think of it as a gift from S. S." She leaned toward me and said, "If you had any idea how much he's paying me . . ."

"Okay, all right," I said, frowning and nodding. "Since you put it that way . . ."

A woman said, "If you need any help, please don't hesitate to ask."

I turned quickly, startled by the sound of a voice other than ours.

Behind the counter stood Vanessa Roberts. She held her baby and gently rocked him. She was wearing a plainly cut blue dress and a black bonnet, and her face was free of makeup. By her eyes and the way she began bouncing her baby faster I could tell that she recognized me. Lucy took hold of my arm. She, too, recognized Vanessa from the photo I had been flashing.

My first impulse was to demand the money she owed me for the breast pump. My next impulse was to use Lucy's cell to call Lauren Castle with the hope of catching her before she boarded her plane in Cedar Rapids. I could gloat over the phone: *See? I'm not as worthless as you think!* But then another option came to me, a possibility that hadn't, until this very moment, crossed my mind: What if I let it all go? The money. Vanessa Roberts. What if I pursued none of it? Ironically, it was this prospect that brought me the most relief. Letting go was something I had never been able to do until S. S. had physically excised my novel from my life, treating it like the malignant tumor it was.

I carried the typewriter up to the counter and set it down.

"How much?" I asked.

Vanessa didn't look at it. She maintained eye contact with me. "It's free," she said. "Please. Take it."

"Oh, no," Lucy said, "we want to pay for it." She reached into her purse, but I placed my hand on top of hers. A deal had been struck: the typewriter for my silence.

"It's all right, Lucy," I said. To Vanessa, I said, "Thank you. I mean that." I picked up the typewriter and said, "Good luck, okay?"

Vanessa nodded. She peered down at her baby and rubbed his cheek with her finger. She cooed at the child, then tilted her head back, peering down her nose at the child and saying, "Oh, what is it? Hm? What is it, sweetums?"

A man came out from the back room, joining Vanessa and the baby. He was dressed in traditional Amish garb, except for the Rolex that glinted on his left wrist when sunlight momentarily filled the room.

"My husband," Vanessa said.

"Glad to meet you," I said.

Outside, I popped the trunk and placed the heavy typewriter inside, and then Lucy and I drove noisily back to Iowa City.

38

NSIDE MY APARTMENT, with the cast-iron typewriter sitting next to my laptop, Lucy said, "Ready?"

I slid a sheet of paper into the feed roller and cranked the knob until the top of the paper revealed itself. I typed my name. The ribbon was dry, and the letters weren't as dark as they should have been, but I could read my name well enough to get by until I found new ribbons for it.

"Ready," I said.

Lucy, standing beside me, said, "Today, I want you to write a generalization—something you think is true of most people that's also true of you."

I faced my typewriter and placed my fingers on the keys, but Lucy said, "Wait until I'm gone, okay?"

"You're leaving?"

"I'm going for a walk," she said. "I'll be back for dinner, though. My treat." She put on her coat and slipped on her pink cashmere gloves. She rested a hand on the top of my head for a moment and said, "Good luck."

I waited until she had left the apartment, and then I waited until I heard the front door downstairs creak open and shut. I took a deep breath, held it, and hammered out my assignment:

Most people fail to recognize the moment they've touched the ceiling of their potential, that point at which they've reached the height of their intellectual prowess or the summit of their popularity.

I breathed out. I stared ahead for a good fifteen minutes. Then I tapped the space bar twice. I still felt Lucy's hand on my head, encouraging me to keep going. I typed:

It can happen anywhere, at any point in their life—away at college during a study session the night before a final, or on a high school football field while catching the game-winning touchdown.

I was about to strike the space key again when someone pounded on my door. *M. Cat,* I thought, sighing. I considered not answering the door, but the knocking came again, harder this time.

"Yes?" I said, opening the door, but it wasn't M. Cat. It was a man dressed in drab-colored clothes, a stranger. He sported a beard without a mustache, the way the Amish do, and yet the shiny new wristwatch and the incongruously hip black-framed eyeglasses, the exact same kind Tate Rinehart wore, told me that this man was not Amish. He stood in the hall, clutching an age-worn leather satchel.

"Are you the writer?" he asked.

I knew, in that instant, that this was the fellow who had saved M. Cat's life. In exchange for having been rescued, M. Cat had offered him my editorial services. The satchel looked over a hundred years old, a beloved heirloom that held only the most precious of one's possessions. The sight of this poor man, who clearly had no idea what he was getting himself into, holding onto his satchel—it nearly broke my heart.

"Yes," I said. "Yes, I'm the writer."

"My name is Amos Claussen," he said.

"Please," I said, stepping aside and smiling. "Please come in."

I lived in the same apartment that I had lived in when I first moved to Iowa City, and as I opened the door wider, it was as though I were fourteen years younger, when each day stretched endlessly before me and the jewels of the world were still mine for the taking.

"I've been waiting for you," I said, blinking away the wetness in my eyes, and Amos Claussen, taking hold of my hand and pumping it vigorously, said, "And I for you."

ACKNOWLEDGMENTS

William Lashner and Fritz McDonald's quotes are from *The Workshop: Seven Decades of the Iowa Writers' Workshop*, edited by Tom Grimes.

F. Scott Fitzgerald's quote is so famous, it needs no attribution.

John Gardner's quote about writer's block is from *On Becoming a Novelist*.

Flannery O'Connor's quote can be found in her collection of essays, *Mysteries and Manners*.

T. C. Boyle's quote is from an interview conducted by Claire Zulkey and can be found at www.zulkey.com.

James Frey's quote is from the Times Online (London) essay, "The U.S. Antihero: James Frey" by Alan Franks. It appeared August 2, 2008.

I found the Winston Churchill quote online. I have no idea where it came from or if he really said it. One thing I've learned, however: Don't trust everything you read.

The poem on page 223 is from Hart Crane's "To Brooklyn Bridge."

Thanks to my friends who, in ways subtle and not-so-subtle, helped with the writing of this book: Joe Caccamisi, Ted Genoways, Owen King, Scott Smith, Sam Weller, and Eric Wilson.

Thanks to my old Iowa cohort Gregg Palmer for playing so much pool with me all those years ago in Iowa City.

Thanks to my workshop teachers at Iowa: the late Frank Conroy, Madison Smartt Bell, Allan Gurganus, DeWitt Henry, and Tom Jenks, all of whom taught me a great deal. Also, thanks to James Salter for a wonderful class on famous novelists' first novels.

Thanks also to T. C. Boyle, for whom I researched the elusive pygmy sunfish.

Thanks to all those writers I escorted back in the day.

Thanks to Prairie Lights Bookstore and the Foxhead for providing safe havens for me to while away so many afternoons and nights.

Thanks to the Iowa City Police Department for arresting me on a November night in 1987 for public intoxication, thereby allowing me to see the inside of a jail.

Thanks to Jenny Bent for suggesting that I write this book after I told her about my media escort days.

Thanks to Jack Shoemaker, Roxanna Aliaga, and everyone else at Counterpoint.

A huge thanks to Connie Green and Peggy Barrett, unsung heroes where I work, for putting up with me these past seven years. They deserve more than this piddling notice.

Thanks to my father, Bob McNally, for his continued support.

Mostly, thanks to my wife, Amy, and our dogs (Emma, Hailey, and Scout) for listening to me read this novel aloud as I wrote it, providing an instant audience and a reason to keep forging ahead with it.

ABOUT THE AUTHOR

JOHN MCNALLY IS the author of two previous novels, *The Book of Ralph* and *America's Report Card*, and two story collections, *Troublemakers* (winner of the John Simmons Short Fiction Award and the Nebraska Book Award) and *Ghosts of Chicago* (a Chicagoland Indie Bestseller and voted one of the top twenty fiction books of 2008 by readers of *The Believer*).

John's work has appeared in over a hundred publications, including *The Washington Post*, *The Sun*, and *Open City*, and he is a contributing editor to the *Virginia Quarterly Review*. He has been a finalist for the National Magazine Award and the recipient of fellowships from Paramount Pictures (Chesterfield Writer's Film Project), the University of Iowa (James Michener Award), George Washington University (Jenny McKean Moore Fellowship), and the University of Wisconsin-Madison (Carl Djerassi Fiction Fellowship).

Like Jack Sheahan, John is a graduate of the Iowa Writers' Workshop. Also like Jack Sheahan, John was once a media escort in Iowa City. Unlike Jack Sheahan, he has never published a story in *The New Yorker* or *Best American Short Stories*, and he was not a Teaching-Writing Fellow while at Iowa. A native of Chicago's southwest side, John now lives in Winston-Salem, North Carolina, with his wife, Amy, their three dogs, and at least seven cats. He is at work on a new novel.

His middle name is not Hercules.